FRAMED
to death

**The Faith Hunter Scrap This Mystery Series
by Christina Freeburn**

EMBELLISHED TO DEATH (#3)

"A fast-paced crafting cozy that will keep you turning pages as you try to figure out which one of the attendees is an identity thief and which one is a murderer."

— Lois Winston,
Author of the Anastasia Pollack Crafting Mystery Series

"A little town, a little romance, a little intrigue and a little murder. Join heroine Faith and find out exactly who is doing the embellishing—the kind that doesn't involve scrapbooking."

— Leann Sweeney,
Author of the Bestselling Cats in Trouble Mysteries

"A heart-wrenching cozy mystery, it delivers so much more with spot-on character and plot development...Don't miss this third book in this wonderful series by a writer who knows how to make you laugh and cry and be eager for more of Faith's sleuthing."

— Pam Andrews Hanson,
Co-author of the Chesapeake Antiques Mystery Series

DESIGNED TO DEATH (#2)

"Battling scrapbook divas, secrets, jealousy, murder, and lots of glitter make *Designed to Death* a charming and heartfelt mystery."

–Ellen Byerrum,
Author of the Crime of Fashion Mysteries

"Freeburn's second installment in her scrapbooking mystery series is full of small-town intrigue, twists and turns, and plenty of heart."

— Mollie Cox Bryan,
Agatha Award Finalist, *Scrapbook of Secrets*

"[Freeburn] is able to weave in humor, but also suspense, and even a little bit of romance...If you're a series lover like me, you'll be happy to know that is the second in the Scrap This series, and a third is due in 2014."

– CriminalElement.com

"This is a fun series with very likable characters you will want to visit with again and again with every new book. Even if you are not a fan of scrapping (and I'm not – it's about the only craft I never got into) you will enjoy the series as it is not heavy with information about the hobby – as some hobby series can be. And if you are into the hobby, there are hints at the back of the book."

– Rantin' Ravin' and Reading

CROPPED TO DEATH (#1)

"A great read that had me reading non-stop from the moment I turned the first page...kept me in suspense with plenty of twists and turns and every time I thought I had it figured out, the author changed the direction in which the story was headed...and I liked the cast of characters in this charming whodunit!"

–Dru's Book Musings

"Witty, entertaining and fun with a side of murder...When murder hits Eden, WV, Faith Hunter will stop at nothing to clear the name of her employee who has been accused of murder. Will she find the killer before it is too late? Read this sensational read to find out!"

– Shelley's Book Case

"A cozy mystery that exceeds expectations....Freeburn has crafted a mystery that does not feel clichéd or cookie-cutter....it's her sense of humor that shows up in the book, helping the story flow, making the characters real and keeping the reader interested."

– Scrapbooking is Heart Work

FRAMED
to death

A Faith Hunter Scrap This Mystery

CHRISTINA
FREEBURN

HENERY PRESS

FRAMED TO DEATH
A Faith Hunter Scrap This Mystery
Part of the Henery Press Mystery Collection

First Edition | April 2016

Henery Press
www.henerypress.com

Trade Paperback ISBN-13: 978-1-63511-013-5
Digital epub ISBN-13: 978-1-63511-014-2
Kindle ISBN-13: 978-1-63511-015-9
Hardcover Paperback ISBN-13: 978-1-63511-016-6

Printed in the United States of America

*In loving memory of Terry W. McNemar,
one of my best friends, surrogate dad, surrogate big brother, and
one of my most vocal and loyal fans and supporters.*

*I will always be grateful for the blessing and privilege of having
had him in my life. No one was ever alone when he was around.
Wherever he was, Terry not only introduced himself
and offered friendship but always made it a point to say
"Hey, do you know..." connecting people to each other,
setting foundations for a new friendships.*

Terry was a builder...and likely still is.

ACKNOWLEDGMENTS

A huge thanks to my wonderful editor Anna Davis for helping me wrangle my characters back under control when they had preferred to do their own thing. I loved how the story was able to evolve with your guidance and support.

To my wonderful beta readers for being eager to see the early draft of the story and making sure I got the football parts right. I couldn't have done this without Bonner and Teresa, who went above and beyond for me this summer when I was working on the book while my heart was breaking. Thank you.

Also, a special thanks to volunteer firefighter Zachary Freeburn who answered some questions, guided me on where to find needed resources, and was instrumental in giving me the one key detail that I needed to work out a plot point that kept tripping me up.

ONE

I closed out the register, securing Scrap This's receivables in the bank bag. Not bad. Not good either. We were out of the back-to-school slump, when most shoppers found their excess income taken by school supplies, but not yet at the Christmas-is-coming, start-the-crafting time period. I hoped the specialty paper designed with the high school football team's colors and mascot would bring in extra revenue. The order arrived this morning, and my grandmothers planned on unveiling it tomorrow morning with a special event.

If there was one thing the town of Eden loved, it was football: professional, collegiate, but especially high school.

From August to January, the town revolved around the sport. Whenever there was a home game, Eden practically shut down, with only a few restaurants remaining open along with the largest gas station in town. The pastor even knew better than to have a prayer meeting on football night. It was something I hated and loved about Eden—consistency.

Our town not only revolved around the game but also Coach Rutherford, who put our county on the football map by winning the West Virginia State football championship six times. The scuttlebutt around town was that Coach Rutherford was granted an exception to all the rules, so lack of parking, change for meters, stoplights, and speed limits wouldn't get in his way of getting to a game, practice, or press conference on time. I guess every town needed a hero. This year, Eden had anticipated making it three championships in a row and bringing the county to seven total, until a horrific car accident left the star quarterback Brandon Sullivan paralyzed from the waist down.

The phone rang. I briefly contemplated ignoring it, but knew I risked a drive-by checking up by either my grandmothers or whoever Cheryl had decided was the new candidate for her granddaughter's knight-in-shining armor as she yanked it from Steve Davis.

"Scrap This."

"Hi, Faith, it's Charlotte. I have a favor to ask."

Six months ago, dressed like an agent of S.H.I.E.L.D., Charlotte Hanson breezed into town on a Harley. Her daughter, Hannah, had followed behind driving their red, white, and blue extended-cab truck. Some of the residents of Eden were a little taken aback and stayed clear of Charlotte. Not me. I introduced myself and we became fast friends.

She intrigued half the community, scared the other half, and ramped up all the gossips in town. The only thing that quieted the talk about Charlotte's past—which included having a baby at seventeen, a short stint in jail, and a relationship with a semi-famous reality television star—was talk about Steve's family tree. My ex-husband Adam happened to be Steve's cousin. And a murderer.

"As long as it has nothing to do with a guy," I said.

"Well, it kind of does."

I groaned. Ever since I cooled things between Steve and me, my grandmothers and friends had been trying to find a replacement. The relationship hadn't taken a nosedive because of our shared skeleton in the closet, but because Steve knew my secret and never told me about his connection to my ex-husband Adam the murderer.

My family and friends feared I'd return to my hermit lifestyle. They refused to grasp that I needed to sort out my emotions before I entered a new relationship. Not to mention during the last four months, Steve continually found ways to change the subject when I started the we-need-to-talk conversation, so we weren't "officially" over. Unfortunately for him, those manipulations firmed up my resolve to end things rather than changing my mind.

"I'm not trying to set you up. I need you to pop into Polished and check that there are no guys visiting with Hannah and her friends. My appointment with the insurance agent is running over, and I don't want the girls taking advantage of my absence."

"Not a problem. I was heading home in a few minutes, so I can run next door first and make sure Polished is girls only."

"And if you don't mind..." A slight hesitation entered into her voice. "Would you mind hanging around until ten to make sure the girls get out by curfew? I don't want to get fined."

"I thought the town ended it when school started back."

"So did I. The school sent out a message last night reminding us of the curfew and that the only exceptions were for students attending football games or pre-game celebrations. "

"How does that make any sense? The last pre-game celebration involved a bonfire that almost burned down the embroidery shop."

"You know Eden better than I do. I forbade Hannah from attending tonight's rally and agreed to let her have a mani-pedi party at Polished to make up for it. It's tough making friends in a new school, especially when you're a senior."

"I'll make sure the Cinderellas head home before the clock strikes ten."

"Thanks. You can use the key I gave your grandmothers to go through the back door." Charlotte ended the call.

I secured the bank bag in the small safe in the back office, snagging from the desk the Polished key Charlotte entrusted to them after she misplaced hers several times in her opening week. Out of habit, I locked the back door of Scrap This and set the alarm. I wasn't afraid someone planned on lying in wait for me, but so far our store hadn't been a recipient of a good-natured prank—AKA vandalism—from Eden High's football team like some of the others had, and I wanted to keep it that way.

I made my way to Polished, unlocking the back door and

easing it back into the frame. I didn't want to startle the girls and make them think I was an attacker.

"Are you stupid?" a high-pitched feminine voice asked.

The question was followed by a loud clatter.

"Let me go," Hannah squeaked out.

I ran into the room. A teen with long blonde hair held Hannah against a wall. Small bottles of nail polish skittered across the floor. Another girl screamed, diving toward small organza fabric bags that were on a manicure table.

"Faith, why are you here?" Hannah pushed the girl away, tripping her way toward the other teen.

"Apparently to break up a fight." I steadied Hannah, stopping her from reaching the girl attempting to hide the silvery bags under her cheerleading t-shirt.

"You're not needed here." The blonde who'd attacked Hannah flipped her hair over her shoulder.

"I can decide that for myself." The antics of the other girl had my attention more than the trying-to-act-like-a-thug behavior of the one not shoveling items down her t-shirt.

One of the bags escaped the groping hands and took up residence in a corner near the back legs of a chair. A light blue ribbon was tied around the top. I knelt down and reached for it.

"We'll clean up this mess." The girl dropped onto the floor, inching forward on her belly like a caterpillar. The items under her shirt making a crackling sound as she wiggled under the table. "Whitney didn't want Hannah telling everyone we were here."

"Shut up, Kirstin," Whitney, the blonde, said.

"We're excluding others. Don't want to get in trouble for it," Kirstin said, continuing to slither toward the bag from the opposite side. She whacked her forehead on the edge of the manicurist chair and didn't slow down one bit. "I'll get the potpourri."

Right. I hadn't been out of high school so long that I forgot what it was like to be a teen. A lot of acrobatics, physical and verbal, were being conducted over some bags of potpourri. I jumped over Kirstin and quickly brought my foot down on the bag. I had a strong suspicion I was seeing the elusive synthetic marijuana disguised as fragrance satchels. The designer drug hit our community three months ago, and no adults or members of law enforcement had seen it in anyone's possession, though all had heard of it and witnessed some of the aftereffects of its use. Like Brandon Sullivan's accident.

I picked up the unmarked fabric bag. The little pouch of potpourri held a mixture of crumbled red, green, and brown dried leaves. It matched the description I'd read in the paper of the illegal herbal substance, named Janie by the police department. My stomach plummeted. "Where did you get this?"

"I'll say you gave it to us if you don't give it back," Whitney said.

A heavy pounding shook the front door.

Kirstin craned her neck, blanching to the color of vellum. "Run!"

Conroy Jasper, wearing civilian clothes rather than a police uniform, stood at the front door of Polished. He jabbed at the doorknob. "Open up, Faith."

The girls raced for the back of the store.

I grabbed the arm of the closest teen. Whitney. "Not so fast."

She whirled, pointing her smartphone at me, and yanked something out of her jacket pocket. A flash went off in my face, then a liquid squirted at me. Pepper spray.

Screaming, I hunched over, scrubbing at my eyes as tears coursed down my face. The bag containing the potpourri dropped to the floor. Someone leaned down; I shoved at the figure. I couldn't let the girls have the drug.

"Leave it," Whitney said.

"Open up or I'll break down this door," Jasper's concerned voice reached me.

The girls ran past me. The culprits were making a break for the back exit. I headed after them, only managing to run into two tables and trip over the legs of a rolling chair. Everything was a big blur through the tears streaming down my face.

"Stop them. The back door."

Dropping to my knees, I scrambled my hands around on the floor, searching for the illegal substance. My hands and arms itched to scrub at my eyes. I stopped myself from catering to the instinct, knowing that would make it worse. Stopping my hunt, I leaned back, taking in a deep breath. The best choice was waiting for Jasper as I might damage the evidence. Hopefully this would put the police on the path of shutting the drug dealer down.

"What happened?" Jasper's voice carried from the rear of the store.

I gestured at the herbs littered on the floor. "The teens had Janie. I'm kind of hoping it was just buying for personal use, not selling."

"I know about that. I mean, what's wrong with you?" Jasper wrapped an arm around my shoulders. "I heard you scream."

"Pepper sprayed." Either the teens got away, or he thought it more prudent to check on me.

"Let's get you to the sink." His other arm went under my knees.

I swatted at Jasper. "I can walk. I don't need help."

With the world still blurry, my independence was short-lived as I smacked into the edge of the counter.

Jasper wrapped his arms around my waist and hoisted me up. Now, instead of being carried across-the-threshold style, Jasper hauled me toward the back like a tantrum-throwing toddler or a humongous bag of fertilizer.

I curled my legs up to make sure we didn't become tangled and end up on the floor in a heap.

He deposited me near the sink in the manicure section, turning on the faucet and splashing handfuls of cold water onto my face. "What have you gotten yourself into this time?"

Coughing, I moved back. "You're going to drown me. I got it from here."

"You need to get it out of your eyes as quick as you can," Jasper said.

"Trust me, I want it out more than you do." I cupped my hands under the water, working on getting out the chemicals.

"Do you know who sprayed you?" Jasper asked.

"Whitney."

"Last name?"

"I don't know yet, but I will after I call Charlotte. She asked me to check up on Hannah and her friends." I snagged the cordless phone.

"I think you should hold off on calling anyone, especially Charlotte Hanson."

My finger paused over the seven. Bits of dried leaves and flowers coated the floor of Polished, and the room held a slight smell of cloves.

Jasper removed his cell from the clip on his belt, the movement revealing his holster. He showed me a picture on Hannah's Instagram account. "Clive Murphy called and reported that a group of teens high on something accidentally set Lake Breckinridge's flower shop on fire. The fire department and some squad cars are heading there. The parents in Eden want a showdown with whoever is selling this designer drug to their kids. Right now, the only tangible link to where it's coming from is a picture Hannah posted."

The photo showed the bag of potpourri on the manicure station. Poor Charlotte. She was having enough trouble finding acceptance in the community. This wouldn't help her.

"And one just popped up with you holding a bag of potpourri."

Whitney wasn't trying to blind me with her camera. She was implicating me, and Hannah helped her. Why would Hannah do that to me? "I didn't sell the drug to the girls."

Jasper collected the evidence. "I know that. We've been monitoring social media sites for the last few months, knowing sooner or later someone would get careless and post something. This is the most substantial lead we've gotten."

"The girls had a couple of bags of it."

Jasper tucked the re-bagged potpourri under his arm. Opening an app on his phone, he started taking notes. "I need the names."

"Whitney, Kirstin, and Hannah. Hannah didn't bring it into the store either," I added. "That explains why Whitney was so mad. She knows Hannah took a picture."

A disconcerting thought trickled into my mind. I shoved at it, but it settled into my brain, making itself quite comfortable. Had Charlotte suspected one of the girls was bringing the drugs? Was that the real reason, not visiting teenage boys, she wanted me to come over?

"Were you here the whole time?" Jasper swiped his index finger across the phone screen. He flipped it toward me. "This picture shows a bag of Janie on one of the small tables, but no one is in the picture. I don't know which teen brought it in."

"Manicurist station," I said.

Jasper heaved out a sigh. "Fine, manicurist station, though now isn't the time to be worried about those particulars."

"I think the particulars concerning this are important."

"Whether it's a called a small table or a manicurist station, no. The second picture of you handing a bag of Janie to a teen is what should concern you."

"I didn't hand anything to anyone."

"That's not what this shows." Jasper showed me another photo.

It had been taken right before I was pepper sprayed. In it, I was holding the bag of Janie and a hand was reaching for it. Someone could interpret the picture to mean I was giving it to someone. I doubted Whitney would admit she was trying to take the confiscated drug away from me.

"I took it from the girls, and Whitney was trying to get it back."

"I know that, you know that, but what will other people believe?" Jasper said. "I'll need you to come to the station first thing in the morning to make a statement."

TWO

A loud pounding on my front door woke me from a sound sleep. I shook my head, trying to clear the fuzziness and the remnants of a nice, tantalizing dream. I had thought I'd be plagued with nightmares of what was to come after my adventure with the teens and the synthetic marijuana. Instead of dreams of being arrested by the police, I had one involving a detective, the ocean, sand, and candlelight. The loud knocking continued. I glanced at the window. The world outside was still dark. Something must be wrong with my grandmothers. I sprung from the bed, nearly face-planting on the carpet as my legs tangled in the comforter.

I half-ran, half-jumped down the stairs. I yanked the door open, stumbling backwards when I was greeted by a fierce-faced Officer Mitchell, a guy I'd attended high school with, and a contrite Officer Glover. With cheeks blazing, I crossed my arms over my chest. I was wearing a Scrap This t-shirt made out of a thin fabric and yoga shorts, not the most appropriate attire for this visit, though I wasn't up on the proper ensemble for a before-dawn visit from the police.

"May we come in, Faith?" Officer Glover asked.

Before I could answer, Officer Mitchell pushed his way inside my home while removing handcuffs from his utility belt. "You're wanted for questioning."

"What?" I focused on Glover, who appeared as taken aback as I was at Mitchell's proclamation.

"The Chief said there are a few things to clear up." Glover put a restraining hand on Mitchell's arm. "No need for the cuffs."

"You might be okay taking a forced leave of absence, but I'm not. I have a wife and three kids to support." Mitchell turned me around, tugging my hands behind my back. "Chief Moore also said by the book, so that's what I'm doing."

"We don't have a reason to arrest her." Glover removed me from Mitchell's custody.

Once again, I crossed my arms across my front, stepping away from the officer who I'd somehow managed to rankle.

"I'm keeping my cool," Mitchell said. "You're the one who's losing it by playing favorites. I don't want to end up like Jasper."

I faced Glover. "What is he talking about? What happened to Jasper?"

"Complaints were made about the police not taking your involvement in the drug distribution seriously."

"I had nothing to do with it," I said. "Unfortunately, a favor turned into a wrong place, wrong time scenario."

"A bit of a habit for you," Mitchell said.

Two state police vehicles pulled into my driveway. Anxiety built up in me. I tried to talk myself down from the growing panic. I had done nothing wrong. There were no drugs, or even organza bags, in either my home or Scrap This. I'd also call Hannah and her mom. They'd explain what transpired at Polished. This would be over soon.

"Can I make a call? A friend of mine can clear all of this up for me." I was proud of the calmness in my voice.

Glover handed me a jacket hung near my front door. "It's better to just let this play out. It'll be easier for everyone."

The trip to Scrap This had been a disaster. From my vantage point in the backseat of the patrol car, I watched the red lights bouncing off the windows of the businesses we passed on the way to the police station. Some were empty, others filled with displays showing love for Eden High School football. The one my grandmothers had started was now in pieces on the floor. The police had to make sure there was nothing hidden in the lightning bolt piñata. Our new boxes of pattern paper were ripped into, damaging the top sheets. I blinked away threatening tears. No way would I crumble in front of Mitchell, giving the hateful cop what he wanted.

Mitchell had made me watch the search team, consisting of Eden's reigning veteran of the police force, a state police officer, and a newly hired assistant prosecuting attorney, dismantle the store. They searched the restrooms, the break room (including opening sealed boxes of snacks bought for next week's crop/baby shower hosted by our most frequent shopper), and the lock box in my grandmother's office. No one believed that it only contained our money bag, even with the proof in front of them. The disgust for me never left their faces.

I drew in a deep breath, pulling back the tears trying to escape.

Mitchell parked in front of the station and sounded the sirens a few times. Let's wake the neighbors and let them know the drug-selling Faith Hunter has been caught.

Karen England, reporter extraordinaire, stood at the top of the steps of the police station under the outside lights. I had an audience for my humiliation. This day was getting better and better.

"Looks like someone was able to make a phone call, even though I wasn't allowed," I said.

Mitchell pivoted, glaring at me through the mesh wire separating us. "How about showing some remorse instead of a snotty attitude? A woman lost her business today, and a couple of kids are very sick. But if you cared about other people, you wouldn't have a side job selling drugs to kids."

"I didn't sell drugs to anyone."

"Save it for a cop who'll believe you." He exited the cruiser, yanking me out of the backseat a few moments later.

I briefly—very briefly—thought of complaining about the rough treatment, then decided keeping quiet was my best defense. I trudged up the stairs, following Mitchell's pace. Now that we were at the station, or maybe more precisely because Karen was out here, Mitchell wasn't as eager to haul me to jail.

Karen flipped open a notebook. "Care if I ask a couple of questions?"

"Yes," I said.

"No." Mitchell stopped, jarring me to a halt.

"Are your grandmothers aware of what's happening?" Karen asked.

"No. And they better not find out."

"How do you think it's possible that they won't find out?" Karen asked.

"Because I'll be released in a few minutes and back in bed before the sun rises," I said.

"You're rather confident that the police won't detain you for distributing Janie to teens." Karen tapped a pen against her lips. "Why is that?"

"Because I didn't do it. I was taking the substance away from the girls, not giving it to them."

Mitchell grunted out a laugh. "She's been saying that all night."

I glared at Karen. "Ask Hannah." Since the photo was on Hannah's Instagram account, I figured there was no harm giving out her name. It was already out there.

"I have," Karen said. "Matter of fact, the chief has already spoken to them also."

The doors of the station opened and an officer leaned out. "You need to get her inside. Now."

My insides felt cold as Mitchell marched me inside. Hannah knew. Charlotte knew. They decided to let the police believe I was selling the drugs to the girls.

"Chief wants her in his office."

"If I was Chief, I'd have a witness in there," Mitchell said.

As we passed the main foyer, a woman charged toward me, screeching indistinguishable sounds. After a moment, the woman gathered her wits and set her words loose on me.

"Jasper protected you. He should be fired. You should be strung up."

I drew away, pressing my shoulder into Mitchell. He moseyed to the side, allowing the woman to barrage me with continuous insults.

"My son almost died. Because of you. Why isn't she handcuffed?"

"She's not under arrest, Mrs. Sullivan," Mitchell said in a soft tone. "Only brought in for questioning."

Felicity Sullivan was my attacker. Brandon's car accident almost killed him, leaving him paralyzed from the waist down, and stole his college dreams. The teen had been on so many scouting lists, Clive Murphy had set up a how-many-scholarship-offers pool at his pawn shop for the football player. Brandon had been on track to become the biggest story this football season.

"After what she did to my boy? That's all? She's in here for questioning?"

"Her house and Scrap This are being searched. If there's any evidence found, she'll have a nice long stay in prison. I'll make sure of it." Mitchell herded me to the chief's office.

I was thankful Mitchell was dragging me to the station rather than helping with the search. If he wasn't I'd worry he was planting evidence. For some reason he really wanted me to be the guilty party.

Mitchell shoved me into a seat in the chief's office.

Chief Moore pointed at the door. "You can leave now, Officer."

Mitchell looked around the office. "I don't see anyone else in here. Might be better for you if I stayed."

"I need your report in the next hour. The prosecuting attorney will be here then to take a look at it and see how we'll proceed."

I felt lightheaded. Had someone planted something in my house or store? The only person who'd have a clue that now was the perfect time to set me up was Charlotte. The dizziness intensified. "It was a favor. For Charlotte."

"You can leave the door open. Are you feeling all right, Faith?"

Chief Moore came around to the front of the desk and sat on the edge.

"I don't understand what's going on." My voice was barely above a whisper.

"I'm sorry about all of this. With those pictures of Janie—and you—on the internet, I had no choice but to investigate your involvement."

"My only *involvement*," I stressed the word, "was agreeing to do a favor for Charlotte. She asked me to check up on the teens in Polished. I used a key to the back door, which Charlotte gave my grandmothers, to enter the store. Like Charlotte told me to. When I walked in, Hannah was being slammed into the wall by her friend Whitney. When Kirstin saw me, she started hiding something. I went to find out what, and it was Janie. I didn't bring it in there."

"Unfortunately, Whitney and Kirstin have a matching story, and it's different than yours. And Hannah says she was in the laundry room running a load of towels when you came in. She doesn't know if you brought in the drugs or not."

Fortunately, my heartbreak turned into anger. "Hannah's lying because she's afraid of Whitney. The pictures are on Hannah's account. How could she have been in the laundry room?"

"Whitney said she picked up Hannah's phone from the table and used it because her battery was dead. I have two against one. It doesn't look good for you."

I drew in a sharp breath. "You believe those high schoolers. Over me?"

"I can't have bias for a person on a criminal matter," Chief Moore said. "Taking what a friend says on face value can result in an officer being encouraged to take a leave of absence."

"Jasper's in trouble because he didn't haul me in? I was pepper sprayed. Isn't that proof I walked into a crime being committed?"

"Not if two other witnesses state it was a defensive tactic because a drug pusher wouldn't take no for an answer."

There was a light rap on the doorframe. "I have some coffee for Miss Hunter."

"I don't want it." I pulled the ends of my jacket tighter around my body. While I rationally understood the predicament Chief Moore was in, I still couldn't believe he'd accept the statements of three teenagers as truth over mine.

The night dispatcher eased into the room. "There wasn't a fresh pot, so an officer went to the trouble of having this made for you."

If it was Mitchell, I didn't want it.

"Here, no sense letting it go to waste." The night dispatcher jiggled the black thermal mug. The smell of marshmallow with a hint of cinnamon wafted to me: S'more flavor. Only three people knew it was my new favorite: my grandmothers and Ted.

I accepted the offering, rotating the cup so I could grab the handle with my right hand. My breath caught in my throat. With shaking hands, I drew the cup toward me, pressing the small picture of Mr. Incredible against my heart. I closed my eyes, allowing the warmth to seep into me. This was Ted's mug. I had cut the shape out of vinyl and slapped it on Ted's cup a few months ago, knowing he'd be irritated, as I had compared his usual police-detective stance with that of the Disney superhero. He never removed it.

A tear trickled down my cheek. This was a signal. Ted knew my predicament. Another tear followed. And even knowing all the fine points, Ted believed in my innocence.

"Don't forget the napkins." The dispatcher placed a pile in front of me. Words were scribbled on the top one.

I picked it up. In my grandmother Hope's shaky handwriting was the lyrics to the song she made up when I had reached the age when I truly understood what death meant. "When tears come for those we miss, we find a happy time to reminiscence. When you find the smiles in your heart, it'll lead you to love that darkness cannot overcome. The times when I thought it was too much to bear I'd cradle you near, repeating these words for my heart to hold dear. Our Faith is strong, Faith is sweet, our little Faith will always make our world complete."

Sobs shook my body. I rested my forehead on the desk, clutching the mug protectively to my body. The first time I had been hauled into a police station for questioning, I had been alone. In a foreign country. Scared. No one believed I was innocent. The people I thought were my friends acted like I didn't exist.

This time, the dispatcher reached out. My grandmothers sent their love. Ted delivered a heartfelt message.

They all were with me.

THREE

The room was quiet. Deathly quiet. I wasn't sure if the chief dashed out during my crying fit or was playing a game on the computer. I wasn't in the right frame of mind to answer any more questions, or proclaim my innocence nicely, so I stayed prone on the desk, hoping the chief thought I fell asleep. Carefully, I placed Ted's mug on the ground. I was annoyed, but didn't want to ruin the carpet.

Then again, maybe that wasn't a bright idea. Could an innocent woman actually sleep knowing she was about to face drug distribution charges?

"You got some major trouble here, Chief," the dispatcher said.

Chief Moore awkwardly patted my shoulder. "I better see to that. You stay put."

I wondered if that was the chief's polite way of saying I was still being questioned about my involvement in the Janie distribution. I sat up, taking in deep, steadying breaths. The longer he was gone, the better. It was time to pull myself together. I used the hem of my t-shirt to dry my face. The chief's subtle warnings went through my head. There was a limited choice on who I could, or should, ask for help. Poor Jasper was in a heap of trouble and all he did was believe the truth.

Once I was out of here and caught up on some sleep, I'd have a level head to figure out a way.

"Where are you keeping her?" Gussie Buford's voice boomed through the station.

I grinned. My friend, grandmothers' confidante, scrapbooking partner, and one of the most down-to-earth and feared women in

Eden had come to my rescue. I didn't think there were too many other "hers" the police were keeping sequestered in the station. I might not have a plan, but my grandmothers had put one in motion.

"I'm going to have to ask you to leave," Chief Moore's voice reached me before he braced himself in the doorway.

"You asked. I'm answering no." Gussie hunched down, peering at me from under the chief's outstretched arm. "How ya doing, sweetie?"

"All right."

"Your grandmothers and your neighbor, Mrs. Barlow, are watching the cops search your house. They want to make sure no one is adding any decorations to your place."

Chief Moore sat in his chair. "No one would do that."

"We didn't think you'd drag Faith in for this nonsense." Gussie squeezed herself into the metal armchair next to me.

"It wasn't nonsense. There are pictures of Faith in possession of the drug."

Gussie snorted. "And I could go take a picture right now of Mitchell in possession of it. You going to arrest him next? The boy has the bag right out in the open on his desk."

"Not for long." The chief launched himself from his chair and stalked out of the room.

I turned to face Gussie. "How are my grandmothers?"

"Not happy." Gussie patted my head. "It's not you they're mad at. Hope is furious that Randall, or should I say Chief Moore, brought you in and that he didn't call her. Cheryl didn't want her coming because she was certain Hope would've clobbered him with a cast-iron skillet."

Uh-oh. Hope was calling him "Chief." Not a good sign for him. "How did they find out?"

"Like they're not going to notice two police cars parked in your driveway."

True.

"Mrs. Barlow heard everything on her police scanner and ran

over to tell them. She listens to it like it's her favorite radio station."

"Thanks for coming. I'm sorry you were dragged out of bed so early."

"This is normal for me, though it's usually my boys I'm hightailing it to the police station for."

Chief Moore rejoined us. "All the evidence is secured."

Gussie heaved her large purse onto the desk and opened it up. "I have enough to pay the two-thousand-dollar bail. That's the usual amount for one of my boys. If it's more, I can bond her out. The boys and I are now certified bondspeople."

"Faith isn't under arrest. There were just some questions we needed her to answer."

"Then we can leave." Gussie snapped her purse shut, lumbering to her feet.

"There are still a few questions I have to ask."

"We're going to run into a different kind of trouble if she's detained any longer." A new voice entered the conversation.

A jolt went up and down my spine. I knew that slow, know-it-all rumble—homicide detective Ted Roget. My nemesis. Burr under my saddle. Major button-pusher. Pea under my mattress.

And, strangely, my best friend.

Ted stood outside the chief's office, propping his broad shoulder against the door jamb. "No further evidence has been found. We only have one piece of circumstantial evidence."

"Because there isn't any at my home or at Scrap This. I'm not involved," I said.

"Don't forget there are three witness statements," Chief Moore said. "I have enough to arrest her."

Gussie took in a deep breath. I was too stunned to do anything.

"Like I said, circumstantial at best." Ted stepped inside, voice dipping low. "Chief, I understand the bind you're in because of the accusations being made against the force, but we can't keep her indefinitely because parents are demanding it."

Chief Moore stood, palms pressing hard onto the desk, his fingers turning a chalky white.

"Detective Roget, what were my instructions early this morning?"

"I was to stay at home and not get involved in this incident so we'd maintain an appearance of impartiality."

"And you're disobeying that request."

"Even worse than being impartial, Chief, is railroading someone to appease a community. With the fire at Lake's business that spread to Clive's, the searches at Faith's home and store, and Jasper being on leave, I knew you'd be short-staffed. I figured it was my duty to help."

"I'm not finding you helpful right now, Detective."

Gussie's gaze ping-ponged between the now three men, as the night dispatcher had wandered into the hallway and took up residence in a corner.

I stood. "I'm going to end this conversation. I was in the legal field long enough to know I don't have to answer any questions. If you want to charge me, then do it. My next step will be calling an attorney." I turned to Ted. "Do you know a good defense attorney?"

"Don't have any on my contact list, but my brother knows a few." Ted unclipped his cell from his belt. "I'll text Bob and get some names."

"That's not staying out of this, Detective," Chief Moore said. "If word gets out that you're helping Faith, the residents—"

"Will run me out of town?" Ted raised his gaze heavenward and held up his hands. "Praise the Lord and pass me the collection plate, that's one miracle I'll help finance."

Gussie leaned toward me. "You know, I'm starting to like him."

So was I. More and more.

"If you're leaving, Faith," the dispatcher said, making his presence known, "I'd use the side door. There's quite a crowd out front."

Chief Moore groaned.

"I'll escort her out," Ted said.

I shook my head. "No. I don't want anyone accusing you of anything. It's bad enough they've got Chief Moore running scared.

I'll leave out the front door. I'm not slinking out of here like a criminal."

"I'm not scared," the chief corrected me. "I'm being prudent."

"Whatever you want to call it, it's made you force Jasper to take an involuntary vacation. I don't want to make anything harder for you, Ted, or anyone else in this station. I need to leave here on my own."

When I stepped outside of the station, I wished I hadn't been so hasty. A group of people holding signs walked back and forth in front of the doors.

"Cover-up!"

"Stop shielding the guilty!" A woman shook her sign toward the station.

"They're letting her go!" An enraged voice filled the air.

At six o'clock in the morning, shouldn't they be at home getting ready for work or sending kids off to school, not picketing the police station?

The crowd hurled profanities. The hostility around me was almost tangible. It rolled off the crowd. Heated words. Rage-filled faces. My breath clogged in my throat as I battled back fear.

"No surprise, the resident lawman-lover just skips out of jail." Andrew Taylor, a former big-man-on-Eden-High campus, accosted me with his roaming gaze. "Adding the chief to your list?"

Even if it went against my instinct, there were times to keep your mouth shut, and now was one. The crowd was spoiling for a fight and I refused to take the bait.

Andrew's fingers dug into my skin.

"I'm making a citizen's arrest."

"Don't touch me."

I unhooked his grip from my arm.

"This crowd needs to disperse before you all find yourselves saying 'cheese' to our booking camera." Ted positioned himself a few feet away from me.

"Just leave her alone." Charlotte ran up the stairs, using her elbows to clear out the crowd. "This is out of hand."

Who was at fault for that? I glared at her. Never again would I do her a favor.

"She sold drugs to your kid," Andrew said. "Why are you defending her?"

"I confiscated it. I wasn't selling it," I said.

"Are you blaming those poor girls?"

"Let's leave. I'll take you home." Charlotte tried shooing me down the stairs.

I ignored her. I didn't want hate directed at Hannah, but I wouldn't stand by and take the blame for someone else's crime. The first time I said nothing when I was accused of a felony, I was put into jail while my then-husband Adam was free, laying the groundwork to try and prove I'd committed his crime.

"I'm not saying they're selling it, but they are the ones who brought it into Polished. Not me."

"Remain silent, Faith," Ted muttered behind me.

"We should believe you over them?" someone shouted.

"Yes," I fired back.

The crowd took in a collected breath, releasing it out in one angry hiss.

"You don't think we know you were married to a murderer?" Andrew taunted me.

I was positive the news had gone around town about three minutes after Steve and I'd returned from a crop in May. Mrs. Barlow had researched the situation to find out why I—and more intriguing, my grandmother Cheryl—didn't look so adoringly at Steve anymore. "Doesn't mean I'm a liar," I said.

"You two are in this together." Andrew jabbed a finger toward me then Charlotte. "She's trying to confuse everyone by first blaming Faith, and then coming to stick up for her."

The crowd pushed in on us, shouting profanities and threats at Ted, who maneuvered himself in front of us.

"Go into the station, Faith." Ted eased in front of me. "We understand the community has some concerns, but behaving like this isn't helping anything."

"Neither is letting her go. Coach Rutherford told us the superintendent suspended all the players," Andrew said.

"What?" Ted looked at him in confusion.

"That fire last night took out the flower shop," Andrew said. "The fire chief said it was caused by the carelessness of the teens, and he found a bag of Janie there."

So that's what the picketing was really about. The team got wrapped into this issue and now couldn't play. The forfeit ruined their perfect record, and depending on the length of the suspension, could ruin their chances of becoming division champs for the third straight year. Eden had three claims to fame: my sleuthing, an assistant prosecutor having a murderer as a relative, and state football championships. And only one of those items benefitted the town in a positive way.

"The police have nothing to do with the decision the superintendent made," Ted said.

"It's not fair. The team is suspended and nothing is happening to her because she's slept with an assistant prosecutor and now you," Andrew said.

"I'm not sleeping with anybody," I defended my honor.

"You need to go home, Andrew." Steve Davis materialized out of the crowd, placing one foot on a stair, the other on the sidewalk. He leaned forward, arm resting on his knee. "Right now, without uttering one more word against, or to, Faith."

Even from ten feet away, I saw the anger burning in his eyes. Steve was a calm guy. I couldn't recall a time when I saw him enraged, but everyone had their Hulk moment, and I had a feeling Steve was approaching his.

"You ain't my boss," Andrew said.

"But I'm the man who holds all the power over you hearing the game tonight," Steve said. "You insult my girl one more time, I quit."

I bit my lip. Now wasn't the time to force Steve to accept the fact I wasn't his girl anymore.

"Come on, Andrew, leave her alone," a man in the crowd said.

"Good call, Davis," Ted said.

"Do you want Clive or Principal Hanover taking over again?" Steve asked. "You know what a fiasco it was the last time one of them called the football game."

"But there's no game," Andrew said. "That's what Coach Rutherford told us."

"He's mistaken," Steve said.

"You calling him a liar?" With clenched fists, Andrew approached Steve.

"No, he's just not a lawyer. I know the law. He doesn't, and neither does the superintendent," Steve said.

A hopeful smile broke across Andrew's face. "No suspensions?"

"No grounds for it," Steve said. "You can't go making up rules or changing them because you suspect something and want it stopped."

The crowd dispersed. Andrew even muttered an almost-sincere apology to me.

"Faith, I need to talk to you." Charlotte rested a shaking hand on my arm, tears filling her blue eyes.

"I'd rather you didn't."

Steve wrapped an arm around my waist and led me away from the police station. At that moment, I didn't care where he planned on taking me, as long as it was away from Charlotte. I needed sleep and a renewal of my patience before I said what I was thinking.

I shivered. The early morning air held a tinge of the coming coldness as spring left for the coming fall. Steve slipped out of his suit jacket and draped it around my shoulders.

"Are you going to get into trouble?" I pulled the coat closed, hoping to ward off some of the chill from my upper body. Until I exchanged my shorts for pants, my legs were out of luck.

"For what? Walking you to my truck so I can take you home?" He grinned at me.

I didn't want him to pacify me; I wanted the unvarnished truth. I used to love how nothing frazzled Steve, but now I knew it was because he was a great pretender. Feelings were something he locked up tighter even than I did. I was working on being more of a free spirit, or at least taking my heart out of the closet, not quite up to wearing it on my sleeve yet.

"You know what I mean. For coming to the station and taking up for me. I'm sure your boss won't be thrilled with it."

"No," Steve admitted. "But I don't care. They're making a mistake and riling up the town by taking a small piece of evidence and acting like it establishes a complete case. It won't hold up in court...if you have a good defense attorney."

I slammed to a stop, grabbing hold of Steve's arm. "They're going to arrest me? Because of that photo?"

"If the county prosecutor gets her way, yes. She wants to make a grand gesture showing she's taking a firm stance against the drugs and the rising crime rate. It's the only hard evidence we have linking the drugs to someone."

"So I'm turned into the poster girl of the criminals getting their comeuppance."

"Unfortunately, yes."

"Running to my aid puts your job in jeopardy. I don't want you doing that."

That had been my original concern when I realized Steve wanted to date me. I feared my past—having married a murderer and briefly been in jail for having committed his crime—would ruin Steve's chances of moving up in the legal field. I knew Steve had ambitions beyond being an Eden county assistant prosecutor.

"I owe it to you, Faith."

Anger churned through me, warming my blood and chasing away the cold. "You don't owe me."

"Yes, I do." Pain flashed across his face.

The guilt Steve felt, and the responsibility he took for what Adam had done, was what I refused to live with for the rest of my—our—life. I was more upset about that than the fact that Steve had kept a secret from me. I could eventually get over the information withholding, but having Adam's ghost hovering around was a deal breaker. I needed the man out of my life. He had resided in my heart and head too many years after we were divorced.

"No. His sins aren't yours. I don't want you getting fired because—"

"I can't win with you, can I?" Steve ran his hand over his shaved head. "A man stands up for the woman he loves. He puts her first."

"If it's for me, fine. But if it's because you want to make up for what Adam did to me, no."

"That makes no sense." Steve paced back and forth on the sidewalk.

"It makes Adam the deciding factor in our relationship. Not me. Not you." I took in a deep breath. Now was the time to make sure Steve was clear on what I meant. We were over. "Steve, it isn't going—"

A large truck pulled to a stop beside me. The engine revved, sounding like a psychotic cat readying to attack. I recognized those red, white, and blue rims. Charlotte.

She rolled down the window. "Please, Faith, I need to talk to you. Explain everything."

"It's easy to understand. You and Hannah lied to the police."

"It wasn't the first time," Charlotte said.

I gaped at her.

"I don't want to hear this." Steve headed down the block.

I wasn't sure if he meant what Charlotte was talking about or the statement I'd started. Yet again Steve found a way to stop our inevitable conversation. "Steve, we need..."

"I know. Saturday night, dinner, at a nice quiet place."

"Faith? Please?" Charlotte's beseeching voice was getting to me. Along with my curiosity. I felt the warmth from her heater. "I have coffee and cinnamon rolls."

After my run-in with the hoodlums last night, I went straight to bed, skipping dinner. My stomach was begging for some food. "Fine. I'll hear you out, but it doesn't mean I've forgiven you."

I climbed into the truck then took a sip of coffee. Black. No sugar. No milk. I should've clarified what type of coffee before I agreed to the tête-à-tête.

Charlotte pulled away from the curb. "I'm sorry. The officer that spoke to us, some intense guy named Mitchell, had already talked to Whitney and Kirstin before coming to us. Coach Rutherford had called him and said you tried selling drugs to the girls. Hannah and I were shocked."

"Why didn't you clear it up?"

"He had a picture from Hannah's Instagram showing you giving one of the girls the bag of Janie. It threw us off balance. He said since Hannah took the pictures to document the crime and posted them, it proved she wanted to let everyone know the truth. The other girls said Hannah was the hero. All I kept thinking was if Hannah disagreed, she'd be in trouble. I didn't want my little girl going to jail. Whitney Rutherford is considered pure and good in this town."

I remembered the flash going off, right in my face. Whitney had Hannah's phone and took the picture. The situation grew less and less fuzzy. Coach Rutherford had rounded up the people to block me from leaving the police station.

"Why did Hannah post the first picture? Why not just call you or the police when the drug was brought into the store?"

"Hannah knew she needed evidence to prove Whitney bought the drugs. No one would believe her over Whitney."

"Chief Moore would've. And Ted and Steve. I would. I do."

"Maybe. Maybe not." Charlotte turned onto my street. "Whitney is the daughter of the town golden boy. Hannah is the daughter of a criminal. I was run out of our last town."

"You set a garbage can on fire. On the scale of crimes, it ranks pretty low."

"True. But that was arrest number three."

"The first time doesn't count. The guy deserved to be hit."

"It's the extortion rumor that bothered everyone."

"Extortion?" I coughed out the word, and the coffee I'd just sipped.

"Yes. The police didn't believe that the owner of the biggest car dealership in town was trying to sleep with my daughter."

I sat with my mouth wide open.

"So I snuck into his office and swiped his phone. There were a few pictures of him and Hannah at his house. They were having a nice PG-13 time in his pool. I told him he had two choices: jail, or give me enough money to move Hannah out of town."

"I'm surprised killing him wasn't one of the options you offered."

"Hannah needed me. Her dad isn't much of a winner, and I didn't think the police would understand me murdering the man when they refused to believe he was dating her. And as he told me, Hannah was sixteen, the legal age of consent in West Virginia. I told him a sixteen-year-old girl and a forty-three-year-old man would never be legal in my mind." She released a shaky breath.

I rubbed her back. "I'm so sorry, Charlotte."

"Hannah is always looking for a father figure. I wish I'd picked a better man to father my child, but then I wouldn't have Hannah."

I'd been in jail for a crime I didn't commit, and I wasn't going to duplicate that time of my life. And I'd also refuse to allow a browbeaten confused teenage girl to go to jail either. "I'm not selling drugs, and you and Hannah aren't selling drugs, so our only course of action—"

"Is finding the person who is," Charlotte finished my sentence for me. "You're the expert. Tell me what I need to do."

FOUR

I slid out of Charlotte's truck, patting the pocket of my jacket. Scrap it all. I forgot my keys. I wasn't sure if I wanted to hope the police had locked up, thereby keeping out nosy neighbors, or had left my home unsecured so I could go inside without bothering my grandmothers. They'd want to know I was home, but I didn't want them knowing I was up to something.

My contemplation lasted only a few seconds. My grandmother Cheryl opened the front door, shouting over her shoulder, "Faith's home."

Making a plan was going on the backburner.

Charlotte nodded at me, hoisting herself back into her truck. "I'll talk to you later. I have to head home and get Hannah to school this morning. I'd rather she avoid her usual morning ride."

I made a mental note to ask Charlotte which one of the two girls at Polished last night usually took Hannah to school. Chances were that girl was Hannah's closest friend and someone Hannah perhaps colluded with to bring Whitney down.

I hugged Cheryl.

She clasped me close, squishing out all the breath in my lungs. "We were so worried. We wanted to go, but thought it was best to watch your home and keep an eye on what those officers were doing. Heather videotaped all of it."

"I'll tell Mrs. Barlow thanks later." I stepped inside, the smell of sausage gravy and biscuits making my stomach rumble.

"You can tell her now." Cheryl pointed toward the dining room I'd converted into scrapbooking central.

Mrs. Barlow, my across-the-street neighbor and announcer of any and all secrets known, was hunched over the table, the tip of her tongue sticking out. She arranged and rearranged a grouping of pictures. Beside her right elbow was a plethora of choices of my cardstock, ranging from peacock blue to alabaster white. She picked up the top sheet, regular blue, and laid it next to the photos. Shaking her head, she shoved it to the side and plucked off the next choice.

"She's working on a scrapbook album," Cheryl said, a hint of pride in her voice. "Her first one."

I was shocked. Every Friday for the last nine months, Mrs. Barlow came into the store and purchased two pieces of white cardstock. I had anticipated the day when she'd change it up and buy a different color, never expecting her to actually have pictures she wanted to scrapbook. And I'd definitely never expected to see her use my personal cropping space.

"Breakfast is almost done," Hope called out from the kitchen.

"How is she?" I asked, linking my arm with Cheryl's. I figured not so good since Hope was hiding out in the kitchen. She hated me seeing her enraged. Distraught, yes. Disappointed, yes. Worried, yes. On the verge of harming someone, or at least wishing to, no. Grandma Hope found that emotion very unchristian-like and strived to always be the best example for me.

"She broke her date with Chief Moore tonight. It'll be Hope and me again, like old times. He'll have to attend the football game by himself."

"It's not his fault." Not really. He did go a little overboard, and I thought he should've told Felicity Sullivan to take a long walk across the Appalachian Trail, but the man did have the county to answer to. If it was anyone else besides my grandmothers, I'd have been furious if the chief just took their word.

Mrs. Barlow released a loud, long-suffering sigh. She cupped her chin in her hands, glanced over at us, heaving out another woe-is-me exhalation.

"I'll see to that." I tilted my head in Mrs. Barlow's direction.

Cheryl smiled. "I'll go set the table and tell Hope you're right as rain."

"I appreciate you being there for my grandmas this morning," I said as I approached Mrs. Barlow.

"Wouldn't think of doing anything else." Mrs. Barlow held up a stack of photos. "Can you give me a hand? I'm not real sure what I should do. It's so complicated."

"The first layout is always the hardest." I took the pictures, layout ideas already swirling in my head. Mrs. Barlow was a classic kind of woman with a touch of sassiness. Pattern paper with chevrons in distressed primary colors would mix well with neutrals, giving her album a cohesive look. She loved to garden, so flowers with a touch of glitter accents would be a nice complement, adding in some touches of her personality to the pages.

As I flipped through the pictures, my brow furrowed. Flowers might not be the best choice for embellishments as the pictures featured nothing but flowers, in large tubes and vases.

Why in the world was Mrs. Barlow scrapbooking the inventory of Lake's florist shop?

"Lake wants to document her store and knows I shop at Scrap This. She asked if I could make some layouts for her. Her flower shop burned practically to the ground last night, and she'd like to have something pretty to look at rather than just a stack of pictures." Mrs. Barlow blushed. "I told her I was a wonderful scrapbook artist. Truth is I don't know a thing about it."

I was certain Mrs. Barlow also wanted the fresh gossip straight from the source. The fire had happened last night, so Lake must have visited her friend bright and early this morning in the cover of darkness.

"We have a paper line at the store that will showcase these photos beautifully."

"Wonderful." Mrs. Barlow drew the front of her shirt away from her chest and stuck her hand inside. After rummaging around, she drew out three fifty dollar bills. "Buy whatever you think will look nice. Don't worry about putting the pages in a book. Just put them in the page protectors and I'll take them to Lake that way. Do you think you can have the pages done by Tuesday?"

When had I agreed to scrapbook the pictures for her?

"Lake plans on dropping off more pictures this afternoon. I'll just bring them over before I go to the game. You'll be home?"

"Yes. I don't have any plans." But maybe I should. The game would be a good place to talk to the girls that were at Polished last night and possibly get some ideas on who was supplying the teens of Eden with Janie.

The problem with the plan was the cheerleaders would be cheering; not the right time to have a little chat with them. And there was the problem of Coach Rutherford being there. I was sure he wouldn't be too keen on me chatting with his daughter.

What about this morning? The students were just arriving. I had a better chance of Coach Rutherford not being in the student parking lot than him not being at the game. Step one in proving I wasn't a drug dealer was about to commence.

I parked in a visitor's spot at Eden High School. Students hustled from the parking lot toward the door, attempting to beat the impending bell. Walking toward the glass front doors, I scanned the crowd, trying to pick out Hannah. I preferred to get information out of her first. A few gazes shifted my way, though most of the kids were caught up in their phones and conversations.

A large group of cheerleaders were gossiping near the doors. The snippet I heard stopped me in my tracks. I hid behind a large column, wanting to eavesdrop a little more before I asked any questions.

I might get my answers without having to say a word. Just in case the universe was working with me, I pulled out my cell phone to record the conversation.

"I wonder if the police will talk to Whitney," a girl said, tapping on her cell phone. "I heard she was the one buying."

"She told the Scrap This girl to come over to Polished?"

"Someone called her. We all know no one does anything when Whitney's around that she hasn't approved."

"I'd drop it." The tallest girl in the bunch jerked her head toward the student parking lot. Whitney was approaching the group, a scowl on her face.

"The picture Hannah posted went viral. I hope Whitney doesn't get kicked off the team for being there. The school handbook says no drugs." The lilt in a cheerleader's voice told me that was exactly what she hoped would happen.

Whitney stomped up to her entourage, blond hair in a ponytail, perfect curls dancing down her back. "Has anyone seen Kirstin or Hannah this morning?"

"No," the cheerleaders answered in unison, averting their gazes to the cell phones in their hands.

"Did any of you pass on the photos Hannah took last night?" Whitney planted her hands on her hips and glared at the girls.

"Don't know why you're worried. We all know it's not your fault," a petite redhead said.

A couple of the girls giggled. Whitney shot them a scathing look and the merriment ended. "It isn't. Hannah was the one being all snap happy with her phone."

"There's Kirstin." The redhead pointed out a teen slipping out of a rusty red compact car.

"Interesting." Whitney tapped her cell against her chin. "Hannah's not with her this morning. I guess Charlotte shut that friendship down." Whitney started toward her.

A young man in a wheelchair moved into Whitney's path, a determined look on his face. He gripped the rim of his wheels, making small corrections to match every sidestep Whitney made. The pair made eye contact. He shook his head, raising his left hand toward his mouth like he was holding a cigarette.

I quickly snapped a photo. I was certain the kid was Brandon Sullivan. Why was he making that gesture?

"I'll talk to her later." Whitney about-faced, snapping her fingers in the air. "Let's go."

The cheerleaders turned as one unit and entered the school, singing and chanting praises to the football team.

My sleuthing gene kicked into high gear at Whitney's reaction. Was his gesture a veiled accusation that Whitney had something to do with his car accident? The scuttlebutt around town was that Brandon had smoked Janie right before the wreck that paralyzed him. Brandon denied it, and as nothing was found in his system, no charges were filed against him. Of course, the synthetic drug wouldn't have shown up. Felicity was certain something besides fatigue had caused her son to fall asleep at the wheel.

Brandon wheeled into the school.

Kirstin's attention was on her phone. Perfect. I hurried into the lot, stepped into her path, and planted myself firmly, bracing for impact.

She smacked right into me. The cell tumbled to the ground. She leaned down and picked up her phone, checking the screen to make sure it wasn't cracked. "Sorry. Good thing I bought this case."

"Why did you lie about me?"

After opening and closing her mouth a few times she muttered, "I didn't."

"The police told me they had witnesses saying I arrived with the drugs."

She shoved her phone into her back pocket. "I don't have anything to say to you."

"Whitney and Hannah aren't going to save you when the truth comes out. And it will."

"Says you."

I took hold of her arm, stopping her from running into the school.

"Once the police look at the timestamp of when that picture was posted and when I set the alarm for Scrap This, they'll know the drug was already there when I went into Polished."

"Let me go," Kirstin whispered, not putting up a real struggle.

I wasn't sure if she wanted me to force the truth out of her or didn't want any attention directed her way for some other reason.

"I don't care who brought the drugs into the store. I want to know who sold it to one of you girls."

Kirstin heaved out a sigh. "You don't think it'll get around that I snitched?"

"People's lives are in jeopardy."

A buzz filled the air. First bell.

"What does it matter?" Kirstin's gaze darted to and fro, looking for a savior. "This will all end soon and you'll be off the hook."

"How do you know that?"

Kirstin heaved out an anxious breath, brows drawing down over her worry-filled gray eyes. "I just do. It's not like you can smuggle potpourri into your regular inventory. You guys don't sell it."

Into your inventory. Did Kirstin just let something slip? "Which store is?"

She blanched. "I don't know. How would I know?"

"You said we couldn't smuggle it into our inventory. And you're quite certain this will go away. That gives me the impression you know who is selling it."

Kirstin bit her lip, looking around nervously.

"If you know something, you have to tell the police. People's lives are being ruined. Someone could get seriously hurt."

Tears filled her eyes. "You don't understand. You don't need the Rutherfords to like you to have a job. My mom does."

"Who do you think is going to be blamed next when I'm cleared?"

Kirstin smiled. "Hannah."

"No. You. The police have your and Whitney's statement. Hannah was in the back doing laundry when the drugs were brought into the store. Remember?"

Kirstin's eyes widened, and we stared at each other for a long moment. Finally, she spoke. "If Whitney isn't at cheerleading practice or a game, you can find her at Upcycle Wear, Made With Love, or Piece A Pie."

"I didn't know Piece A Pie was still a teen hangout."

"It's not." Kirstin checked the time on her phone. "I have to go."

"How did Hannah get wrapped up into this?"

"Because Brandon almost died."

Coldness swept the back of my head. Someone was watching me. I slowly turned, trying to act casual and not like I was up to something. Principal Hanover stood right outside the front door of the school, gaze zeroed in on us. Had the final bell rung? The man had the same stern expression I remembered seeing every day when I was in high school. He had just been hired as the new principal, coming up from the elementary school. Students in my class were thrilled, assuming the principal for a bunch of babies would be a pushover for them. We hadn't thought he'd last long on the job, yet fifteen years later he was still in charge of Eden High.

Principal Hanover strode over, staring at my hand lingering on Kirstin's arm. "You're thirty seconds away from being tardy, young lady."

I placed my arms behind my back. "It's my fault. I wanted to ask her a few questions—"

Principal Hanover held out a hand. "I'm sure you do, Miss Hunter. Kirstin, go inside and pick up an excused tardy slip from the secretary."

She scampered away.

"I hope you're not trying to browbeat any of the students into changing the statements they made to the police."

"Just trying to get to the truth."

"Which from my understanding, the police already have."

"No, they don't," I said.

"I'm sure that's what you'd like everyone to believe." Hanover settled a disapproving look on me. "I'm asking you to stay away from school grounds. Parents will not be pleased to find out you were spotted here talking to the students."

"I'm not doing anything illegal."

"That will depend upon everyone's interpretation of what you were doing here. Seeking the truth, or selling drugs."

He had a point. As long as my name was in the running as Eden's drug dealer, parents would automatically think the worst of my being here, especially when I was lurking behind columns and conversing with students in parking lots.

FIVE

I couldn't get a hold of Charlotte on her cell, so I called Polished. While I waited for her to answer, I planned out my stops. Upcycle Wear. Made With Love. And even though it meant backtracking, I'd save Piece A Pie for last. I'd get there around lunch time and pick up some pizza along with information.

Charlotte finally answered. "Polished—"

"It's Faith. I have three places on the 'most likely to have sold the drugs' list. I'm heading to store number one."

"Not alone, I hope."

"It's not like I can bring along police backup or my grandmothers."

"Let me see what I can work out. What's your first stop?"

"Upcycle Wear."

"Okay, I'm going to finalize a few things and then head over."

"Is it a good idea for you to close your place?"

Charlotte let out a small bitter laugh. "I've had one visitor all morning, and all they wanted was to use my restroom."

I hung up and headed over. Upcycle was a small store in a new shopping plaza near the high school. Most of the store fronts for rent in the center remained empty, and the high traffic time was on Friday nights when there was a home game at the football stadium and the large parking lot was used for overflow parking. Eden had tried morphing itself into a business-friendly town, wooing owners to open up shops here, but it hadn't worked. Our proximity, or rather, lack of it, to the interstate hadn't brought in droves of entrepreneurs like the town council thought.

Like usual, the lot was almost empty. I parked near the front door of Upcycle. The front doors were decorated with hanging clothing. Most of the apparel was little girl t-shirts turned into ruffled dresses adorned with cartoon characters. The items were cute, but I didn't have anyone in my life who fell into that age category. Maybe Ted would like one for his daughter, though I didn't know if our friendship was at the level where buying his daughter a gift wouldn't be seen as something more—like that I'd showed up at a store to snoop around.

Unfortunately, Ted knew me so well that he'd know within a second I'd been out and about trying to prove my innocence and that Upcycle was on my list.

A bell jingled as I walked into the store. The front counter was littered with fabric remnants, ribbons, and business cards of all shapes and sizes. An attractive man wearing an Eden Volunteer Fire Department t-shirt tapped a business card on the glass counter. He looked over at me. Sally, the proprietor and seamstress, was nowhere to be seen.

I walked over to a display of dresser drawer satchels. There wasn't much else I'd think a high schooler would be interested in. The small tulle bags were filled with potpourri. I picked one up, inspecting it from every angle. It was a little heavier than the ones the girls had in Polished, but I was sure the owner wouldn't have the illegal substance out on display. I sniffed it.

"She has other scents in the back room," the guy said.

"I'm just browsing right now. Thanks though." Was there a way for me to get back there?

"I'm not sure—" Sally stepped out from the back, growing silent as her gaze found me. Her skin paled and she shot a worried look at the guy.

Seconds later, the door opened and Felicity stormed in. "I should've known it was you. I called the police. They'll be here in a second."

The owner exchanged another look with the guy. He rolled his eyes and let out a huge exasperated sigh.

"Don't count on it, Felicity," the guy said.

Felicity grabbed one of the satchels from the display and dropped it into her oversized purse. "Once they test this stuff in the lab, they'll be here to lock her up."

"You have to pay for that first or you're stealing," I said.

"No, I'm not. I'm confiscating contraband items." Felicity clamped her arm against her purse.

"She can have it. Just get her out of here." Sally practically collapsed against the glass counter. "And you too. I know what you're doing here, Faith."

"I'm here to look for a present...for a little girl." I blurted out the first good reason my mind conjured up. I hoped Ted's daughter liked ruffled dresses.

"I'm not stupid. My shop is the closest to the high school. I sell potpourri." Sally picked up a newspaper and waved it around. "And the front page news story is about how the Scrap This owners' granddaughter was taken to the police station for questioning regarding the distribution of Janie."

I drew back a little. I wasn't surprised it was news; I was surprised I hadn't considered that happening. My sleep deprivation was worse than I thought.

"Daniel Burke being here is more proof." Felicity stamped her foot.

Daniel, the guy in the Fire Department t-shirt, crossed his arms, looking with sympathy at Felicity. "And why's that, Felicity?"

"Because you were at the bonfire the football team held the night of Brandon's accident. Don't think Brandon hasn't told me how often you show up."

"I was there because the owner of Made With Love asked me if I could make sure the kids put the fire out correctly. He was afraid his place would burn down. I warned him about letting the team have the after-graduation celebration behind his property, but he thought it would bring in some business. Parents being grateful."

"And did it work?" I asked.

Not that I wanted a bonfire behind our store, even if we had the proper set-up. Our "backyard" consisted of asphalt and dumpsters.

"The teens asked about holding one in the clearing behind my store since it's close to the high school," Sally said. "That's why Daniel is here. I wanted his advice."

"I don't believe either of you," Felicity said. Daniel and Sally continued with their conversation, not carrying about Felicity's opinion.

"Not a good idea," Daniel said. "The field out there gets really dry and with all of these empty buildings, it could spread quick."

"I guess my merchandise isn't something that would interest teens anyway. It's not like I'd get a bump in sales for it."

I looked around the store. Upcycle had a lot of cute clothes, most of them geared toward the preschool and elementary-school set who were in love with princesses. I examined the clothing closer. The stitching was intricate, each piece with a different pattern. "Have you thought about giving classes? Some scrappers love sewing on their pages, and you have some beautiful stitching on your pieces."

Sally smiled at me.

"That's a wonderful idea. I can whip up a sample board and some ideas for one."

"Sounds great. I'm working on some new classes for the fall. Drop it by and I'll talk to my grandmothers. I'm sure they'll go for it."

"Why are you helping her?" Felicity asked me through gritted teeth. "She's our enemy."

Our?

My confusion apparently showed on my face as Felicity rushed into an explanation. "Charlotte told me to meet you here so I'd see you weren't the one selling the drugs. You were just a victim of circumstance."

"I'm not the dealer," Sally screeched.

Daniel patted her hand. "Don't worry. Two weeks ago, she was certain it was Andrew Taylor and got him suspended from the volunteer fire squad. By tomorrow, she'll have a new choice as the town drug dealer."

"He deserved it. Norman never should've let him join. He knows his son-in-law is a drunk."

"Doesn't make him a drug dealer," Daniel said.

"He was also at the bonfires. And I know that's where those children are getting the drugs."

"Then why let Brandon attend them?" Daniel leaned against the counter.

"It was a team event. I believed he'd be protected. But no one cared about him." A tear snaked down Felicity's reddening cheeks.

"Why didn't he call the police and tell them?" I asked.

"He didn't think it was harmful," Felicity said. "And he didn't plan on ever using it."

"He changed his mind?" The anger coming from Felicity seemed to come from something deeper than just her son using the synthetic marijuana.

"No. Someone tricked him into taking it."

"What?" the three of us shouted together.

"Brandon had too much to lose if he started taking drugs. He knew he'd have scholarship offers coming in. It was his only way to go to college." More tears cascaded down her face as her whole body trembled. "We can't afford to send him."

"Who would've done that to him?" I placed an arm around her shoulders.

She shrugged.

"Are you sure?" Daniel asked. "The football team is rowdy and has gotten away with vandalism, but I don't see Coach Rutherford ignoring teammates drugging each other."

"I have it on good authority," Felicity said.

"Who?" I asked.

"My son. Brandon swears he didn't take it, but says someone did give him a cigarette that night. He was told it was just tobacco."

"Tell the police," I said.

"I have. Chief Moore doesn't believe me."

The boy, or in this case, woman, who cried wolf syndrome.

"Give him the proof," I said.

"There isn't any." Felicity's shoulders collapsed forward. "Just 'she said, she said.' And the other she has a better standing in the community."

"Which she?"

Felicity left the store without dropping a name.

Felicity sat in the passenger seat of my car as I drove to Made With Love. She was so distraught, I couldn't in good conscience leave her to drive herself home. Besides, I had a feeling she'd show up there herself. Not a good option either. I also hoped bringing Felicity with me created some trust between us, and she'd share the name. And it would be good to have her to act as a distraction while I looked around. If there was one thing Felicity had proven, she was good at disruptions.

Made With Love was located on the edge of town, near the bridge leading residents out of Eden and into Maryland. The two-thousand-square-foot two-story house was on the right side of 220 on a small incline. The house was painted a cream color with light blue shutters, holding onto its original quaint charm.

"When we get there, I'll do all the talking," I said.

"No. I have the right to confront them myself."

"And that's the problem. We don't want to confront them, we want to talk. You catch more flies with honey."

"I don't want flies. They're nuisances and have no redeeming value."

I stayed silent. She had a point, though not a very good one.

The front and side gravel parking lots were empty. Paper cups, plastic sandwich bags, and empty matchbooks littered the area. Using the tips of my index finger and thumb, I snagged a couple of the sandwich bags and tossed them into my backseat.

If these bags had contained some Janie, the police now had real evidence. I also took a few photos on my phone of the ones I left behind. I wasn't quite sure if Ted would—or even could—take my word for it.

And I was even less sure that having Felicity Sullivan as my back-up witness worked in my favor.

We walked into the store. The walls that had separated the main area into living spaces were knocked down, turning the area into a thousand square feet of retail space, most of it empty of merchandise. There was a wrought-iron spinning rack near the door with handmade scarves hanging from the hooks. Bookshelves held a few children's and recipe books, but otherwise they were bare. On the wall behind the register area were tall shelving units filled with small bottles of essential oils and organza bags filled with potpourri. The bags were similar in style to the one I saw at Polished.

With a pile of papers in front of her, Dawn Carr hunched over a granite countertop, fingers shoved into her hair.

I approached her, wanting a closer view of the fragrances.

Dawn's attention was so focused, she didn't hear us come in or Felicity's heavy stomping. The papers were for an insurance policy for the store. I should ask my grandmothers where we kept ours. It was another part of the business I didn't know anything about, and while I hoped we'd never use it, I should know where it was for safekeeping.

"May I see one of the bags of fragrances?" I asked.

"Sure," Dawn said, without taking her gaze off the paperwork. She plucked a bag from the rack and handed it over.

The scent of roses and lemon wafted toward me. Tiny bits of lemon peel were in the bag, along with rose petals. This type of potpourri wasn't ground as much as Janie. The organza was a pale blue, the texture the same as the Janie satchel.

"What are you doing?"

A furious Chad Carr snatched the pouch out of my hand. His tattered jeans hung low on his skinny frame, and his Eden High School t-shirt was two sizes too large for his lanky frame.

"Shopping," I said.

Where had Felicity wandered off to? I didn't see her in the main part of the building.

Dawn gathered up the papers, shoving them into a cardboard box. "Honey, Faith isn't doing anything wrong."

"She's playing Miss Innocent." Chad grabbed my arm. "I want her out of here."

"Why? Are you hiding something?" Felicity wandered over with a blinged-out lighter in one hand and something similar to an electronic cigarette in the other. "Do you just add the potpourri mix into this contraption and light it?"

"Why don't you ask your son?" Chad sneered at her. "I'm not stupid. You two are here to blame me for his accident. I already told you I didn't give your kid anything."

"I know it's you." Felicity threw the vaporizer at Chad's head. He easily swatted it away. "Brandon attended your bonfire—"

"It wasn't my bonfire, you psychopath," Chad said. "It was the football team's party. I just supplied the venue."

"And the refreshments. Including the Janie," Felicity said.

"Take your crazy friend out of here before my wife calls the cops." Chad motioned for her to pick up the phone.

"Come on, let's go home." I took hold of Felicity's shoulders, steering her toward the door. "We're not going to get any answers."

"No." Felicity weaved away from my control. "He hurt my son. I won't let him hurt another child."

"I didn't hurt your kid," Chad said. "He hurt himself."

"You're a liar. A drug dealer. A dream crusher. A life stealer." The open lighter shook in her hand like she was driving over a mile-long stretch of potholes. She clamped her teeth together, breaths hissing out of her.

Chad looked more amused than stricken by the list of insults Felicity heaved at him. His smile enraged Felicity further. She rubbed her thumb viciously over the steel roller. I was close enough to hear it click. No flame. I exhaled in relief, hoping it was either broken or, better yet, out of fuel.

"My son's life is ruined because of you." Felicity held the

business end of the lighter at Chad. "He almost died. He's paralyzed. Lost his scholarship. Won't be able to go to college. He could've been in the NFL, and now he won't ever leave Eden. You. Ruined. His. Life."

Chad pursed his lips and mimicked the sound of chopper blades. "Maybe if you worked instead of helicoptering over the kid, he could've gone to college."

Felicity brought the lighter to life, moving it toward the scarves. "How dare you blame me."

Crop it all. I should've made her stay in the car. Heck, I should've left her at Upcycle Wear and let the police deal with her. Why in the world was Charlotte out to get me? I didn't need an unstable mother tagging along.

"You're blaming me." Chad fisted his hand and swung at Felicity.

I snagged her around the waist and twisted. Unfortunately for me, I reacted at the same time as Chad and received a sharp smack to the back of my head. My face slammed into the back of Felicity's skull. The lighter clattered to the floor. I released Felicity and spun around.

"Chad, leave them alone." Dawn pushed herself into our melee, dragging Chad away.

Chad blinked a few times. "That was on her. She got in the way."

"You think it would've been better if you hit Felicity?" I gently rubbed the sore spot on the back of my head.

"I was defending myself and our store. She threatened to set the place on fire."

"You're an evil, vile man." Felicity's hands were hooked into talons. If she was a few steps closer, she'd be able to rip out his eyes and heart.

Chad raked a look of superiority over Felicity. "Just call me Satan."

"Oh my God." Dawn paled, hands cupped around her mouth.

I smelled smoke.

Chad cursed, running for the area marked restroom. "The scarves are on fire."

A small flame leapt from one scarf to another, the silk ones quickly catching on fire while the wool smoked. I toppled the display over and stomped on the blaze, while Felicity turned into a frozen statue. Dawn hightailed it over, brandishing a broom above her head.

Between my jumping and her swatting, we had the fire almost out when Chad heaved a bucket of water onto us and the scarves. "Where's your fire extinguisher?"

"Not working," Chad said.

"I didn't mean for that to happen," Felicity said.

"Right." Chad took the broom from his wife and shoved the sodden strips of wool toward the door. "Just leave before I call the cops."

"Why don't you?" Felicity crossed her arms and smiled smugly. "I'd love for them to come by and check this place out."

And I'd rather not be there when they arrived. This situation wouldn't bode well for me.

"We're leaving." I hooked my arm through Felicity's and forcibly dragged her out.

"But...but..." Felicity's anger took away her ability to speak.

"We're not going to find out anything now," I said.

"So we're back where we started." The look Felicity fixed on me sent a chill through my body. I was back to being the villain.

Felicity's grieving heart desired someone else to blame rather than face the fact that Brandon likely created his own nightmare. Someone in this town knew the truth. I just had to find the right mix of indignation, barely contained anger, and nervousness to get the gossip started. The majority of the town attended the high school games, so that was where I'd go for answers.

SIX

I spent the remainder of the afternoon at Scrap This having a very uneventful and boring day. Our business was below a trickle. My grandmothers had assured me, while giving me the evil eye, that it had nothing to do with my "visit" to the police station. They figured out I'd spent the morning investigating, not resting, and not even one teeny-tiny, glitter-sized piece of happiness was in them. They were certain one day I'd antagonize Ted into arresting me for my own good.

If they spotted me at the game, they might request he do it tonight. Of course, at the speed I was driving now, the game would be over when I arrived.

The traffic sloughed toward the high school like a snake stuck in deep mud. I craned my neck, looking for an accident or anything else responsible for the holdup. No one was honking or sending gestures toward other cars. The southbound lane was free, and every once in a while a car drove past. I had always assumed everyone went to the home games as nothing else happened on a Friday night, and today I found out my guess was correct.

The drivers in front of me started parallel parking along the street. Great. All the parking spots at the high school and across the street at the shopping plaza were taken. It was going to be a little bit of a hike to the high school stadium. Sighing in complete drama queen fashion, I followed suit, easing toward the curb. A car zipped in front of me, taking my "parking space."

"Idiot." I showed much restraint by not adding a gesture to the label. In my rearview mirror, I noticed a beat-up, rusted muscle car trying to pull up behind the spot stealer.

"Oh no you don't." I quickly backed up, wedging my Malibu into the slot, the front end of my car sticking out. It wasn't the best job I've ever done, but there was no way I was going to drive down the road to turn around.

The other driver flipped me off and pulled back a few feet. After they parked, I'd straighten my car so I wasn't creating a hazard. I pulled out a bit, not wanting some other driver to swipe my spot, then inched my car back. Nope, not quite. I tried again. Same result. I'd parallel parked before; why couldn't I get it right this time?

A steady honk accompanied every movement of my car. The drivers behind me were getting restless.

"I'm trying. I'm trying." Looking over my shoulder, I started the process over again.

Someone rapped on the window, startling me. My foot slipped from the brake, and I bumped the curb. The evening was just getting better and better.

Daniel Burke motioned for me to roll down the window.

"Is something wrong?" I shoved the gear shift into park, hoping the fire department wasn't called because someone believed an emergency caused the holdup.

"You're stopping people from getting to the game."

"I'm having a little trouble parking." I smiled. "I'll get it this time."

Daniel glanced back again. I followed his gaze. Numerous people stood beside their cars, and none looked happy.

"How about I park it for you?"

I hated being treated like a damsel in distress, but everyone looked ready to run me out of town if I wasted any more time. I hopped out of the car. "Give it a go."

I felt a little vindicated when it took Daniel three times to get the vehicle into the spot. For some reason, no one honked at him.

"There you go." He deposited the keys into my hands.

"Thanks." I took my camera bag out then locked the door. Holding the bag over my head, I wiggled between my car and the one in front of it. I thought it better than walking down the long line of cars parked on the side of the road.

Daniel placed one hand on the hood of my car then vaulted over it. "I'll walk with you."

"Don't you need to park?"

"I already did. I heard a call come through about there being a drunk, or a bad driver, blocking traffic, and I said I'd check it out."

"I'm surprised a police officer didn't show up."

Daniel grinned. "Once the description of the car and license plate came through, Detective Roget started grumbling, so I offered to help you out."

"Just what did he grumble?"

Daniel's grin broadened. "You can ask the detective."

There were some things I'd rather not know. "Thanks for coming to my rescue."

"Anytime." Daniel held out his arm, blocking me from the road, looking both ways before beckoning me to follow him.

I huffed and puffed up the hill leading to the high school. The place was packed. The scent of hot dogs and hamburgers filled the air, reminding me I'd skipped dinner. When we reached the school parking lot, I saw a large section of choice spots were blocked off with rope and traffic cones.

"Shouldn't someone be manning the handicapped parking?" I asked. "It might be difficult for the driver to get out and remove the blockade."

"Those spaces are reserved for Coach Rutherford's family. There's a section right at the front gate for handicapped parking."

Apparently having a quarterback son and coaching for the division-winning team came with a lot of perks.

We paid for our tickets and went inside. Most of the spots on the bleachers were full. I knew my grandmothers would make room for me, but I hadn't told them I was attending and didn't want them to know. The moment they spotted me, they'd know I came here for a reason besides watching the football game. As we walked, I noticed a roped-off section in the best viewing spot.

"Those for Coach Rutherford's family?"

"Yep. They don't like having to fight the traffic so the reserved seats give them the option to arrive just before the game starts."

"I hope I can find a place."

"Want to sit with me?" Daniel asked.

"No, that's okay. I'm going to wander around and check everything out. I've never been to a game before."

"Have fun." Daniel climbed up the metal steps.

I headed for the area near where the football players entered the field. Eden High School cheerleaders were standing there holding a large hoop covered with butcher paper. Whitney ordered the other girls into the proper positions, switching two of them around. I placed my bag on the ground and took out my camera. Since I was here, I might as well document the event. Sometimes the local paper ran contests for photos taken by citizens, and since this was the first football game I was attending, I wanted to document it in my scrapbooks.

The steel bleachers were filled. Latecomers would have a hard time finding a spot amongst the masses of bodies. One side of the stadium looked like a sea of black and gold, while the other was filled with blue and white. Spectators shook mini pom-poms on sticks, and a few had homemade signs raised. A battle using printed words. I snapped a couple of photos of the crowd and the decorations on the Eden side of the field. I wanted to duplicate some of them in Scrap This and have them up for Homecoming in a few weeks. My grandmothers usually handled the decorations for town events, but I should step up and stop pretending football didn't exist.

I was also ashamed that I had never known about Steve's role as announcer. When I thought about it, there were a lot of things about Steve's life I didn't know. That should've been a big clue to me about our relationship. I never asked, and he never mentioned anything. If I'd thought about it, instead of being relieved I didn't have to reveal my "secret" to him, I'd have come to the conclusion long ago that Steve also had something huge he was withholding. No sense ruminating on the past. It never worked for me before and just meant I was once again spending more time there than in the here and now.

I focused my lens on the cheerleaders standing in front of the cement foundation for the bleachers. Their skirts billowed in the wind. Bright smiles lit up their faces, highlighting not only the teenagers maturing into adults, but also the childlike innocence still left. Using her arms, Whitney made broad arc motions in the air. Four of the girls held up the large sign hanging from the silver hoop, while the other eight girls stood, four on each side, and shook their pom-poms. The gold and black vinyl strips whipped back and forth. I took some shots.

A drumroll began. Hooting and hollering, the cheerleaders shook their pom-poms and stomped their feet. A boo came from the other side of the field. I heard the crowd behind me rise, and soon after, feet stomped on the bleachers. I kept my camera trained on the paper-covered hoop.

Masculine voices joined the cheerleaders in yelling chants. A few uniformed players left the small covered entranceway between the bleachers while the rest remained in the darkness. The sound grew louder. The stomping increased. The metal of the bleachers clanged, making me fear the whole structure might collapse into a million pieces, even though Eden had spent a fortune to build the stadium a few years ago.

Coach Rutherford and the team ran through the hoop covered in butcher paper.

Steve's voice filled the air. "Eden High School has taken the field."

A shiver danced down my spine. I'd always found Steve's voice sexy, and that feeling was still strong. There was just something about his particular mix of West Virginia twang and sophisticated lawyer that got me every time.

"Eden won the toss and will receive."

The game started, and I tried keeping my attention on it, but nothing made much sense. One team went after the other team who had the football. Bodies fell on top of each other. I wasn't sure if all of the shoving and smacks were a true part of the game, or sneaky ways of getting back at the rival team.

A large heavily padded player wrapped his arms around a smaller player wearing the black and gold uniform, crashing them both to the ground. I squeezed my eyes shut, wincing. Why in the world would parents allow their sons to play football? Seemed violent to me.

Says the woman who involves herself in murders. I guess everyone had a less-than-safe activity they engaged in.

While I waited for a break in the game, I scanned the crowd. Nearly everyone in Eden was in attendance; I thought it might be interesting to see who wasn't here. I switched to my zoom lens and moved the focus back and forth across the crowd. My grandmothers were seated in the middle, wearing black and gold garb from the top of their heads to, I suspected, their feet. I doubted they'd don black and gold-brimmed straw hats and black shirts with Eden written in gold glitter across their chests only to put on just any old pair of shoes. They waved pom-poms in the air. Chief Moore sat a few people down from Hope, a wistful expression on his face. Poor guy. I hoped my grandmother forgave him soon. My grandfather had died eleven years ago, and I was happy to see Hope might have found someone to share the rest of her life with. I know Grandpa Tom would want that for her.

Chad was talking to someone standing in the shadows between the sets of bleachers. He gestured wildly, almost striking the other person in the face while they stood calmly. I took a few shots, then snuck my way over to the duo. People didn't conduct meetings in alleyways unless they were up to something. And what better place to hand off illegal drugs to kids than at a football game, where most people's attention was on the field?

I flattened myself against the wall, hoping I blended into the gloom.

Chad accepted something from the man, taking a few tries before he successfully shoved it into his back pocket. "People are looking, but it's perfect timing."

The man in the shadows nodded.

"Has to be tonight."

A roar echoed in the gangway.

Chad's gaze flicked in my direction. I held my breath. He weaved his head back and forth.

Rocks skittered behind me. Both men turned and exited from the side closest to the restrooms, away from me. I released the air in my lungs and turned. Brandon Sullivan was struggling with his wheelchair on the gravel.

"Need some help?" I rested my camera on my chest, the strap tugging at my neck.

"I got it." He jerked forward, knuckles turning white as he gripped the rims of the wheels tighter.

Heat flashed across my face. He was probably tired of people walking up and doing things for him, implying that simple tasks were beyond his ability. "Sorry."

"Kind of a bad day for me. No need to take it out on you." He wheeled away.

I'm sure it was. Instead of being the star quarterback, he was on the sidelines in a wheelchair because of an accident everyone assumed he'd caused.

I ran after him. "Can I ask you a question?"

His gaze skittered around the stadium. "I don't think that's a good idea."

"Your mom said you attended the bonfires and that's where the kids are getting the drugs. Who sold it?"

Brandon turned his chair to face me. "I don't know."

"You didn't see anything?"

"Sometimes it's best not to see or hear things. I never touched it when it was passed around."

"Were other kids smoking it around you? Maybe someone gave it to you and told you it was a cigarette?"

"I don't know what you're trying to prove, but the help's not coming from me." Brandon spun his chair and wheeled toward the concession stand, where I saw Hannah waiting for him.

My foot almost slid out from under me. I had stepped on something near where Chad had stood. I picked up a business card. Using the light from my cell I took a look at it. The words Vulcan Catering were framed by wisps of curling smoke, and the edges had a distressed finish. An open grill was in the left corner. I pocketed it.

Cheers and boos shook the stadium. I wandered out of the alleyway, turning my attention to the game.

"You don't miss those," Coach Rutherford yelled.

One of the Eden players on the field shrugged.

The cheerleaders moved closer to the bleachers and formed a human pyramid. Their chants were almost loud enough to drown out the taunting and barbs being slung to and from Coach Rutherford.

I backed up a few paces to get some shots of the pyramid. The girl on the top was still just out of my viewfinder. I took a few more backward steps.

Someone careened into me, knocking me onto the field. A whistle blew. Two helmeted players were charging each other, readying for a near-the-sidelines tackle, and I had stepped between them. Placing my hands over my eyes, I screamed, knowing it was going to hurt.

A hand wrapped around my arm and dragged me backwards into a hard chest.

I was scooped up and set down on the spectator side of the football field. The whistle blew again and again. Someone was getting a time-out, and I had a feeling it was me.

"Your water guy needs to be more careful," Ted said.

"It's her own damn fault," the coach said. "Spectators shouldn't be that close to the sidelines."

"Coach, the ref is coming over here," a player said.

A very unhappy referee gestured at me.

"Keep your photographer off the field. Next time, Eden will get a penalty."

"She's not ours," Rutherford said.

"Trust me, a penalty is the least of her worries." Ted took hold of my arm. "I'll see to it that she finds a spot away from the field."

I didn't want to create any more of a scene, so I didn't argue and followed.

Ted escorted me away from the sidelines and out the front gate.

"I didn't do anything wrong, and I paid to attend the game."

Ted pulled out his wallet and handed me five dollars. "Go home and try not to stir up any more trouble."

"I wasn't."

"Please, give me a break and go home."

"I was actually taking photographs."

"With no other ulterior motive for showing up at a football game? Good night, Faith." Ted stood right at the gate and watched me walk past the baseball field connected to the football field and into the parking lot.

Grumbling unflattering things about Ted under my breath, I dug my keys out of my pocket. They slipped out of my fingers, falling onto the asphalt. I leaned over to pick them up, my camera clunking against me. I'd left my camera bag near the bleachers where the football players entered the stadium.

I could either risk Ted's ire and go back into the stadium, or call Charlotte and see if Hannah could grab my bag for me. For once, I went with the better, and least likely to contribute to Ted's bad mood, choice. She answered on the first ring.

"I'm here. I'll get it for you."

"Then I'll forgive you for partnering me with Felicity."

"I was trying to help you. If Felicity had new information to go on, she'd stop ranting to the cops about you."

"I don't think it worked out for me." I ended the call, shuffling along the parking lot. The dim light made it hard to see any ruts. Crickets chirped and then stopped. I paused, squaring my shoulders and looking around me. Cheers carried over from the stadium. Steve announced the score: Eden 21, Hazard 10. I kept walking.

Coldness pricked my scalp. I glanced over my shoulder toward the ticket booth. I couldn't see anyone there, but it was possible Ted was still watching. I turned on the flashlight app on my phone. It settled my nerves. A little.

The strap of my camera dug into my chest and shoulder. Screaming, I lurched sideways as someone jerked at it, dragging me across the lot. My heart pounded. I didn't want to lose my camera, or more importantly, my life. Car lights turned on, highlighting the thief, wearing all black with a stocking cap tugged over their face.

"What's going on over there?" Karen England called out.

The person inhaled a sharp breath and pulled out a knife. I dropped to my knees, trying to shove the strap off of me. The knife arced down, cutting through it. I was freed, splayed on the ground. The person ran off with my camera.

The pounding of my heart made me lightheaded. I took in calming breaths, dusting off my hands and pushing myself up from my knees.

"You okay?" Karen helped me to my feet.

"Yeah. Thanks for saving me." I dusted myself off.

"No problem. I thought you were being assaulted."

"I was. My camera was stolen."

"We should tell Detective Roget what happened," Karen said.

"I think he has enough going on." Or rather had had enough of me. "I'll report it when I get home. There's nothing the police can do about it now."

Karen linked her arm in mine. "Let's go to my car. I'll drive you to yours."

"I prefer to walk." I tried to slide my arm from hers.

Karen pressed her arm to her side so we looked like Siamese twins. "I don't think that's wise, considering what just happened. Whoever that was might decide you have money on you."

She was right. I liked being independent and relying on no

one, but I liked being smart—and alive—even more. "Sounds like a plan."

"Good, because it's also the safest place for us to talk."

"About what?"

Karen refused to say any more until we got to her car.

The moment I buckled in, I twisted my body to face her. "Start talking."

"You don't know everything that's going on." Karen expertly pulled from the spot where she had parallel parked. I wished it was so easy for me. "And you should stop trying to dig it up."

"What are you talking about?"

"I know about your visits to Upcycle and Made With Love. If you think you're going to clear your name by tarnishing someone else's, it won't work. I won't let it."

I opened my mouth a few times, finding it hard to come up with the right words.

Karen turned onto the main road. "Where are you parked?"

"On the right side, just past the grocery store. I'm not going to let anyone railroad me into a drug charge. No matter what you threaten," I said.

"I'm not threatening you, I'm just giving you notice." Karen pulled over, keeping the engine running. "Stop dragging others into your mess."

There was something going on with Karen and I wanted to know what. She wasn't overly fond of me—or I her—but we'd never wished ill on each other. There was an intensity in Karen's eyes and a tightness in her body that told me this was personal to her.

I rifled through my memory for a family connection between Karen and the key players. Just because Karen changed her last name from Pancake to England didn't make all her family connections disappear. Change of name. Before she married Allan Sullivan, Felicity was a Pancake.

Great. I'd dragged Karen's cousin into a figurative—and literal—fire. I'd just made the woman in control of dispensing the information in Eden an even bigger enemy.

"Felicity came on her own free will. If you want to help her, find out who's selling Janie to the kids, and who gave some to Brandon."

"I'm working on the story. So stay out of my way. If you ruin this for me, I'll ruin you."

SEVEN

I rummaged in my kitchen cupboards for something sweet. I'd already tried my old standby comfort food of grilled cheese, and my mind was still stuck on driving by Made With Love or playing tit-for-tat with Karen. Being threatened made me want to delve in deeper, not back off. Fortunately, there was a sliver of common sense in my head screaming neither idea was a good one.

The sound of an engine drew me out of the kitchen and to the front window. Leaning over, I pulled the curtain back a smidge and peered outside. A truck pulled into my driveway, darkness making it hard to tell the color. A feminine figure slipped out from the driver's seat and hustled toward the front door. Charlotte.

My doorbell chimed, followed by an insistent pounding. I answered the door.

Charlotte tugged me out the door. "Come on."

I held on to the doorknob. No way was I following Charlotte blindly. "Where and why?"

"Made With Love. An impromptu midnight celebratory bonfire was announced through social media. Hannah snuck out to attend. There's a reason those kids are heading over there tonight. I want you to take pictures while I get Hannah out of there."

Chad's words haunted me. "Perfect timing. Has to be tonight." Was he getting a delivery of Janie tonight? Whatever was planned, I was sure it wasn't a good idea for unwanted guests to arrive.

"Let me grab my cell. My camera was stolen, so I'll have to use it." I ran back into the kitchen, plucking my phone off the counter. "We should probably let the police know."

"No," Charlotte said. "I don't want Hannah getting into trouble."

"If the drugs are making an appearance tonight, Hannah is already courting trouble. The police can stop it."

"Hannah will be blamed."

"Not if she didn't bring it."

"Those kids will never turn on Whitney. I know Hannah's going there to try and get proof that Whitney's involved. Hannah feels bad that her first attempt landed you in trouble."

And her second attempt might get her hurt. "Chad Carr is planning something for tonight. I'm not sure what. I only caught the end of a conversation."

"I'll take care of him." Charlotte pushed up the sleeves of her black and gold hoodie.

I was sure she would. Charlotte was the poster child for Mama Bear. She had spent some time in jail after setting her ex-husband's garbage cans on fire, and was photographed having a knock-down slap fight with a former boyfriend who'd been on *Naked and Afraid*.

From the expression on the man's face, I think he'd rather have spent another twenty-one days out in the swamps, trying not to be eaten alive by an alligator, than go up against Charlotte again. He did have it coming to him for hitting on Hannah, who'd been almost sixteen at the time. It was amazing how long pictures and stories are stored on the internet.

"It's still best if we call the police, let them know what's up," I said.

"They're monitoring social media. If they want to come, they'll come. You don't need to be a reason for them to show up."

"A reason?"

"If you're there, Detective Roget and Steve Davis will arrive to help you." A twinge of bitterness entered her voice.

"And that's a bad thing? Helping?"

"Helping you, not everyone else."

I locked my door then followed Charlotte to her truck.

"Ted and Steve wouldn't frame someone for me."

"I'm not saying that, but they'll dig until they find out the truth. And I'll go to jail again to keep Hannah out. I've done it before."

I remained quiet as Charlotte unburdened herself on the drive to Made With Love.

"Hannah started the fire at her dad's place. I lied for her."

I should've guessed last year there was something scandalous in Hannah's past to have Charlotte move in the middle of her daughter's junior year in high school. Most families would wait until graduation.

"Her dad had no problem with her visiting him whenever she wanted, until his young girlfriend moved in. She was only a few years older than Hannah. After that, Hannah had to get permission to stop by and see him, and he quit paying child support because the girlfriend convinced him I was using the money for my truck payment. The night of the fire was Hannah's birthday. Her dad was supposed to take her out to dinner. Instead, he told her he was taking out the girlfriend that night because she was feeling sad."

My mouth remained closed. The last thing I wanted to do was react in a way that silenced Charlotte.

"She was devastated and acted out. She thought they had already left when she set the cans on fire. Her dad called the police."

"If they saw Hannah set the fire, how did you get arrested for it?"

"I agreed to confess to it. The girlfriend changed her story, saying it was possible she really saw me because Hannah and I look alike from a distance. It worked out better for them. I lost my job, so we had to move. Now she wouldn't have to share any more of the deadbeat's time."

A deep blare, like a foghorn, sounded from behind us. I looked out the back window. A fire truck bore down on us. Charlotte moved to the far right, the truck whizzing past us at almost the same speed as the red swirling lights.

"You don't think..." Charlotte choked out the words, all color drained from her face.

She must think her daughter got into an accident or was responsible for a fire. I squeezed her hand. "I'm sure she's okay. It's probably another poorly planned bonfire. The team needs to find a better way to show school spirit."

After last night's uncontrolled bonfire that destroyed Lake's florist business and damaged Clive Murphy's pawn shop, Chief Moore might be able to get somewhere with Coach Rutherford and Principal Hanover to stop the tradition. And it might make it a little harder for the teens to buy the synthetic marijuana.

When we turned down the road leading to Made With Love, my breath caught in my throat. Every fire truck owned by Eden, and possibly ones from the neighboring counties, lined the road. Charlotte slowed the car, inching past the emergency vehicles and the burned timber that had once been Made With Love.

"Oh my God." Charlotte slammed the truck to a stop. "I'm going to find my daughter."

"They weren't in there." Bile snaked up my throat. I slid out of the truck. Charlotte had already disappeared into the darkness.

The scent of smoke clung to the air, filling my lungs and setting off a coughing fit. Everything smelled burnt. Not the good burn like a blackened marshmallow, but one of destruction.

Crime scene tape created a forty-foot perimeter around the entire store. The giant square was working to keep the arriving lookie loos away from the burnt building. Lights from the cruisers and the fire trucks flashed red on everything and everyone. I spotted Officer Mitchell talking to Chief Moore. A small movement to the right side of the burnt-to-a-crisp building caught my attention.

I squinted, straining my eyes to make out if the shape blending into and then out of the small grouping of trees was a shadow cast by the lights or something more. I leaned toward it, certain I'd spotted someone poking around back there. Tucking my chin to my chest, I slowly backed away from the fire scene.

It got darker the farther away I walked from the remains of Made With Love. The smoke smell lessened, making it easier to breathe. I focused on the movement near a grouping of trees. Were some teens hiding, afraid to come out after another bonfire destroyed a building, or was my imagination creating something from the night and white wisps of smoke?

My arm was snagged and I was whipped around.

"What the hell are you doing here?" The lights from the emergency vehicles allowed me to see Officer Mitchell's fierce look in full ominous view. The man looked even scarier with his expression highlighted by the rotating red lights.

"I saw the fire truck heading this way." I made up the half-truth on the fly, feeling a twinge of guilt immediately.

"How would you know it was headed this way?" Mitchell still held my arm, his other hand resting on his handcuffs.

"It's really easy to follow a fire truck with flashing lights at night," I said. "Besides, the football team posted all over social media that they were having a midnight celebration bonfire near Made With Love. It was easy to put two and two together and come up with this location."

"Of course you'd know where the kids were hanging out. I bet you're bringing some party supplies for them." Mitchell twisted my arm, bringing it behind my back. "How about we go search your car?"

Which was at my house. I just talked myself into a huge mess. I didn't want Mitchell knowing I came with Charlotte.

"I didn't bring those drugs into Polished. The girls did."

"You mean your friend's daughter?" Mitchell glanced around. "I think I see her truck. So you both showed up. I wonder what that means."

"It means she has a teenage daughter. Maybe she wanted to make sure she wasn't here with the football team." I struggled to get free.

"You're blaming those kids?" Mitchell tightened his hold, arcing my arm up higher.

Fear tumbled through me. I hadn't been this scared of a police officer since an MP banged on my apartment door in Germany. I hadn't been too thrilled when Ted questioned me after Michael Kane's murder, but I was never afraid he'd hurt me. This officer I wasn't so sure about.

"I'll take it from here, Officer Mitchell." Ted wore a firefighter's helmet with the face shield pushed up. Soot dotted his face.

"I bet you will," Mitchell said.

"I'd release her before you get slapped with an assault charge. The public doesn't like it when the police manhandle people. Especially women." Ted rested his hand on Mitchell's wrist.

"They like it even less when we allow drug dealers to hover around their kids."

Mitchell reluctantly released my arm.

I stepped back, cradling my arm.

"You all right, Faith?" Ted asked, gaze locked on Mitchell.

"Yes."

"Taking up with the enemy again, Roget?" Mitchell said. "Hasn't the chief already warned you about showing your bias?"

"And hasn't the chief warned you about keeping your temper in check?"

"Officer Mitchell," Chief Moore's voice carried over to us. "You're needed for crowd control."

More residents had shown up at the scene, straining their necks to see what little remained of Made With Love. Where were Chad and Dawn Carr?

"I'll start by repeating Mitchell's question. Why are you over here?"

"Why are you at a fire? Are you volunteering for the squad?" The department had been recruiting lately, but I wouldn't think Ted would want to take on a high-stress volunteer gig, since he already had a high-pressure job.

"I ask the questions, you answer them." Ted readjusted the helmet on his head. "Why are you over here?"

I knew when it was time not to push anymore. And if I wanted to get any help from Ted once I found Hannah and Charlotte, I needed to do some cooperating and behave like a law-abiding citizen. "I saw a shadow and wanted to get a better look at what it was. I thought maybe it was the person responsible for the fire. I figured Made With Love didn't just spontaneously combust."

"Where did you see someone?"

I waved toward where I'd believed I saw the movement.

"Show me." Ted took hold of my elbow and turned on a flashlight I hadn't seen in his hand.

I looked at the ground, trying to avoid tripping over anything in the dark.

"Was the area near the store or farther away?" Ted asked.

"Near the trees on the edge of the property."

Ted stopped me. "What was the size of the shape?"

I shrugged. "I was too far away. It was just more of a sense of movement, something going in and out of the shadows. Could've been the light."

"Why did you come here tonight?" Ted's voice hardened.

"Some teens were coming for a bonfire and—"

"You wanted to talk to them."

"Actually, I wanted to catch them, or the dealer, with the synthetic marijuana. It's been made clear that I need more than my word to prove I'm innocent."

"Stay out of this case. It's dangerous."

"I don't want to go to prison for something I didn't commit."

"You won't. I wouldn't let it happen. Or Steve." Ted's voice changed a fraction when he mentioned Steve. I couldn't decipher the meaning of the new tone.

My heart dropped. What if the earlier fire had reignited? Felicity and I hadn't stuck around to make sure all the embers were put out. "How did the fire start?"

"I can't say. It's an ongoing investigation."

A throat cleared from behind us. Wayne Buford, a member of the volunteer fire department, stood behind us, a helmet in his hand. "The fire chief recommends everyone stay out of the building until the inspector clears it in the morning. The tape will remain up, and we'll help guard the structure."

"Thanks," Ted said.

"Do you think the person who did this will come back?" I asked.

"We're more worried about nosy kids exploring or homeless people deciding it'll make a good place to sleep for the night," Wayne said. "No sense in anyone else getting hurt or killed."

Anyone else? My heart pounded. Was Hannah okay? What about the other teens who had shown up? I started to speak but a rustling sound quieted me. Ted's right hand rested on the butt of his service revolver. Wayne signaled someone near the structure with his light, then stepped in front of me.

"Go back," Ted whispered, motioning at me. "Ask the chief to head over here."

I took a few steps, a wail stopping me in my tracks. Ted directed a light toward the sound.

"I want to find my mom!" Hannah clung to the arm of Daniel Burke. The volunteer firefighter dragged the distraught girl toward us. "She was coming to pick me up."

"I parked at the far end of the building, near the bonfire," Daniel said. "I saw the kids were having one tonight and wanted to make sure none were still here. Found her wandering around."

"I have to find her." Hannah broke free from Daniel's hold and ran toward me. "I can't find my mom."

I caught her in my arms and held on tight, doing my best to soothe her.

"I need her to come with me." Ted's hand rested near his handcuffs.

He thought Hannah set the building on fire. I pulled her into a protective embrace. "There were other kids at the bonfire."

"I'll need you to come with me to the station." Ted attempted to untangle Hannah from my grasp. "There are some questions you need to answer."

"No, she doesn't." Charlotte's voice emerged from the woods. "I left Hannah at home and came out here. Since you wouldn't look for the synthetic marijuana, I came here to get it. Someone has to do your job and protect these kids."

She was lying to Ted. I made a startled sound, earning a shut-the-hell-up look from Charlotte.

"Is that so?" Ted crossed his arms, flicking a gaze in my direction.

Charlotte stood in front of Ted. "Yes, it is."

"We have been doing our job." There was a bitter edge to Ted's voice. "The public interfering is what's hampering it."

"Charlotte, don't," I said.

Charlotte placed the car keys into Hannah's hand, sending another warning look my way. "Have someone bring the bike home tomorrow. I rode over on it. Hannah brought Faith here in my truck. The place was burning when I got here. I was the one who called 911."

The ease Charlotte had in making up a convincing story, giving her a perfect reason for handing over the "bike" keys to Hannah, which I knew were the truck keys, was ingenious and a little unnerving. If Charlotte could lie so smoothly to the police, how much easier could she to me?

"You can explain it all at the station." Ted took hold of Charlotte's arm.

Hannah sobbed, falling into my arms.

My heart battled itself over the truth. Charlotte feared Hannah set the fire and was willing to take the blame for her daughter. Should I allow her? I couldn't. Could I?

"You should get her home." Daniel turned Hannah and me toward where the truck was parked. "Go on."

"I'm sorry my daughter dragged you into this, Faith," Charlotte said. "You're the best friend I've ever had."

I wasn't so sure about that.

EIGHT

The light seeping through a slit in the curtain told me I was on the verge of being late for work. I bolted upright, looked at the clock, and sank back into the pillow. Good. Plenty of time. My need for coffee overrode the lingering tiredness, so I pushed myself out of the comfort of my bed. And now that I was awake, the demons from last night returned full force. I'd lied to Ted. Or let him be lied to. Not that there was much difference between the two in this case.

I turned on the Keurig, waiting for the water to heat up. I should've told Ted that I arrived with Charlotte, not Hannah. I was sure the mother-daughter team would've backed each other. Would Ted have believed me over them? What reason did I have to lie? Getting even with them for not telling the truth about who brought in the Janie. Saving myself from going to jail.

Ted wouldn't believe I'd do that...but other people in the community I wasn't sure about. I rubbed my eyes.

The machine blinked the magic words "Ready to Brew" and I pressed the button. While the coffee brewed, I opened the front door and reached for the newspaper. In all the commotion last night, I forgot to ask Ted who died. Unfolding the paper, I scanned the front page, looking for the answer. I blinked once and then twice. The headline stayed the same. "Murderer or Savior?"

Under the caption was a set of pictures: the charred remains of Made With Love, an angry Chad Carr, and then a big question mark inside of a box.

Karen England started with the basic facts of the fire. The volunteer fire department received an anonymous call, later identified as from Charlotte Hanson, regarding the fire at Made With Love. When the squad arrived, the store was engulfed in flames. After the fire was contained, Chad Carr's body was discovered in a back area of the store. An unidentified source revealed that the police were looking into the fire being a result of arson, and that an illegal substance marketed as Janie was found under rotting floorboards in the building.

"The death of Chad Carr brings safety to our community. The real question this morning isn't who killed Carr, but if they are a villain or a saint."

Wasn't that nice of Karen? It was horrible to blame the man, considering he was dead. He couldn't defend himself. I shut the door, dropping the paper into the recycle bin.

I checked my voicemail and email. No word about my stolen camera. I had called in a report last night and the night dispatcher, who also took the non-emergency calls, said an officer would follow up with me on Monday.

A rustling sound by the front door drew my interest. Standing on my tiptoes, I looked out the peephole, spotting a woman with gray hair rummaging around in the weeds by the front door. A ring twinkled on her wrinkled hand.

I opened the door. "I already brought in the paper, Grandma, and read the front page."

Hope straightened. "Promise me you'll stay out of this mess now that the real drug dealer has been identified."

"How convenient for the town, the murdered guy is to blame."

"Would you rather everyone still suspected you?" Hope's voice held more sass than I ever heard her use.

I held the door open and waited for my grandmother to come inside. "I think we should talk."

"Yes, that we should." Hope scanned my living room. I fought back an eye roll. No matter my age, she still checked my "room." I hadn't been a slob as a teenager, but keeping things organized wasn't one of my favorite ways to spend time, unlike Grandma Hope. She always felt Grandma Cheryl was too lenient on what cleaning my room meant. Cheryl and I were cut from the same piece of pattern paper on that matter; as long as no dirty clothes were on the floor, clean clothes were put away, and no food was left in the room, all was good. What were a few books and random notes on the floor? I wasn't sure what Hope loved more about scrapbooking: the actual process of making pages, or sorting and putting all the goodies into proper categories.

"Charlotte wasn't at the scene when the fire started. She and I arrived together."

"I know. I saw her pull into your driveway last night."

"I took the easy way out. I let her talk and didn't correct the information." I plopped onto the couch. "She'll go to prison."

"Maybe not. I spoke with Randall this morning. He said Charlotte was released because there was nothing to hold her on. Arriving at the scene and calling 911 isn't a crime."

"Who do the police think set the building on fire? A man died."

"Don't do it, Faith." Grandma Hope's voice held a steel quality, sounding more like Cheryl than herself.

"Do what? I'm just asking questions."

"That's exactly what you shouldn't do." Hope sat on the edge of the couch, worrying her hands together. "Questions have a way of putting you in danger."

I wrapped my arm around her thin shoulder. My grandmothers had always been larger than life to me. They were my rock, my solace, and they kept me in line with iron fists and soft hearts. Now Hope looked small and anxious.

"It just doesn't seem right to blame the man who died."

"Drugs were found on the property," Hope said.

"The whole building burnt down, but not the drugs? Doesn't that seem a little odd?"

"No. I'm sure he would've put it in some weatherproof box in case of flooding or if the police brought a drug dog in."

"Grandma, you believe this story without any proof. Just because Karen is reporting it doesn't make it the truth. Undisclosed sources? Why doesn't she just name the person?"

"Because she doesn't want to get the officer into trouble."

"A police officer told her?" Jasper popped into my head. He was in love with Karen. The only person in town who didn't seem to realize that was Karen. Or maybe she did and used it to her advantage. "How do you know? Did Chief Moore tell you?"

"Who else would know? Let the police do their job, and you do yours."

I stopped arguing. My grandmother would do anything to keep me safe, including accepting the easy answer.

I drove to work, thinking about the Carrs. Poor Dawn. How was she handling the accusation against her husband? And what would she do without her store? She had no income. My mind pictured the nearly empty store. There hadn't been much merchandise to sell. The business wouldn't have lasted much longer...unless the couple had a product that wasn't on their shelves.

When I neared the shopping complex of our store, I was surprised to find the parking lot almost full. The only spaces available were the ones at the back of the lot near Home Brewed. What was going on? The only clue was a line snaking out of Polished. I had a feeling it wasn't a sale that had a quarter of the population there. Keeping my head tucked low, I hurried toward Polished. I don't know why I tried playing covert operative; my grandmothers knew what I looked like. I doubted hiding my face would stop them from recognizing me.

"If you're here for an appointment, please come inside." Hannah held a clipboard in her hand, motioning in the proper direction. "If you're here to schedule one, please wait in line."

Two women stepped out of line and went to the front. I stood at the end of the eighteen-person-deep line. I had questions; I didn't need my nails done. Would the women get upset if I went up front? Most were playing games on their phones or reading. Everyone seemed calm.

Hannah waved at me, more together than last night.

"Great, you're here for your appointment, Faith. Come on in."

It appeared that Charlotte wanted to talk to me as much as I wanted to chat with her. I stepped inside.

The walls in Polished were painted a soft shade of turquoise, making the place look cheerful and inviting without being overly bright. In a corner near the front door was a coffee station with a Keurig and coffee, tea, and hot chocolate pods. The manicure stations at the back of the spa were a burnished nickel with yellow leather cushions, and the chairs in the waiting room were the same color as the ones in the stations, except with orange and yellow fabric covering them. The far wall had wooden shelf units attached displaying nail polishes in a multitude of hues and shimmers.

Hannah pointed at the polishes. "Why don't you pick out a color and I'll let my mom know you're here for your pedicure. Felicity, can you man the desk while I get the station set up? Mom appreciates you coming in to help out today."

"As I told her, I can always use the extra money." Felicity placed a pile of towels on the counter and took over scheduling appointments.

Pedicure? Why not? I browsed the collection of nail polishes, my gaze drawn toward the ones containing glitter.

Hunched over, Lake Breckenridge shuffled into the store, looking left, then right. Lake was in her early forties and had never had a problem with her back. Did she get injured in the fire the other night, or was she up to something? I watched her inch toward the customers sitting in the waiting room.

Lake reached behind a woman, dropping some glossy flyers onto a table with magazines. Instead of landing on the table, the leaflets scattered over the floor and onto the woman's lap. With her cheeks blazing, Lake ran out of the nail salon, nearly colliding with Hannah.

"She's getting bolder."

The woman crumbled up the flyers in her lap and dropped them into a nearby trash can.

I picked one up. It was a pitch for a direct sales company that sold nail wraps. The back of the flyer had a handmade label with Lake's email and address on it.

"Her business has been struggling, and the fire Thursday night isn't going to help her much." Felicity limped over, slowly bent down, and collected the papers on the floor.

"It's still not right for her to advertise her new business venture here." The woman helped Felicity gather up the remaining flyers. "Why don't you see if your husband can speed up Lake's claim? Didn't she switch her insurance over to his company?"

"Allan filed it already," Felicity said. "There's not much else he can do."

Hannah touched my elbow. "My mom can take you now."

A few of the customers in the waiting area grumbled.

"After I take you back, Mom asked me to run over to Home Brewed to get some coffee and pastries for those waiting. Our treat." Hannah spoke in a loud voice.

The rumbles of discontent stopped.

The phone rang, causing Felicity to shuffle toward the counter. Leaning over, she picked up the receiver then made her way into the closed-off hostess area. "Thank you for calling Polished. How may I help you?" She tapped her finger onto the computer screen. "There's nothing available today; the soonest I can get you in is Wednesday morning."

"My mom is waiting for you." Hannah pointed over her shoulder.

Charlotte was sitting in front of a chair at the far end of the store. At the base of the chair was a tub filled with water. The large leather seats looked inviting. A control was on the left armrest, offering choices of different speeds of back and shoulder massages.

"Have a seat." Charlotte added a peppermint scent to the water.

The crisp, clean scent washed over me, bringing to mind Christmas and relaxation. I'd never had a professional pedicure before and was looking forward to it.

Charlotte pulled a tray closer to her. "I'll take the polish."

I handed it to her, removed my socks and shoes, and then hoisted myself into the raised chair. The line was growing, even as Felicity tapped away at the keyboard, occasionally pausing to stretch her fingers. The moment Felicity hung up the phone, it rang again. Business was booming for Charlotte. Was there a local event tonight I didn't know about?

"Put your feet in the water."

I complied, then took them immediately out of the almost blistering water.

"Sorry, I'm a little distracted today. I'll add in some cold." Charlotte turned on a tap and cold water rushed out.

"You have to tell the police everything. You don't want to take the blame for Chad's murder."

Charlotte huffed out a breath, twisting the spigot off. "I'm fine. Don't worry about it. It's all taken care of."

I leaned forward, almost tipping myself out of the chair. "Being labeled as a murderer is taking care of the problem? You're okay with that?"

Charlotte gave me a tiny nudge back and turned up the bubbles. "Faith, let it go."

I scooted forward so I could whisper. "You lied. I lied. Chief Moore will find out."

"It's all cleared up." Charlotte used the back of her hand to smooth some tendrils of blond hair from her forehead. "I already spoke to Chief Moore this morning. I explained about the fire at my ex's, in case his new wife decided to call the chief or the prosecutor and tell them. I also didn't want you getting into more trouble because of us. I told him I threatened you to keep quiet."

"Your ex-husband's girlfriend would change her story again?"

"She's his wife now." Anger flooded Charlotte's face. "My ex is so wrapped around her finger, he'd let his daughter go to jail if it made his wife happy."

"That's awful."

"Tell me about it."

"People are going to speculate," I said. "The truth needs to come out. Do you really want to spend the rest of your life thought of as Chad Carr's murderer?"

Felicity limped to the back and returned carrying a pile of towels.

"You okay?" I asked Felicity.

"Of course I'm okay." Felicity clutched the towels to her bosom. "Why would you ask?"

"You're limping."

She gave me a tight smile. "New shoes. They're a little tight."

"You can put the towels on the chair." Charlotte pointed to the one beside me. She lifted up one foot and dried it off. "Look around you. Do you think there's a debutante ball going on tonight? The reason my business is booming today is because people think I had something to do with that man's death. They're here to show they approve of me taking out the drug dealer."

The salon was filled, in my opinion, past maximum occupancy. Women were crowded around the counter, some booking appointments and others picking polish and other nail care supplies from the store. Even a few men had come inside and browsed the items for sale.

"And you're okay with people thinking you're a killer?"

"No." Charlotte twisted off the top of the polish. "But people can assume I'm a murderer if it means I can pay for my daughter to go to college."

"You have an alibi. Hannah doesn't."

Charlotte looked up from my toes and glared at me. "How do you know? Were you following her around?"

"No. But the other teens at the bonfire might say something," I said. "What will people say once it's known Hannah was at Made With Love, not with me?"

Her hand jerked. The brush left my nail and colored the end of my big toe. "Those kids aren't going to say anything. They don't want anyone to know they were there." Charlotte rubbed her forehead, leaving a thin line of pink over her eyebrow. She placed the wand down and swiped at the polish with the hem of her shirt.

I plucked a towel from the chair beside me and handed it to her. "That means Hannah doesn't have an alibi."

Charlotte scrubbed the polish from her forehead. "Tell people she was with you all night, then you won't have to worry about Hannah anymore."

Something in my chest tightened. I did not like where this conversation was going. "I can't. It's not true."

"If you can't do that for a friend, then just don't say anything, and stop asking questions. You're not a police officer."

"A man is dead."

"Don't you get it? No one cares that Chad Carr died. It's best to leave this all alone before someone innocent gets hurt."

"I'm sorry." Felicity's voice carried over to me. "We don't have any openings until next Friday evening."

"Saturday," Charlotte called out. "I'm going to the game."

"Chad Carr was murdered," I corrected. "And there's no proof he was guilty of anything."

"Murdered. Self-defense. Dead." Charlotte grabbed my other foot and yanked it from the bubbling water. "It doesn't matter the term used, the outcome is the same."

Her nonchalant answer stunned me into a momentary silence. Charlotte finished painting my toes.

"What if one of the kids she was with killed Carr and is afraid a friend will rat on them? The police have to know the truth."

"Faith, drop it. No good will come from you poking around."

"The truth would come out."

"What makes you think anyone wants the truth?"

NINE

"I was getting my nails done." I sat on the rolling chair, removed my sock and shoe, and wiggled my smudged pink toenails at my grandmothers. "Whoever told you otherwise was mistaken."

When I strolled into Scrap This, the place was abuzz with excitement over Chad Carr's death. The majority—at almost hundred percent—believed the man had received proper justice for supplying the teens with drugs. I originally thought the customers' behavior—and not mine—had irritated my grandmothers.

"I can't deal with this right now, Faith." Hope turned from me, heading down the hallway leading to the office and employee lounge.

"There's nothing to deal with. I promise." I sent Grandma Cheryl a beseeching look and crossed my heart.

"I wish I could believe that." Cheryl dropped a stack of orders on my desk. "For a girl who wants a quiet life, you sure do have a way of working yourself into someone else's mess. Check these product numbers against special order requests and what's currently on the shelf. We've been putting too much product on the clearance tables."

"I verified those yesterday."

"Double-checking never hurts."

"This is busy work." I knew what was going on. There was a mystery brewing in Eden, and Cheryl wanted me busy at the store, not gallivanting around town.

Cheryl muttered something under her breath and followed

after Hope. I wasn't sure if it was to console her best friend or conspire with her on a way to lock me in a tower.

"Have you found anything good?" Mrs. Barlow rushed into the store, panting and clutching at her side.

"There's nothing good about Chad's murder." I fixed a displeased look at Mrs. Barlow. "I have nothing to say."

"Chad Carr?" Mrs. Barlow tilted her head to the side, looking like a confused soulful-eyed puppy. "I was asking about Lake's album. A fire inspector is coming on Monday, and she'd like to have something to show him."

"Sorry. It wasn't very nice of me to accuse you of being here for gossip."

Mrs. Barlow's eyes twinkled. "But since you brought it up..."

From my purse, I pulled out the stack of photos Mrs. Barlow had given me and walked away. I'd browse our products and find something to enhance pictures of Lake's inventory. In the back of the store, a line of distressed pattern paper caught my eye. I picked out a few sheets and placed photos of roses in a gray vase on it. It would work. My gaze roamed the walls. This project was perfect to try out the new mosaic templates. I'd create a lovely collage using what were to me boring snapshots.

I totaled up the purchases on my phone, subtracting my employee discount. I was still within the budget.

"I wonder what she wants," a customer stage-whispered.

"It'll be interesting for Faith."

Pushing down a sigh, I rummaged in my mind for one of the hundreds of I-know-nothing quotes that would work best with Karen. I knew she'd show up sooner or later to question me about being at the fire and bringing Hannah along for the ride. Or so the story went. I wasn't up to talking with her. Fortunately, I had a good distraction at my fingertips. "Karen's here to talk to me about what I saw this morning. If she spots you, she'll interrogate you too."

Mrs. Barlow beamed.

"That's a wonderful idea. I should go speak with Karen about what I heard on the scanner last night. But she's not here right now."

I glanced out the large picture window. A disheveled and angry Dawn Carr paced up and down the sidewalk, muttering and gesturing wildly. I already had all the drama I needed for one day. There was no way I wanted to tangle with a raging, grieving widow who was also a suspected drug dealer.

"Can you go to the office and ask Hope to call the police?" I asked Mrs. Barlow.

The bell above the front door jingled. Dawn stepped inside and stared right at me. Mrs. Barlow scurried for the office, a gleam in her eye and a bounce in her step. There was nothing she loved more than drama: real or self-created. My grandmothers were encouraging her to start writing fiction in hopes it would contain her drama to paper rather than creating a ruckus at basket bingo or during Bunco games. So far, Mrs. Barlow still liked dabbling in real-world drama.

"You set my husband up. That's why you came to my store Friday afternoon." Dawn clutched a cell phone in her hand. "Admit it."

I looked her in the eyes. "I think you should go home."

"Why? So people can keep talking about me and my husband like we're criminals and treat you like Miss Innocent?" Her body shook so hard, her teeth chattered.

Two women standing near the back wall of stickers edged forward. Not a smart move on their part, but I guess the promise of good gossip outweighed safety.

"I'm sorry about your husband and what you're going through," I said.

"Then fix it." Dawn leaned over the counter, sinking her nails into my arm. "Tell the truth. You were at Made With Love on Friday, along with Felicity. You left the drugs there."

"You really think I crawled under your building and left drugs?"

"The kids didn't just hang out at our store, they hung out here too. There was a picture on Instagram. The potpourri was here, not at my store."

The bell tinkled and another customer came into the store. Drat. Not Ted. The women paused by the front display, tilting their heads toward us.

I squeezed Dawn's wrist until she unclenched my arm. "No, it wasn't."

"I have proof." She ran her finger over her phone's screen. Pictures flipped by. "See here. This is you."

How long would that picture of me confiscating the drugs lurk around? "That's me, but I was at Polished."

"That's a lie!" Dawn spun around and kicked one of the paper racks down.

"Stop." I hustled around from behind the counter. "I'm not lying. I set the alarm before I left. The security company can verify that time. And I'll show the police my bank records. They'll see the only income I have coming in is what I make here."

After every sentence, Dawn went after another rack, tossing it onto its side.

A flash went off. I spotted Hope and Mrs. Barlow standing at the entrance to the hallway leading to the back office and employee lounge. Mrs. Barlow used her cell to get another photo. I had to calm Dawn Carr down before she hurt herself or someone else, or I had to hurt her to stop the rampage.

"You set us up." Dawn grabbed a case of pens and heaved it toward the front window.

I stepped into the path of the pens; picture windows were expensive to replace. I'd rather deal with a bruised body than a shattered window. The customers fled out the front door. Good choice.

"I'll stop you." Dawn snatched up some packages of embellishments, preparing to heave those at me.

"Why would I set you up?"

"To clear your own name. I'll prove I'm not a criminal."

"And how is this tantrum helping you?"

She stopped in mid-throw, dropped the package, and raced out the door, crushing the three-dimensional flowers under her feet.

I looked at the destruction around me: a bent wire rack, crushed embellishment packages, and crumbled and torn decorative paper. There was at least three hundred dollars of ruined merchandise on the floor. She'd better pay for all of it. I took off after her.

Dawn scrambled into her car. I sprinted. Grabbing hold of the passenger door handle, I yanked it open, jumping into the seat. "Not so fast. You—"

The rest of the words left me as Dawn crumbled against the steering wheel, soul-crushing sobs erupting from her.

The woman's husband died—was murdered—and the majority of the community's response was "good riddance." What were a couple of pieces of damaged paper?

The words in my head felt insignificant under the circumstances, and I didn't know if Dawn would even believe me.

"He didn't deserve to die like that." Dawn sat up, wiping her eyes and nose on the hem of her t-shirt.

"No." Whether Chad was guilty or not of selling the illegal substance, I had to agree. Burning a man to death was cruel; a lot of hate had to churn through a person to do that to another human being.

Dawn gripped the steering wheel and stared at the shopping complex which held Polished, Scrap This, and Home Brewed. "Why are people so heartless?"

The intensity and grief in her eyes scared me. I placed one hand on the door handle, readying to bail in case she planned on doing something really stupid, like ramming the wall. "I don't know."

"Chad didn't sell drugs to kids. He sold potpourri."

"That potpourri was synthetic marijuana. It's illegal to sell."

Dawn shook her head. "Not what we sold."

"Show the police your inventory and order records."

"I can't. They were destroyed in the fire."

"Ask the companies and the local crafters to send you a copy of what you bought."

Dawn dabbed at her wet cheeks. "I don't know who Chad bought from. He took care of all of that. How am I going to save my husband's memory and reputation? I have nothing to prove his innocence. It was all destroyed."

"There has to be something. At the bank? Safe deposit box? At your home?"

"We lived on the second floor of Made With Love. I have nothing. No one cares."

"That's not true."

Huge tears trailed down her pale face. "Pastor Evans is hemming and hawing about Chad's funeral. He keeps saying he doesn't know if there's a date available next week or the one after."

My face heated as anger raced through me. Chad was looking like a bad guy, but to deny his widow a funeral service for her husband was horrific. Shameful.

"The police will uncover who killed your husband."

"They don't care. Don't you get that? Chad's a drug dealer to them. He almost killed Felicity Sullivan's son. Crime was rising. Chad's death means it all stops."

"The truth is important to them. They won't drop the case because Chad might not have been a law-abiding citizen."

"The world isn't so noble, Faith. The kids at the bonfire last night were football players. Cheerleaders. Two of them Coach Rutherford's children. Officer Mitchell has basically told me they think Chad set the building on fire himself."

"Why?"

"Why not? It's a good excuse to close a case. Drug dealer sets his building on fire and kills himself in the process. Just did the world a favor."

"Mitchell should never have said that."

"It's not just him." Dawn's shoulders slumped forward, all energy seemingly leaving her body. "I have no pictures of Chad and me. No memorabilia. We couldn't have children. The only thing I have of my life with Chad are my happy memories, and the murderer and this hateful town are taking those away." Dawn's voice broke on a sob.

"We'll find the proof." If Chad was innocent.

"We?" Hope shone on her face.

"Yes. We."

TEN

The computer's hum added a serene background noise to my search. My stuffed animals stared down at me from the shelf above my head. I gazed fondly at my beloved teddy bear that Ted's ex-wife had repaired for me after a murderer slashed it open and ripped out the stuffing. Ol' Yowler jumped onto the desk, stalking over and settling his rump on my keyboard. The once-upon-a-time-stray tabby cat resettled himself, now using my hands as a resting place for his hiney.

Maybe I shouldn't have insisted the cat move inside. I yanked my hands out from under his plentiful rump. "Give me a break. I have some investigating to do. Time is of the essence."

He eyeballed me with that look of superior indifference only a cat possessed.

For as long as I'd lived here, Ol' Yowler was the neighborhood prowler. Many before me had tried coaxing the cat inside to live, and all failed, as the tabby seemed born to wander. It wasn't until this year's awful winter that Yowler decided to accept my offer of a warm place to call home. He claimed the office as his own, treating me like an unwanted guest barging into his domain.

I scrolled through the pictures on Hannah's Instagram account, trying to find the date she first suspected Whitney was involved in selling—or at least giving—drugs to Brandon. Most of the pictures on her account were everyday teenage girl stuff: celebrities, memes of angst and woe over parent-controlled life, food, and selfies.

Not one of a football game or bonfire. Either Hannah never

took photos at them, or she never went to one. How would she know about the cigarette Brandon smoked? I checked her list of followers. Time to browse Kirstin and Whitney's photos.

Now I was getting somewhere.

"Whitney loves to party. And Kirstin loves taking photos." Once this mess cleared up, I needed to get her into scrapbooking. If we won one teen over to the hobby, we'd have more joining in. The hobby was on a downswing and desperately needed a resurgence in interest before all scrapbooking stores closed.

On Kirstin's page, there were pics of roasting hot dogs, bag of marshmallows, stumps used as seats, and teens passing a hand-rolled cigarette. I zoomed in. There was no way to tell if the cigarette was tobacco or synthetic marijuana. None of the pictures showed what the group used to fill the cigarettes. If there had been an organza bag lying around, I'd have something to pass on to the police.

Ol' Yowler plopped his hefty body onto the keyboard, flashing the pictures at warp speed.

"Knock it off." I prodded at the cat. He made himself more comfortable. Finally, I wrangled him onto my lap, where he seemed content for the time being.

I brought the cursor back to where I had left off, pausing when I spotted a picture of the lot beside Made With Love. The next photo was a selfie. Kirstin beamed and the teens in the background looked like they were having a good time. A rock circle contained the bonfire. The flames were about six feet into the air, highlighting all the faces of the kids huddled around it. Near the edge of the woods was a girl. Whitney.

I zoomed in. Andrew Taylor was half in, half out of the wooded area. What was he doing there?

My cell rang, startling me and Yowler. My sudden jump earned me claws in my thighs. I removed the sharp nails from my legs and deposited the cat onto the floor. I scribbled "make a cat bed" in my calendar. The phone trilled again.

Mrs. Barlow. I debated not answering it but knew the woman

would come over. She could see my car in the driveway. "Hello."

"Your grandmothers said you were working at home today," Mrs. Barlow said. "I hope that means my project for Lake is almost done."

Ugh. The scrapbook of Lake's inventory. I'd forgotten all about it. The photos and scrapbooking goodies were on my crafting table downstairs. I had planned on working on it this evening. Dawn's crisis sidetracked me.

"I still have some pages to complete." Like all of them. I saved the photos of the bonfire get-together to my hard drive. I'd make a copy and give them to Ted.

"Lake needs them Monday morning."

"As soon as we hang up, I'll get to work."

"Lake would like the title page to show the front of the shop. She had the brick front repainted and a new sign made."

While I was talking to Mrs. Barlow, Yowler returned to his perch on the keyboard. I left him there. Maybe his tapping on the keys would find something concrete to tie someone else to the drugs. I wasn't so sure that Andrew's presence made him the dealer. The man had been on the volunteer fire squad. He might have been there to ensure the fire was put out properly, and just did a horrible job at it.

I took a slight detour to the kitchen and brewed myself an iced mocha. It wasn't as tasty as the ones made at Home Brewed, but it was easier on my budget. I brought my travel mug over to the craft table and stared at the mix of pictures, pattern paper, and embellishments scattered everywhere.

I arranged Lake's photos by themes. There were pictures of every type of flower she sold, ribbons with varying widths and shades of black and gold, football balloons, even her cash register, and a small basket of satchels with dried rose petals, but not one of any of the hundred and sixty-four pictures were of flower arrangements she'd made.

Why hadn't Lake taken photos of those? She could've used them in a book to help sell her creations to customers. Maybe that was one of the reasons she struggled so much. She had nothing displaying her talent for clients to see, and she had incredible skills when it came to flower arranging. She had such a creative eye, she could put her own book together. All she needed was a gentle nudge, and someone to give her the confidence to try.

I reached for my cell, knocking the pictures to the floor. Leaning over, I gathered them up, noticing the date on the back was Wednesday, the day before Lake's shop burned down. Why would Lake pick that day to get the pictures printed? Coincidence?

When it came to crime, I didn't believe in coincidence. I studied the front of the pictures, hoping to see a date stamp on one of the pictures. The windows were clean and the prominent colors of ribbons were gold and black with football balloons floating in the background. A black ribbon slashed through a small wreath made of blue and white buttons. Hazard High School colors. The pictures were taken the day before the fire. The day before a home game, Lake always hung up a wreath using the opposing team's colors. Why had Lake decided to take photos that day? Had she just finished doing the work to the outside of her shop? Or had she been worried the bonfire might cause damage?

There was only one woman with the answers. I called Lake.

"Lake Breckenridge, how can I help you?"

"It's Faith. I have a few questions about your scrapbook."

"Heather passed my project off to you?" Lake sounded incensed.

"Mrs. Barlow was worried her skills weren't up to showcasing your pictures for the insurance adjuster. Is there a certain style you'd like for the whole project page? Linear. Shabby chic. Abstract. Or do you prefer every page is unique and has a cohesive feel by using the same color scheme and embellishments on each page?" I rambled. The more I talked, the more the project woke up the conspiracy theory gal residing in my brain. Why did Lake want an album? Was it to prove she had these pictures for a long time and not just taken them?

"I prefer you give my photos back to Heather."

"I started on the album." Kind of. I moved the pictures into groupings. "Would you like a collage of your inventory? Do you have any shots of your arrangements?" I really wanted to keep her pictures until I studied them. Her behavior was odd.

"Give them to Heather. She knows how I want it done."

"I can consult with her if you'd like." Someone rapped on the front door, then rang the doorbell.

"I don't want you touching my photos," Lake said. "Heather is on her way to get them back."

"Did you tell her—" I stopped the question. Officer Mitchell stood on my small front porch, tapping a rolled-up sheet of paper against the frame.

"I have to go. The police are here." I reluctantly allowed Officer Mitchell to step inside, pocketing my phone.

"According to this police report, you were at the football game Friday night." Mitchell unfurled the document, showing me the date on the top.

It was my report about my stolen camera. "Yes, I was. I was returning to my car when someone stole my camera."

"Let me see if I understand all this. You attended the game Friday night. For the first time ever. You were so close to the players, you were jostled onto the field."

"Shoved," I corrected him.

"When you left, someone stole your camera."

The word "stole" held a completely different tone than when I said it to him.

"And then Friday night, there was a hasty bonfire celebration put together, Made With Love burned down with Chad Carr inside, and lo and behold, Janie was found under the floorboards, in a location where someone could've entered through the crawl space at the side of the building."

When he listed everything out, it sounded more like I was engaged in committing a crime rather than trying to solve one.

A crash coming from my office caused us to look toward the stairs. Darn that cat.

"What's that?" Mitchell headed for the stairs.

"My cat." I raced in front of him, planting myself on the second step, and holding out my arms. If he saw what I had on my computer, he'd have something else to add to his list of "Faith's dubious behavior." "His favorite game is pushing my collectibles off the shelves."

"I really should check it out. Maybe someone broke in."

"With a cop car parked out front? I don't think so."

"Maybe they got here before me." Mitchell tried shoving past me. I held my ground.

"I'm sure it's my cat." Fortunately, Yowler decided now was the time to demonstrate the reason for his name. The guttural squall reverberated through the house. "See? Cat."

"Or an injured burglar."

Mitchell really wanted to get upstairs and check out my office. He must be hoping he'd find something to use against me, but without a warrant he needed a good excuse to go up the stairs.

The front door burst open, and Mrs. Barlow charged inside, a woebegone look on her face. "I need those photos back. Lake is having the hissy fit of all hissys." The excitement in her voice cancelled out her expression. This was making the older woman's day.

"I have a doorbell," I said. "I'd appreciate you use it instead of barging in."

"I saw you had company. Didn't think I should interrupt. I figured I'd sneak in and get Lake's items for her." Mrs. Barlow fixed a captivated gaze on Officer Mitchell. I wasn't sure if it was because the man was attractive—though not likeable—or because there was a member of law enforcement in my house who wasn't Ted.

"You are interrupting." I remained on the stairs as Mrs. Barlow gathered items from my craft table.

"My apologies. Lake was just so insistent I retrieve her photos, I allowed my manners to slip. Why don't you two carry on with your conversation? I'll pack up the items for the album lickety-split. I'll be so quiet, you won't know I'm here."

Mitchell switched his gaze from me to Mrs. Barlow and then back again. He grinned. "Sure. Why not? So you were at the football game, near the bleachers for the Eden High School players, the very night there was a fire at Made With Love that burned it down, and police were finally able to locate drugs in the building. That happened the day after there was a picture of you handing a bag of Janie to a teenage girl."

"But Faith wasn't at the bonfire with the players and cheerleaders." Mrs. Barlow hoisted the strap of one of my totes onto her shoulder.

"Is that so?" Mitchell leaned against the banister, moving his attention to Mrs. Barlow.

"Yes. Obviously you're not monitoring Instagram." Mrs. Barlow raised her nose into the air, narrowing her eyes into slits as she pranced by.

"We'd be able to close this investigation if some people weren't protected." Mitchell made it clear he was talking about me.

"As I recall, I was questioned at the station. It's nice that some officers know they can't hold an innocent person responsible for the crimes of another." I went up another stair for some personal space.

"I know you're trying to hold those teens responsible for what you've done. I won't let it happen."

The doorbell chimed "It's a Small World."

Mrs. Barlow yanked it open. "Good thing you're here, Steve. There's an officer accusing Faith of being a drug dealer when we all know it was Chad Carr."

Steve. I forgot about our dinner tonight. Steve wore a charcoal suit, white shirt, and a purple-striped tie. He had planned for a fancy dinner out, while I still wore the t-shirt and jeans I'd tugged on this morning. His choice of attire also told me Steve believed we were getting back together. Why would a man dress up for a woman who was now in the category of "just a friend?"

"Actually, we don't know that either," I said, feeling a need to defend the dead.

"Change your mind?" Steve asked.

"I've been preoccupied." I tilted my head at Mitchell, putting all the blame on the officer rather than my sleuthing.

"Is there a problem, Officer?" Steve asked.

"Just here to follow up on Miss Hunter's complaint of a stolen camera," Mitchell said. "There was a crash upstairs and I offered to investigate it. Miss Hunter is very insistent I not go up."

"It's just Yowler being obnoxious."

"Thanks for your diligence, Officer Mitchell, but I'm sure you have more pressing matters. I can check out the noise." Steve maneuvered around me.

"Are you coming, Officer?" Mrs. Barlow held the door open.

"Yes." Mitchell took the heavy bag off of Mrs. Barlow's shoulder and slung it on his own. "How about you show me the pictures taken at the bonfire?"

Mrs. Barlow batted her eyelashes at him. "I'd be delighted."

After the duo left, Steve gave me a good onceover. "I think a change of plans is in order. How about pizza?"

Piece A Pie. After the fiasco at Made With Love, I totally skipped visiting Whitney's other hangout. And Chad's murder shoved it even further down into my memory. "Sounds perfect. Tell you what, I'll meet you at Piece A Pie. I'd like to get cleaned up a little." And turn off my computer, in case Mitchell found a way to wrangle a search warrant from a judge.

Steve opened his mouth, I figured for an argument, and then closed it. "Fine. I'll get us a table."

I wanted to tell him I didn't think we'd have any trouble as business had been slow at Piece A Pie for a while, but I wanted to drive myself, so no sense giving him a reason to wait around for me. It wasn't that I didn't trust Steve; I just believed it would be easier for him—and me—to go home in separate cars once I told him friendship was all I wanted.

I changed out of my t-shirt into a light sweater and switched from sneakers to boots. At least I looked a little spiffier. I didn't want to go overboard, but didn't want to act like I didn't care at all either.

When I arrived at the pizzeria, Steve's car was the only other one in the lot. The nonexistent lines on the asphalt made it hard to differentiate one spot from another. A lone lamppost was on near the front of the restaurant, an outline of a dumpster barely visible in the faded light. Out of habit, I parked near the lamppost and hurried inside.

A buzz sounded when I opened the front door. Jim Ryland, the owner of the pizzeria, ran from the kitchen to the small hostess stand blocking the entrance into the dining area.

"Welcome to Piece A Pie." He wiped his hands on a stained apron, then grabbed a dusty menu. "Let me seat you."

"I'm joining Steve." I pointed.

"Okay." He held out the menu. "When you're ready to order, hit the bell on the table."

Using my fingertips, I accepted it. I must've looked surprised, because Jim launched into a long explanation of his wife's illness, followed by other reasons for the bell.

"I can't afford extra help right now," he continued on. "I'm making the pies, waiting tables, running the cash register, and taking care of any maintenance issues."

"I'll ring the bell." Maybe Steve and I should find somewhere else to eat. Even with the place empty, it might take a long time to get our order. Then again, we couldn't find a much more private place to eat than here.

Steve was entertaining himself by spinning an empty cup on the table.

"I got here as quickly as I could." I sat on the vacant side of the booth. The faux leather creaked as I tried to make myself comfortable.

The walls were devoid of art or any other decorations, and paint peeled off in chunks. The jukebox in the back corner of the pizzeria was cracked and unlit, the plug dangling half in, half out of the wall. A light flickered at the table right behind us.

When I was in high school, Piece A Pie was the favorite teen hangout. The decor on the walls changed seasonally, often including posters made by students at the high school, usually about upcoming sporting events and dances. Now the walls were blank and everything looked sad.

"I'd recommend plain cheese pizza and soft drinks," Steve said.

"I agree. Keep it simple." I rang the bell.

Jim ran from the back, pencil and order pad in his hand. "What can I get you?"

After Steve placed our order, I jumped right into the heart of the matter, or at least the one concerning Chad Carr's murder. I figured it was better to broach the other topic once I got some needed answers. "What did your boss think about Karen's article? It doesn't seem like the police are very interested in finding the murderer. Everything has been relatively quiet in Eden, considering a second business burned down and one of the owners died."

"What are you talking about?" Steve nodded a thanks as Jim placed our bottles of soda on the table.

"The whole murderer or savior angle to her story. I haven't heard there are any other suspects."

Steve twisted the tops off the bottles. "The police have another suspect in mind, but there's some disagreement on how to handle the situation."

"What does that mean?"

"It means it hasn't been decided if it was even a murder." He took a swig of his soda.

"What else could it be?"

"Why not ask your new boyfriend? I'm assuming you two are an item now since you've been avoiding me."

I didn't like the sarcasm in Steve's tone. I wrapped my hands around my bottle. The condensation made my hands clammy. "He's not my boyfriend. He's a friend. That's it." For now. "I told you I needed some space to sort things out. Not to mention I've been busy. I wanted to prove to my grandmothers I can handle the business on my own. They want to take a cruise and are worried about it."

"You are turning into a woman of excuses." Steve fidgeted, moving over to the right.

The smell of the pizza baking churned my stomach. I took a small sip of soda, hoping the carbonation would settle it. "Those aren't excuses. I have been trying to be a better employee."

"And how's that coming along now?"

"It's a little harder when I'm still being viewed as the town's drug dealer."

"That's only by one officer."

"One officer too many."

"Better than the rest of the town thinking so."

"That could change if I help Dawn prove Chad is innocent," I said.

Steve's eyebrows rose. "Why would you do that?"

"Because Dawn believes her dead husband is being railroaded. She doesn't want his memory tarnished and no one else will listen to her."

"That doesn't mean you have to."

"It does. Ten years ago, I was at the same crossroads. I needed help and only one person listened to me. Thank God they did or I'd be sitting in prison." Instead of your cousin.

"I agree that no one cares much that Chad Carr died in that fire, besides Dawn and the insurance company, but it doesn't mean you should risk your life and reputation. Poking into this matter is only going to make Officer Mitchell suspect you more." Steve turned sideways and rested his back against the brick wall instead of the booth. A little bit of light glinted off the springs poking out from the leather. No wonder he squirmed around.

"Your pizza." Jim placed the steaming cheese pizza in front of us.

The phone rang. With hope in his eyes, Jim spun toward the sound.

I reached for a slice and stopped. "We don't have any plates."

"Sorry, I'll go get some," Jim said.

The phone rang again.

"I need to answer that, then I'll come back with your plates." Jim ran for the register area.

I picked up a slice, using a napkin as a makeshift plate until Jim brought a couple. I took a bite. The cheese tasted fresh, though it was a little skimpy on the sauce, and the crust had the right mix of crunchy and softness. Next time I felt like pizza, I'd stop here instead of getting one from the freezer section. It would be nice to help out a fellow business owner.

Jim's excited voice carried over to us. An order, a huge one from the sound of it, was being placed.

Steve finished one slice, reaching for a second. "Think about it, Faith. Searching out the truth could easily be construed as you setting someone up."

"Not if I have solid physical evidence and not just a verbal statement saying 'I didn't do it.'"

Steve took an inordinate amount of interest in the remaining slices. It wasn't like he needed to count the pepperonis and snag the one with the most pieces. "Then I'd be careful taking other people's words at face value. They may have an ulterior motive in wanting to be proven innocent."

I paused with my hand an inch from my chosen slice, the one with the most browned cheese. "What?"

"For a couple with money troubles, Chad sure was insured for a hefty sum."

"How much?"

"Four million."

I sucked in a breath. "Where would they get the money for the policy?"

"Something or someone was financing the policy."

Janie. I was sure those sales were kept off the books and paid for in cash, which meant Dawn knew her husband was selling the synthetic marijuana. How else would she know they had the funds available to pay for a large life insurance policy?

A throat cleared near us. I looked over. Jim offered a shaky smile and put two plates on the table. Steve and I had to be careful.

The place was empty customer-wise, but not totally devoid of other people. I didn't want Steve getting in trouble for giving me information.

"I just got a large order," Jim said. "Do you need anything else? I'm going to be busy in the kitchen for a while."

"We're good," Steve said.

Jim nodded and went to the back.

I picked some cheese off a slice of pizza. "Are you insinuating that Dawn is using me because she had something to do with her husband's death and wants me to prove she's innocent?"

"That's an accurate assessment. Let's just say it's likely Chad didn't know about the policy his wife—more correctly, estranged wife—took out on him."

"Are you sure? Dawn's devastated. She's not faking her grief. And I saw them working on the policies together when Felicity and I were there. The insurance stuff was on the front counter."

"She wasn't living with her husband."

"Who told you that?"

"Did you get a good look at the documents? Was it personal life insurance, business, fire?"

I glared at him. He was ignoring my question. "I didn't get that close of a view. I just saw the title on top of the document. They were using Allan Sullivan's insurance company for the policy."

"I wonder why Mrs. Sullivan didn't mention that when she was questioned."

"Felicity was questioned?"

"Faith, stay out of it."

Worry crossed Steve's face.

"You tell me I'm probably being used by Dawn and she's a suspect in her husband's murder, then that Felicity was questioned, and then say stay out of it. Why? So Dawn can be blamed for Chad's death? Does the town, and the law, believe that if Chad was a drug dealer, she must be one too?"

"You're not being fair. Drugs were found on the premise, and there's much more that you don't know about."

"So you're only able to tell me the details you can use to control me. It won't work."

"That's not it, Faith." Steve reached for my hands.

I pulled back.

Old feelings stirred in me. Moments of my relationship with Adam merged into ones I had with Steve. All the times Adam convinced me what I saw wasn't the truth whirled in my mind: the moments he recounted conversations I was certain we never had, the checks he insisted I had signed but I didn't recall, the day Adam swore he had come home at a certain time when he hadn't. It was the last lie that was almost my downfall. While I had vouched for Adam being home with me, he told the police he was at a bar with friends and those friends lied for him. Everything Adam had ever said to me, or asked of me, was to help himself.

"I worry about you. Nothing has changed for me." Steve placed his hand on mine.

"It has for me." I drew in a deep breath, gathering all the strength and resolve I'd need. "I won't be controlled. Not by you, my grandmothers, or by myself, trying to pretend the past doesn't exist. Not anymore."

"I'm not controlling you." His voice rose. Quickly, he lowered his tone. "I love you, so I worry. I want to make sure you're safe. That's not controlling you."

"Yet you were willing to hand me information to help yourself out. You're like everyone else in town who want nothing to do with bringing to justice the person who killed Carr. You're willing to take the answer right in front of you because it's the easiest to believe. I've been that easy answer, Steve. I won't stand by and let you or anyone else do that to Dawn."

All the emotion left Steve's brown eyes. I wasn't sure if it was because I caught on to the manipulation, or if he hadn't realized that was what he was doing.

"I'm not Adam," he said.

"I know you're not."

"Do you?" Steve gripped the table, his fingers whitening from the pressure. "Everything between us changed when I told you Adam was my cousin. You're doing to me what you feared everyone would to do you."

"That's not true. Everything changed because you lied—"

"I didn't lie."

"Lie. Withheld. Same thing." I stood.

"You lied." Steve relaxed his hold on the table.

"I was keeping something about myself private, because I was afraid people would judge my grandmothers and me. It was why I hadn't wanted to date you. I was afraid dating the ex-wife of a murderer would ruin your career. The whole time you knew and kept that from me. I was scared and confused, twisting myself up in a knot, and you could've relieved all of that. You knew what I was holding back, and instead of telling me, you played a game with the truth."

"I wasn't toying with you, Faith. I wanted you to tell me."

"I didn't need you to test me. You knew what I was struggling with, and you sat by and watched." I felt tears well in my eyes but refused to cry. "I always believed you were helpful, the one person I could trust to have my back. Now I don't know what to believe about you anymore. What else do you know, or think you know, that you're silent about because you're waiting for me to mention it first? I won't go through that again."

"Tonight wasn't about a new start, was it?"

"No. I never said it was."

"It would've been nice for you to have said something."

"I've been trying. You wouldn't listen."

Steve slid out of the booth. "I was hoping you'd give me another chance."

I knew what he wanted from me. I couldn't give it to him. Part of me wished I could, but I was done wishing my life away. I wanted to live it in the here and now. "We can be friends, Steve. I can give that."

"That's not enough for me."

He walked out the door, leaving me with an aching heart and

the bill. That wasn't the way I'd hoped it would go, but one couldn't control another person's reaction. I didn't want Steve entirely out of my life. He'd either change his mind, or I'd get used to this new reality.

Clanging came from the kitchen. Jim was still busy getting the order ready. I waited at the front. More banging was followed by a crash and some choice words. I spotted the order pad by the phone and decided to help Jim out. I found our order, took a menu, and wrote down the correct prices. After a few taps on the calculator on my phone, I had everything added up, including the tax.

I pulled twenty-five dollars from my wallet, starting to place it on the counter. A set of headlights flashed in the parking lot. I didn't want to leave the cash out where someone could snag it. Leaning over the counter, I checked out the register, noticing it was a vintage one without all the bells, whistles, and security devices like the one we used at Scrap This.

"Jim, I tallied our bill. I'm going to put the money in the register."

After pulling up the latch and lifting the opening in the counter, I stood in front of the register. I hit the correct buttons and the drawer popped open, snagging the corner of a business card. I untangled the card Jim had placed in the slot for twenties. Vulcan Catering. Identical to the one I found in the alleyway at the stadium. Was Jim branching his culinary repertoire to barbeque? I yanked my fingers away before the register was slammed shut.

"What are you doing?" Jim's face was red, sweat beaded on his brow.

"Putting money in the register."

"I'm closing. You need to leave." Jim grabbed my arm, dragging me away from the register.

"I'm sorry." I struggled to get out of his grasp. "I was trying to help."

"I have an order to deliver. You need to leave. Now."

"I'm going."

I pulled away from his grasp.

Jim yanked the door open and watched me every step of the way to my car.

A small light flickered in the cab of the truck still in the lot. The only additional detail I made out in the dark was the roll bar attached to the bed. I started my car and left the parking lot, a shiver working through me. I swore the person in the truck stepped out to watch me leave.

ELEVEN

The sun bounced off the white cross on the steeple, creating a welcoming halo around the church. I whipped into the crowded parking lot as the bell pealed. The usual stragglers were wandering through the open doors of the sanctuary. Time was running out for me. I hated getting the Sunday lecture from my grandmothers and it wasn't looking good for me to beat the final dong of the bell.

I scuttled into the church and snagged a bulletin from the greeter's hand. I hadn't seen so many people in church since Easter Sunday.

"You'd better hurry," Mr. Murphy grumped. "Your grandmothers are getting in a tizzy, especially Cheryl."

"How's your pawn shop?"

Mr. Murphy ran a handkerchief over his balding head. "Okay, considering what could've happened. Young punks started themselves a bonfire behind Lake's store. It jumped from hers and went to mine. Thankfully, my sprinklers worked. I think that's the only thing keeping the fire inspector off my back. Poor Lake isn't having such an easy time. The man the insurance company sent sure is hot to prove she did it on purpose."

"Why would they think that?"

"I guess it looks all kinds of wrong because Lake got the policy approved a few days before it happened. I figure the company ain't liking the fact it has to dish out a huge chunk of change to a new customer. And it don't help none that Lake gave the kids permission to have the bonfire back there. I told her it wasn't a bright idea but she thought it would make the parents come running to her store. Homecoming is around the corner and she wanted the business." He turned me by the shoulders. "You better get inside. Cheryl is giving me the evil eye."

"One more question. Did anyone contact you about buying a camera?"

"Nope. Upgrading yours?"

"Trying to get it back."

Mr. Murphy shook his head in sympathy and patted my arm. "Tell you what, darling, if someone brings one by, I'll let you know and notify the police."

"I thought you were closed?"

"The Buford boys are letting me use their plumbing office until my place is fixed up. I can't make money if I'm not open. If someone brings in a camera, I promise to call. I usually do a good job of making sure my merchandise is free and clear, but things can get past these old eyes."

"Thanks." I headed for our pew. No one actually owned any of the pews in the church, but every member of the congregation always sat in the same spot.

I craned my neck, trying for a view of the fifth row from the front, otherwise known as Dawn and Chad's spot. No Dawn. Was she skipping church this morning? I walked a few more feet, getting a good look at the pew, and heaviness filled my heart. Handbags took up the spaces where Dawn and Chad usually sat, the owners of the accessories looking pleased.

Sobs came from behind me. Dawn sat in the back row alone, hands pressing into her face as she squished up against the end of the pew. Empty except for her. As I backtracked, congregation members sent each other knowing looks, thrilled smiles on their faces, and a few even added a slight nod when my gaze clashed into theirs.

They thought I was going to confront the widow and were pleased. Would everyone's opinion toward Dawn change if she *was* the one who killed her husband? Everything Steve told me last night rushed into my brain. Were Dawn's tears real heartbreak, or a show for the congregation, the police, and the insurance adjuster?

The choir members left the pews and walked onto the stage at the front of the church. If I didn't want to be considered late and receive a lecture, I needed to sit down before the first note left Gussie.

Hope sat up taller. Cheryl glanced at her watch then turned her head. I met her gaze and nodded toward Dawn, sliding into the pew and dropping myself next to Dawn. The thin red cushion shifted as Dawn created a little more personal space between us. Ted was sitting behind my grandmothers and frowned at me.

Gussie tapped her throat and rubbed at it, signaling she needed water. Gussie got a little diva-ish on church days. She had a beautiful singing voice, and a look that terrified the congregation into submission, so what she wanted Pastor Evans rushed to get her.

Today, I knew her actions bought me more time. I owed her one. Unlike other members in the congregation, I knew she wanted to give me time to comfort Dawn. I rummaged around in my purse and found a clean tissue, then placed it on Dawn's lap.

With a shaking hand, she picked it up and wiped her face. Her red-rimmed eyes and the devastation in her blue gaze told me everything. This was real, cut-into-your-soul grief. Her husband was murdered, and her community turned on her.

I clasped her hand. It was ice cold.

"Go sit with your grandmothers." Dawn wiped her eyes. "I don't want you to help me anymore. If you do, the town will hate you."

"I don't care if they do." I pulled a hymnal from the holder and stood. "No one should pay for someone else's sins."

"My husband isn't guilty." The sadness left Dawn's expression, replaced by a steely resolve.

I wasn't so sure about that, but I did know what Chad committed was on him and not anyone else. Even if Chad sold the illegal substance, it didn't mean his wife should be shunned by the town.

What if she knew?

Gussie gave a nod to the choir director and the hymn began.

I locked the thought up for the meantime. Three songs later, Gussie pivoted sharply to the right and the rest of the choir followed suit, trailing her off the stage.

Pastor Evans climbed the stairs. He opened a bulletin, placing it on the podium. "Please be seated for announcements."

Murmurs floated around the sanctuary, papers rustled, and pews squeaked as the congregation settled back onto the cushions. Dawn clutched a bulletin in her hand. Something about it made her unhappy. Listed in the bulletin were the names of the women working in the nursery this week and the volunteers for next Sunday, the date for the next cleaning party, the code phrase for the menfolk who trimmed the bushes and mowed the lawn. At the bottom of the page was a list of prayer requests.

Pastor Evans droned on, reading the bulletin verbatim. I pretended to listen as I tried decoding the pamphlet to find out what irked Dawn.

Beside me, Dawn pulled bulletin after bulletin from her large bag.

Pastor Evans finished reading and gazed around the sanctuary. "Is there anything I left out?"

Dawn stood, pressing an armful of bulletins to her chest. "Yes."

Pastor Evans searched the sanctuary for someone else other than Dawn. He let out a nervous laugh. "This is the first time I haven't forgotten anything."

"I said yes," Dawn said more forcefully.

The entire congregation swiveled in their seats to face Dawn.

"We're running behind. If there's time at the end of the service you can mention your news," Pastor Evans said.

Standing, I did what I did best and stuck my nose into the business at hand. "There was enough time a few minutes ago. Why isn't Dawn allowed to speak?"

Hope and Cheryl smiled.

"It looks like she has a lot to say," Pastor Evans defended his position.

"Then let the woman speak," Gussie said.

"Go ahead, Mrs. Carr," Pastor Evans said. Was it my imagination or had there been a sneer in his voice?

"Why wasn't Chad's death announced in the bulletin? That's what usually happens when a congregation member loses a loved one." Dawn raised her arms and dropped the pile she held. Bulletins rained down to her feet.

Pastor Evans loosened his tie. "It appears there was an oversight. My apologies."

He didn't sound very sorry to me.

Dawn's eyes narrowed. "Can we also narrow down the date for my husband's funeral? Since Saturday wouldn't work because of a prior engagement that couldn't be changed."

"We can discuss this later, Mrs. Carr," Pastor Evans said. "I don't have the church calendar with me."

"How about you or your wife get it?" Dawn pointed at the back door. "The church office is right next door, so it won't take long at all."

"We're in the middle of a service." Pastor Evans opened his Bible.

"I want to make sure I get my request in before something else more important comes up," Dawn said.

"Please don't make me ask the ushers to remove you," Pastor Evans said.

"Doesn't your husband's body have to be released first?" Karen asked. "I was told it's still at the morgue because there are questions concerning his death."

A sigh of relief floated around the congregation.

Ted sprang to his feet. "Enough, Miss England."

"What? Doesn't this town like the truth?" Karen crossed her arms and sent a smug look in Ted's direction.

"There's a time and place for certain details, and in the middle of a church service isn't it. Some of those details aren't meant for the general public." Ted narrowed his gaze onto Jasper, who sat beside Karen. Smiling, Jasper shrugged.

It appeared Jasper was spending his forced leave talking with Karen. I hoped his sharing didn't result in his leave becoming permanent.

"Here we go again, the police hiding information." Karen inspected her nails.

"Or someone twisting the truth to shift blame," I muttered.

Karen spun around. "What did you say?"

"I think you know."

Karen crossed her arms. "Do I?"

"Yes. It was along the lines of people using their position to play games and turn an opinion into truth." I gripped the back of the pew. "Let the police do their job."

"You're one to talk," Karen said.

Snickers filled the room.

"Fine, I admit it. I don't always listen, but at least I'm looking for the truth, not actively creating a different one."

"Face the facts, you're helping a murderer." Karen pointed at Dawn.

"Time to leave." Ted stepped out from the pew and headed for Karen.

Loud brittle laughter stopped Ted in his tracks. I gaped at Dawn and slid a couple of inches away. The woman sounded like she was about to lose it.

"If I killed my husband, don't you think I'd say so?" Dawn grabbed the handle of her purse and hoisted it to her shoulder. "'Cause if I did, I'd receive some sympathy from this town instead of a cold shoulder."

I stared at the remnants of the items for Lake's scrapbook. Mrs. Barlow had cleared most of the items from my table, but a few lingered here and there. I gathered up some errant sticker gems, a thin roll of pink ribbon, and some photos of crystal vases. I stacked the pictures, then tapped them on the table to even the pile. Two business cards slipped out. One was from Lake's shop, and the other was for Vulcan Catering.

My mind flickered to the business card with the burnt edges and grill graphic in Jim's cash register. Vulcan Catering. He hadn't been happy at me seeing it. Why? It wasn't like it was against the law for him to have two food businesses in town. More questions rolled through my head. Why did Lake have one? Was she helping Jim? Was he drumming up business? Why hadn't I seen the cards around town or Jim drop one off? We held a lot of events at Scrap This. My thought trail brought me back to why Jim was upset that I saw the card.

The front door opened, wafting the smell of chicken and dumplings to me.

"It's your grandmas," they called from the foyer.

I swept the pictures off of the table into a tote bag. "I'll go set the table." And make sure I had enough clean dishes.

I gathered up bowls and napkins and took them to the table.

Hope took silverware out of the dishwasher. "We believe Dawn is innocent. We want to help you."

Help me? I didn't want my grandmothers involved in solving a murder. There was no way I wanted to introduce my grandmothers to a murderer. "No."

"We're not asking your permission, young lady." Cheryl scooped spoonfuls of chicken and dumplings into the bowl. "Hope and I are adults and can make our own decisions."

"Just like you do."

Hope had a smug smile on her face.

They both looked rather pleased with their copycatting. I didn't like it one bit. "It's too dangerous."

"If you can handle it by yourself," Cheryl said, "then we can handle it as a team."

Hope nodded.

Stirring my lunch to cool it off, I pouted. This wasn't going my way at all. There had to be some way to convince them that sleuthing at their ages wasn't a good idea. But if I said that, I'd guarantee their involvement, and possibly my destruction.

"Don't be a poor sport, dear. That's not how we raised you."

"I'm not being a bad sport, I'm worried. Most of what I'm hearing is gossip. I have to dig around and ask questions to sort the fact from fiction. I know how you both feel about gossip."

"We don't like it," Hope jabbed her spoon in my direction, "and you shouldn't either."

"I don't like it. It's just how information comes to me. People aren't forthcoming with Ted or Steve either. Not that Ted shares with me."

"Steve does?" Hope asked.

"A little. I don't think he's too keen about prosecuting whoever killed Chad Carr."

"No one in town cares a whit," Cheryl said.

"All they want to do is judge Dawn." Hope wiped up a spot of sauce from the table.

"If she had killed him," I said, "they'd throw her a parade."

"But she didn't."

"Steve hinted the police are looking in her direction," I said.

Cheryl paused with a spoonful of chicken halfway to her mouth. "Why?"

Quickly, I told them about the insurance policy taken out on Chad and the store. "Then there's the rumor that Chad and Dawn were separated."

They put their utensils down, giving me their undivided attention.

"Steve's the one who mentioned it. Maybe the reason only Chad died in the fire was because he was living there alone."

Hope and Cheryl exchanged a knowing, and somewhat guilty, look.

"There's someone you need to talk to." Grandma Cheryl pulled her cell phone from her sweater pocket and handed it to Hope.

"I don't think Dawn wants everyone to know her business," Cheryl said. "But keeping this secret isn't going to help her."

"Hello, Nancy," Hope said into the phone. "I was wondering if you'd like to come over to my granddaughter's place. I have an apple pie cooking and chicken and dumplings on the table. I'd like you to tell Faith what you know. Dawn's life in this town depends on it."

Cheryl went next door for the pie while I set another spot at the table and Hope paced around in the living room.

"I won't repeat what she says," I said.

Hope stopped and faced me. "I don't think you would do that at all. It's just that Nancy will also have to tell the police. Someone is likely to get in trouble. What will happen to Dawn?"

Happen to her? Had Dawn been committing another crime while her husband died in the fire? That was a good alibi, but it was one a person wouldn't want to get around if they were trying to stay out of jail.

Though the community was more likely to forgive and forget if Dawn had murdered her husband.

"What does Nancy know about Dawn?"

"Nothing nefarious. Nancy works at the nursing home where Dawn's mother has been living for the last four months."

That was around the time the synthetic drug started being sold. It would be easy for the guy to start selling an illegal substance without his wife knowing about. She had a lot on her plate.

A car pulled into my grandmothers' driveway, and a woman in her mid-fifties slid out. Her hair was slicked back from her face and twisted into a messy bun, and she wore a fall-themed nurse's smock. Cheryl exited her house holding the pie and directed Nancy to my house. I had chatted with the nurse a few times when my grandmothers hosted Bunco at their house, but didn't know much about her besides her occupation and love of card games. My grandmothers always invited me to play with them. I never stayed long as I wasn't interested in the game, just the snacks they served. I opened the door for Cheryl, Nancy, and the pie.

Once we sat down at the table, Cheryl wasted no time filling Nancy in.

Nancy picked at her food. "I wanted to say something once Chad died and the rumors started, but Dawn wants us to keep quiet. I heard what happened at church. Such a shame."

Hope tsked in agreement.

"Simply horrific and very unchristian behavior," Cheryl said.

"Even worse because the pastor took part in it," I said. "He's supposed to be the best example."

"Even if the pastor behaves unkindly doesn't mean all should follow suit." Hope placed a bottle of water at Nancy's place. "We all know right from wrong, and just because someone else started walking down the path of wrong, it is never a good reason to skip along behind them."

Nancy pushed her plate away.

"I'm not very hungry."

Hope went to the cabinet and took out a plastic container.

"What do you know about Dawn and her husband?" I asked.

"The Carrs lost their home a few weeks ago through a foreclosure."

"But they lived on the second floor of the store. That's what Dawn told me."

"They moved there after the foreclosure, but the second floor isn't livable," Nancy said. "They wanted people to think they chose to live at the store to save money and let the bank have the house."

Dawn lied to me. "Were Chad and Dawn sleeping in the store?" The fact that the one night she wasn't there Made With Love went up in flames wasn't something the police and insurance adjuster would overlook.

"Chad stayed at the store, while Dawn slept on the floor in her mother's room at the nursing home. Chad liked everyone believing he was a business guru and didn't want to lose their respect, so he did everything possible to keep it quiet. Dawn was preoccupied with her mother, so she went along with his opinion on taking out loans and branching off into new items."

"Like potpourri?" I asked.

Selling drugs to teens was probably more profitable than

handcrafted items. Unfortunately, Nancy's testimony was adding more evidence to the "why Dawn killed her husband" column.

"Yes," Nancy said.

"Dawn didn't want him at the nursing home?" I asked, hating the fact the nurse's words proved the couple was on the outs.

"No, *we* didn't. It wasn't easy for us to let Dawn stay in the room; two people was pushing it. The first night Dawn stayed over by accident, her mother didn't have any night terrors. So the next night, I pretended I didn't see her hiding behind the curtains, and again her mother had a calm and restful night. Since Dawn's mom having a restful night meant the nurses had a calm night, we decided to let Dawn stay. If the director found out we allowed an extended overnight visitor, our jobs would be in jeopardy. That's why Dawn didn't want us to say anything even if it gave her an alibi."

"You were being kind to a homeless woman," I said.

"It probably won't matter. Dawn doesn't want to repay our kindness by getting us in trouble," Nancy said.

"We know," Cheryl said. "That's why we want to help."

"But we're talking about a murder charge," I said.

"That's also why I came." Tears filled Nancy's eyes. "She shouldn't have to suffer because of what her husband has done."

"Has done?" The delicious lunch soured in my stomach.

Nancy glanced down at the table, running her finger through a spot of condensation that dripped from the water bottle. "Chad used to come by and talk to Lucy, Dawn's mom, for hours. She adored the man. I overheard him telling Lucy things were turning around. He found a way out of his and Dawn's money troubles. Soon he was going to have enough cash to take care of her and her daughter like queens. Her mother is non-verbal, so he had no worries she'd tell anyone what he said."

"Do you think he meant he was selling Janie?"

"I do now," Nancy said.

"Have you told anyone else your suspicion?"

"Dawn. You. Your grandmothers." There was a long pause

before Nancy added another name. "And Coach Rutherford. I figured if anyone could stop Chad from selling drugs to the kids, it was the coach, so I told him."

TWELVE

I turned down the street leading to Ted's house, crafting the introduction to our conversation. The police were left off of Nancy's people-in-the-know list, and I insisted they be added. I was elected for the role. I hoped I got through my whole spiel before Ted threw me out or arrested me.

Ted lived in a nice subdivision close to the south side of town. The street was quiet for a late Sunday afternoon. Two teenagers played basketball in a driveway; otherwise the neighborhood was empty.

Ted's house was a single-family home tucked into the corner on the cul-de-sac. It was a charming house build in the 1920s. The porch had recently been updated with a fresh coat of paint, and a bucket of tar was by the garage door. The driveway must be the next item on Ted's home improvement list.

I parked, took in a deep breath, and slowly let it out, repeating the process while I waited for my nerves to settle down. Nope. My hands still shook and the smell of the pie, a peace offering my grandmothers contributed, was more an annoyance than a comfort. I wasn't confident about Ted having a pleasant reaction to my impromptu visit.

The front door opened and Ted stepped out barefooted, wearing faded jeans and a Pittsburgh Steelers jersey. I'd interrupted him during a game. Hopefully he wasn't an avid football watcher. I rolled down the window as Ted walked over. "Hi."

Ted propped his arms on the window ledge. "Well, what do you know? There is some chick parked in my driveway."

"It's unusual for you to have a woman visitor?"

Ted raised a hand. "Thanks, dude."

A teen dribbled a basketball by us and lifted his chin in greeting. "Thought you'd like to know. Lot of crazies been coming by."

Ted snorted. "Little does he know."

"You think I'm crazy?" Temper. Don't ruin your mission before you even get out of the car.

"More like aggravating, which drives me crazy." Ted opened my car door. "Let's get this over with."

"What over with?" It was a habit for me to explain away what I was doing. It was the one constant in our relationship, besides his flirting and subtly, and sometimes not so subtly, mentioning more developing between us. That seemed to have disappeared from our relationship lately, and I was growing concerned. Why had it changed? Was it because of the favoritism talk surrounding me? Or had Ted got tired of waiting for me?

"Whatever you came to talk to me about. I doubt this is a social call."

"It could be. I brought pie." I reached for the container on the floor in front of the passenger seat.

"But it's not." Ted held out his hands. "I'll take the pie. I might as well get something positive from this visit."

I handed him the token for future forgiveness and followed him into his house.

Ted's living room was decorated in a tasteful and sparse manner. There were two leather recliners with a small table separating them, and an area rug in maroon, gold, and burnt orange warmed up the laminate wood floor. A fireplace was on the main wall, a flat screen television hung above it. The art on the walls were pictures done by his daughter, showing the progression of her style as each picture had the grade she'd completed the project in the right-hand corner.

My gaze rested on a large terrarium. An empty large terrarium. I moved behind Ted, grabbing his waist, as I scanned the floor for any slithering going on. "What belongs in there?"

"Twinkle, my lizard." Ted pried off my grasp.

"Okay." My disposition brightened. Lizards I could handle, snakes not so much.

"Want to tell me why you stopped by?" Ted plopped onto a recliner and snagged the remote, turning down the volume on the television.

I shifted from foot to foot, not knowing if it was okay for me to take a seat or if I should wait for the invitation.

"Can you get on with it? I'm missing the game." He aimed the remote at the television. "It's a close one, and I'd like to watch it."

"I'm glad you're planning on being a gentleman." I waited for Ted to ask me to sit down. For some reason, it became important that Ted ask me, and the only thing I chalked it up to was I wanted him to want me there.

"Why wouldn't I be?" Ted's eyes were on the television.

Usually, Ted would've followed up that question by hinting that him not being a gentleman could be more fun for us, so either he was really into the game, or the feelings he'd had for me evaporated. Maybe once there was no competition for me, Ted decided I wasn't worth it.

I dropped into the other recliner. "You might want to turn that off. This is important."

"With you being involved, I know I'll need the distraction." Ted settled into the recliner and turned his head to look at me.

"What does that mean?" I kind of hoped Ted had a bordering-on-inappropriate comment for me.

"It means I'm sure what you're going to reveal to me will irritate me. It's best for my temper if I have something to divert my attention."

"I don't even know why I came." I crossed my arms. "All I wanted to do was help you."

"No doubt." Ted leaned forward, eyes wide. With a

disappointed moan, he collapsed backwards. "I thought he had that ball."

"The Carrs' home was foreclosed on. That's why Chad was living at the store. Dawn didn't throw him out. She was staying at the assisted living center when Chad died, so she has an alibi. She didn't burn down the building to kill him. The large life insurance policy recently taken out on him is a coincidence."

Ted paused the game. "Who told you this?"

At least now I had his undivided attention, though with the anger making his green eyes blaze, I wished I didn't. I gave him Nancy's name, then filled him in about Coach Rutherford.

He rubbed his eyes. "Contrary to your belief, I don't need outside help on this case."

"You needed a little. Neither Nancy nor Dawn planned on coming to you."

"Then Dawn could've sat in jail and faced a murder charge. That wouldn't have been my problem. How about we watch the game and have some pie?" Ted held the remote out and pressed a button. "I'm advising you to stay out of this matter. If it weren't for this game, I'd be hauling you in for questioning."

"On what grounds?"

"You were at Made With Love when the fire happened, not to mention you were photographed holding the synthetic marijuana, and you were at a football game, an activity you never attended before, the very night the team decided to hold a celebration after a win. Something they had never done before. Should I go on?"

"You sound like Officer Mitchell." I slunk down in the chair.

He froze the game with the quarterback in mid-throw. "What did Officer Mitchell say to you?"

I told Ted about the Saturday visit from the officer and how he pretty much parroted Ted's list of my sinister behavior. "If Steve wasn't there, I'm sure Mitchell would've barged upstairs to search my office."

"Steve was over when Mitchell arrived? I'm surprised he didn't shut the officer down immediately."

"No. He arrived later. We had dinner plans."

"I see." Ted resumed the game.

I sat quietly and watched the game, or at least tried, as I had no idea what was happening on the field. "I'm going home."

"Suit yourself," Ted said, gaze remaining on the screen.

"I will."

Ted's cell made an awful noise. He snatched it up and turned off the television. "Detective Roget." His face reddened, then whitened. "On the way."

Ted opened a drawer in the table between the recliners. He took out a shoulder holster and secured his service weapon into the holster.

Fear gripped hold of me.

"Jasper was injured." Ted grabbed my arm and tugged me toward the door. "I need you to go to the hospital. His grandmother should have someone with her, and I doubt Jasper's parents are going to make the trip from North Carolina."

"What happened?"

"Karen was interviewing some of the teens, and some parents found out and went after her. Jasper defended her and was beaten."

THIRTEEN

The emergency room doors swished open, and a small shiver ran down my back. The last time I was in a hospital, I'd taken a bullet meant for Steve. I pushed away the bad memories, having spent way too much of my life focused on the painful moments in my past. Gwendolyn needed me now, and I was there for her.

"He's my baby. My grandson." Gwendolyn, wearing mismatched slippers, a duck and a rabbit, stood in front of the nurse's station. She sniffled and raised a balled tissue to her face, dabbing her cheeks with it.

"I'm sorry, ma'am." The nurse's voice was filled with sympathetic understanding. "We can't let anyone back there. The doctor should be out shortly."

"I want to be with him. He's a police officer." Tears ran down Gwendolyn's face.

I draped an arm around her shaking shoulders.

Sirens screamed. Red lights ricocheted around the room. The unloading zone in front of the emergency room was lined with police cars. Gwendolyn's trembling increased. I tightened my hold on her, watching and praying that there were no other injured officers being brought to the hospital.

Ted jumped out of a cruiser, yanked open the passenger door, and hauled out Coach Rutherford. Chief Moore clambered out of another cruiser and repeated the process for the passenger seated behind him: Andrew Taylor, the fire chief's son-in-law, former volunteer fireman, and the man hiding in the woods talking to Whitney before Made With Love went up in flames.

"They hurt my Conroy." Gwendolyn tightened her fists and moved away from me.

"Mrs. Jasper, I wouldn't say anything to them." I tugged her back to my side.

"That's the problem with this town. No one wants to say anything to Darrel Rutherford."

The doors whooshed open. Ted brought the coach inside, one hand on the man's handcuffed wrists, the other on his shoulder. Coach Rutherford struggled against the grip. His face was bruised in various shades of purple and he yelled obscenities at Ted.

"I was helping that woman and your officer," Coach Rutherford added to the end of the trail of colorful words he had shouted.

A more docile Andrew allowed Chief Moore to lead him into the emergency room. Blood dripped from a gash on Andrew's forehead and he avoided looking at his partner in crime.

Gwendolyn slipped away from me and strode forward. Before Ted had a chance to move the coach out of reach, she slapped Rutherford across the face. "How dare you!"

Rutherford twisted his body, trying to look at Ted. "You going to let the old lady get away with that?"

"With what?" Ted asked. "I was busy checking my phone for an update on Officer Jasper. I didn't see anything."

"I did nothing wrong," Rutherford said.

"You're a liar. Everything you do, those young men do." Gwendolyn waggled her finger at him. "Those boys practically worship you, and you use that for evil. Have them vandalize the town. Assault an officer."

"I did no such thing. I went to help your grandson. He should've known better than to go question those kids without their parents present."

"Known better?" I moved Gwendolyn away from the coach before she took another swing. "His job is to protect the citizens in this town and investigate crimes."

"He was on leave," Rutherford said. "He had no business being there with Karen England. That woman is nothing but a crap-stirrer."

"He's still a cop," I said. "As much as you and others in Eden want to deny it, the team built those bonfires. They hold some responsibility."

"I made sure they were put out," Rutherford said.

"You didn't do a very good job of it," I said.

"Enough, Faith." Ted pointed at a row of chairs against the wall. "Go have a seat."

"If you want to hit someone, hit him." Rutherford used his chin to point at Taylor. "He's the one who set everyone onto your grandson."

Andrew's eyes widened. "But I went there because you called me."

"Shut up, Taylor." Rutherford glared at him.

"We'll sort it all out at the station after we get you two checked out," Ted said. "The parents are all giving us different accounts."

"Ask the reporter. She was recording everything." Rutherford sat tall in the chair, while Andrew hunched down.

"We're looking for her," Ted said.

Gwendolyn clutched onto the chief's arm. "No one will tell me anything about my grandson."

Chief Moore walked over to the counter. "I need these two checked out. Also, is there any way Conroy's grandmother can go back with him? I'm sure he's worried about her. It'll do him a world of good to see her."

"I'll have someone check with the doctor."

Two nurses helped Ted and the chief escort Rutherford and Andrew to examination rooms while a doctor shepherded Gwendolyn to her grandson. The moment Ted and the chief's shadows disappeared, Karen rushed into the waiting room.

"Is Conroy okay?" Her gaze skittered from me to the area just beyond the nurse's station.

"I don't know. Gwendolyn just went back to see him. The police are looking for you. What the heck happened?" I asked.

Karen sank into a chair. "I contacted Whitney Rutherford to talk to her about some pictures I saw."

"Taken at the Made With Love bonfire?"

Karen nodded, leaning her head against the wall. "Whitney and I agreed to meet at the high school parking lot. She said she had a Sunday practice."

Highly unlikely the coach would schedule a practice on a day the Steelers were playing. "Let me guess, she didn't come alone."

"No. She didn't come at all. It was a set-up. Her father and a host of parents were waiting for me."

"How did Jasper get involved?"

Karen heaved out a sigh. "I invited him along. He was supposed to stay hidden in the car and only watch. When the fathers surrounded me, I panicked and yelled for him."

"Are the other parents at the station?"

"I think so. Jasper pulled me out of the circle and told me to run. I did." Karen swiped away the tears trickling down her cheeks. "I hid across the street at the shopping plaza and called 911. I should've stayed and helped him."

"What you should've done was leave it to the police." Ted stood in front of us.

"I was working on a story," Karen said.

"Is Conroy going to be okay?" I asked.

"He's being kept overnight for observation. He'll be bruised and sore for a few days, but he'll recover with no lasting injuries," Ted said.

"That's good." I squeezed Karen's hand. She looked devastated.

"I'm so sorry," Karen said. "I didn't think the parents would lose it like that."

"Your story was putting their children's futures in jeopardy. Some parents will do anything to protect them." Ted knelt down in front of me and Karen. "I need you two to let the police handle the murder investigation."

"From what I'm hearing," I said, "there isn't really an

investigation. The only thing happening is Chad and Dawn's names being dragged through the mud."

"Dawn's name is in the dirt because that's where it belongs," Karen said.

I jumped up, clenching my hands. "That's not true."

"Chad is...was a drug dealer. There's no question about it." Karen stretched out her legs. Dirt coated her jeans. "If you knew—"

Ted directed his barely contained fury onto Karen. "You've created enough problems tonight, Miss England. I don't have the patience for any more of your so-called truths."

"It was the truth," Karen said meekly. "I am sorry about this. I didn't think any of this would happen."

"I'm sure you didn't mean for anyone to get hurt," Ted said. "Both of you need to stay out of this. You don't know what your actions are going to cause."

How did I get dragged into this? My mind replayed my afternoon. Oh yeah, that.

"Dawn is shifting the blame for the fire from herself to my cousin," Karen said. "I can't let that happen. Dawn told the investigator Felicity started a fire earlier that day and it must've reignited."

"Well," I said, ignoring Ted's "remain silent" look, "Felicity did set a rack of scarves on fire at their store."

The doors slid open, a cold blast of air accompanying a furious Felicity into the waiting room. She pointed a crooked finger at Karen. "I told you to knock it off. But no, you wouldn't listen to me."

"It's good to know someone in your family has sense." Ted stood, giving the space up to the fuming Felicity.

"Now you've given me no choice." Felicity trembled from head to toe.

"I told you to stay at home," Karen said.

"This has to stop." Felicity braced her hands on the arms of the chair. Pain flickered across her face. "I didn't want to do this. I didn't think I had to...but it's time."

Karen touched her cousin's arm. "Please. Don't."

Felicity took a wobbly step away from Karen. With her eyes locked on Ted, she moved forward, each step more controlled and firm. She held out her thin wrists. "I did it. I killed Chad Carr."

"No!" Karen popped up from her chair like a jack in the box.

"We should finish this conversation at the station." Ted placed a gentle hand on Felicity's back and headed for the door.

Felicity spun around, holding out her wrists. "Handcuff me in front of everyone."

"I don't think that's necessary," Ted said.

"Take it back, Felicity." Karen stood in front of the doors, arms spread apart. "What will this do to your family?"

"Get out of the way," Felicity said. "Don't make me knock you over."

"I'm helping you."

"No, you're helping yourself, Karen." Felicity swatted at Ted. "You don't believe me? Is that why you're not cuffing me?"

"No. I just don't want to get mobbed when I take you outside."

The crowd in the emergency room parking lot had grown. Men, women, and a couple of teenagers peered inside, none daring to break through the barricade that consisted of Wayne and Wyatt Buford.

In the corner by the right side of the door, Gussie sat in a vinyl outdoor folding chair, aiming a hose at the crowd. Was she planning on using water from the fire hydrant or whatever liquid her boys had sucked out from plumbing and sewage jobs? The crowd must've wondered too because they stayed well back from the doors and Gussie.

"I expect you to write a darn good story about my arrest." Felicity squared her shoulders, raising her chin in a defiant manner. "And it better be fair to the police. I want the town to know I'm ready to face the consequences for my actions. Take some pictures too."

"I don't think so." Ted turned his back to Karen.

"I also want you to promise, Karen, that you'll stay out of this."

Felicity pointed a trembling finger at her cousin. "Promise me."

"I promise." Karen took out her cell phone, tears rolling down her cheeks. Half-heartedly, she took a few snaps. "Faith, tell her this isn't a good idea. Being arrested and charged for murder isn't some game."

No, it wasn't. A confession was nearly impossible to take back once uttered.

FOURTEEN

When I arrived at work Monday morning, a crowd was growing in front of Scrap This. I knew it had less to do with an aching need for scrapbooking supplies and more about the drama everyone wanted to hear. Karen had not only used a photo she took last night of Felicity, head held high and holding her wrists toward a headless man in a Pittsburgh Steelers jersey, but also wrote her cousin's confession verbatim. Since the Steelers were one of the professional football teams Eden claimed as their own, no one was quite sure which officer arrested her, so there was no public outcry against Ted. Of course, Felicity's confession might have helped with that.

"It doesn't make any sense." Marilyn fiddled with the cardstock in the racks, arranging and rearranging the colors.

I agreed. Felicity's admission took everyone by surprise, especially Ted and Chief Moore, who hadn't known what to do with the determined woman.

"I don't know what she was thinking," Marilyn continued. "I did my damnedest to get out when I was thrown in jail, and she told Detective Roget to lock her up."

"Maybe she's guilty. I mean, she had tried to burn Made With Love earlier that day," I said.

"Then why wait to say something until yesterday?"

I divvied the change into the correct slots in the register. "Maybe her conscience got the better of her. If I was hiding something and other people were getting hurt because of it, I'd confess too."

"Burning a man to death doesn't seem like something Felicity would do. She's such a soft-spoken, tender-hearted woman."

The curtain separating the store from the storage room fluttered. I watched the curtain, nervousness racing through me. The air conditioning wasn't on, so there was no reason for it to move. Fingertips wrapped around the curtain. My grandmothers said they'd come in at noon, and Sierra wasn't scheduled to work today. Who had entered through the back, and how? Did I forget to shut the back door?

I grabbed a pair of sharp-tipped scissors from the wall and ripped open the package. "I think we have an intruder."

"Who's there?" Marilyn called out, picking up the phone receiver at the front counter.

Great idea, give them a warning. The curtain opened, and my grandmothers stepped into the store. I placed the scissors down as my heart rate returned to normal.

"We didn't expect you so early." Marilyn hung up the phone.

"After Felicity's arrest, we figured the store would be busy today," Hope said.

"Gossip is what they came for, not scrapbook shopping," Marilyn said.

Mrs. Barlow stood in front of the glass window with a decorated container embraced in her arms.

Now what was going on?

"She's here to ask you to put out a collection jar," Cheryl said.

"What?" I exchanged a confused glance with Marilyn.

"Didn't you read the paper?" Hope typed the password into the register.

I shook my head. For once, I deliberately avoided it. The pictures on the front page said all I wanted to know.

"Karen England wrote there's a fund being started for Felicity Sullivan's legal expenses. There's been some site set up to take donations," Hope said.

Cheryl crossed the room, flipped over the sign, and unlocked the door.

"Welcome to Scrap This. Please let us help you fulfill your crafting needs."

Women spread out across the room.

"Here you go." Mrs. Barlow banged the container onto the counter. "The church is collecting money to set up a scholarship fund for Brandon. Poor boy. Paralyzed in a car accident, and now his mother is going to the pokey."

"Technically, she'll be arraigned for a trial first. Prison comes later," I said.

Mrs. Barlow didn't look amused by my correction.

"I'll put in the first donation." Marilyn took ten dollars from her wallet and dropped it into the slot.

A nice-looking man with short cropped blond hair hovered around the front sale table. In one hand, he carried a leather case the size and thickness of a children's chapter book, in the other he held a pack of stickers. He tapped the package on the edge of the table, then put it down. A few minutes later, he picked it up again and placed it back onto the pile. Either he needed a lot of help with picking up something for the scrapbooker in his life, or he was here for an entirely different reason.

"Hi, I'm Faith. Can I help you?"

"Faith Hunter?" He opened the leather case covering his tablet.

"Yes."

"Then you can." He pulled out a business card and held it out to me.

Charlie Powell, Investigator, Full Life Insurance Agency.

"Dawn Carr requested I speak with you. She said you could clarify, and also confirm, much of what she has told me." He unclipped a stylus from the side of the cover and tapped away on the large screen. "According to Mrs. Carr, you were not only present when the fire started at Made With Love, but also when the arsonist confessed to killing Chad Carr."

All other private conversations in Scrap This ceased.

"That's not quite the way I'd word it," I said.

"Then how would you?" He stopped tapping and sighed. "I don't have all day."

"Wouldn't it be better to have this conversation in private?"

The women in the store became louder, but they weren't fooling me. They were making an attempt at background noise so the investigator and I would think it was safe to chat again.

"Yes, I think you're right. How about we take a field trip?"

"Fine with me, as long as we take separate cars." I'd nosed around enough in investigations to know it wasn't smart to get into a car with a stranger. A printed business card was not proper identification.

Seeing the charred remains of Made With Love in broad daylight made me want to cry. The grass was dead around the building, leaving a burnt circle that formed a boundary more menacing and heartbreaking than the yellow crime scene tape the police strung across the remaining trees. Half of the building remained partially upright, held up by two scorched and leaning support beams. I didn't know if it was memories of the night or the slight wind that tinged the air with the smell of smoke.

Staring at the ground, Charlie walked around the area, taking notes and pictures on his tablet. There was a scorch mark on the ground he took particular interest in. It looked like it went around the entire area where Made With Love had been.

"Do the police know we're here?" I walked up the hill to the burnt remains of Made With Love, doing my best not to step on anything Ted might claim was evidence.

Charlie flipped the case closed on his tablet. "They know I'm in town talking to possible witnesses. I want to know where you were standing Friday so I can get the best picture of that night in my head. There are some details I do not quite understand."

"I don't know how much I can help. When I arrived, the police and fire department were here and had most of the area blocked off."

"I'm talking about earlier that day. When," he opened the case and tapped on his tablet, "Mrs. Sullivan threatened to, and then did, set the building on fire. Mrs. Carr told me you had a front-and-center view of the whole incident, and I could trust you to be forthcoming with information."

"That was an accident."

"An accident?"

I kept it short, making sure I only told him what I saw without adding any elaborations or unneeded details. I was sure all the investigator wanted was the facts of what went down, not the commentary.

Without looking down, Charlie tapped the stylus on the virtual keyboard on the tablet. I hoped the man was getting everything down correctly. One small mistake in his note-taking could mean Dawn went to jail for fraud rather than receiving an insurance check. "The night before, there was also a fire at a flower shop and a pawnshop. Has there been any talk about those being the work of an arsonist?"

I frowned. Why would he ask that? "No. Most people are blaming it on the football team not putting their bonfires out properly."

"Has the community done anything to curb this activity?" Charlie asked.

"Not that I'm aware of." If it was the bonfire, would the kids be responsible for Chad Carr's death? Was that why Felicity confessed? Had Brandon been there?

"I'll do a little checking on that."

"Karen England, the reporter who handles the big stories in town, might have more information."

He jotted down the name.

"Can I ask you a question?"

"Sure. I can't promise I can answer it."

"Why do you need to know where Felicity was standing Friday afternoon? Felicity confessed. Doesn't that prove Dawn had nothing to do with the fire and her husband's death?"

"No. There's a very peculiar trail of money, and," he glanced at the mark on the ground again, "some things that aren't quite adding up. There are two points of origin which makes this scene a little confusing, and neither of them was where the fire you witnessed occurred. And then there's the circle around the building."

"Point of origin?"

"Two places where the fire burned hottest. Those spots are where the fire was born."

"And neither was near the front door?" I indicated where the scarf rack had been.

"No. One was in the back of the building, and the other outside." He walked closer to the woods and indicated a patch of ground. "Felicity Sullivan insists the earlier fire wasn't put out all the way. She says she saw some tiny embers glowing under a wooden quilt rack, and tugged the quilt on display down to hide it."

What quilt? I conjured up the room. It wasn't in my memory.

A few feet away large rocks, blackened by soot and scorch marks, were in a semi-circle. Some teens had been at Made With Love that night, though they were leaving when I arrived. Had they started a bonfire and abandoned it without ensuring it was put out?

"You know an awful lot about fires," I said.

A sad smile crossed his face.

"My first job was being a firefighter, and I also helped with arson investigations."

"Too much stress?"

"Injured on the job." He gently patted the side of his head. "Part of a building caved and I was trapped inside. I took a hard blow to the head when a beam collapsed, and my lungs were damaged. I can't go into a fire anymore, and I'm not physically fit for the police force."

"I'm sorry. It had to be devastating, giving up your dream job because of an injury."

"Sometimes you have to find a way to tweak a dream to fit into your life."

"I had something happen that also diverted my original life plans, so I know how it can hurt."

"What did you want to be when you grew up, Miss Hunter?"

I laughed. "I think I still have some growing up to do. My dream was to become a lawyer to help the downtrodden and put criminals behind bars. We didn't have the money for me to go to college, so I joined the Army and figured I'd go to school once I got out. Life made me change those plans."

He nodded. "It'll do that sometimes. Though you are doing it, in a way. You did help bring some murderers to justice, or at least that's what Mrs. Carr told me."

True. It wasn't the way I had originally planned, but I was fulfilling my dreams. The last words I heard Chad speak played in my head. An idea took shape. It was kind of out there, yet still possible.

"What if Carr set the fire himself? If he was going to burn the building down, that would've been the perfect night. I overhead him talking to someone. He said it had to be done that night. Maybe he meant burning down the store." Could the insurance money, not selling the synthetic marijuana, be the way Chad planned on having financial security for his family?

"You might be onto something, Miss Hunter. The hang-up for me is how would the man receive the insurance money? He'd be dead. Thank you for your time. I'm going to head over to the fire station and have a chat with the chief about these bonfires. We insure a lot of businesses in this area, and our company will go under if we keep getting three claims a week."

While he went to talk to the fire chief, I'd stop by the nursing home and find out if anyone else overheard Chad saying something to Lucy.

FIFTEEN

The assisted living facility where Dawn's mother lived was located three miles from the hospital on the south side of Eden. One of the recent improvements in Eden was creating a direct road from the facility to the hospital and allocating a budget for a paramedic to be on staff, allowing the health care workers the option to transport residents themselves. I took a spot at the far of the end of the lot, leaving the closest ones for family members.

I had texted Nancy before I headed over. She met me by the front door with a visitor's badge and an illustrated map of the grounds.

"Everything going okay at work?" I asked, accepting the items.

Nancy adjusted the stethoscope draped around her neck. "The powers that be are discussing what the consequences will be for us breaking the rules."

"I hoped they'd let it go since allowing Dawn to stay helped her mom."

"Management is concerned that when the word gets out, other family members will be upset they weren't granted the same benefit. They have to do something to prove nurses broke a rule rather than treated other patients unfavorably. They're keeping me on duty until I give them the names. They know they won't have any leverage if they fire me now." Nancy held the door open for me.

"I'm so sorry."

"I knew the consequences and felt it was worth it," Nancy said. "Because of the schedule, they know I wasn't the only one. No one will step up and say they agreed to let Dawn stay, and I won't tattle on any of my coworkers. Don't be surprised if the nurses won't speak with you. My job might still be jeopardy, and no one wants to risk theirs."

"Is Dawn here this morning? She'd know who her mom's friends were." Maybe one of the friends or their relatives overheard Chad, not quite realizing what he was talking about.

"Yes. They spend most of their time in the gardens or library."

When I walked into the building, I tried getting the attention of a few nurses. The ones I passed refused to meet my gaze, either busying themselves by pretending to read notes on a clipboard or entering a room.

I ventured outside, stepping into one of the most beautiful gardens I'd ever seen. The two-acre garden was enclosed on all sides by hedge bushes, and beyond them was a ten foot-tall wire fence. The centerpiece of the garden was a three-tiered fountain with a statue of an angel at the top, gurgling water cascading down the side. A decorative rock border encircled the fountain, keeping residents and guests from getting close enough to fall in.

The map showed that the garden was divided into four sections: rose, butterfly, fairy, and vegetable. The fairy garden intrigued me, so I opted to check it first for Dawn and her mother. The little homes were made from wood, moss, and rocks. Tiny roses were blooming in a small garden behind the cottage-style fairy house. I knelt down to inspect the inside; there was a dining table, chair and a recliner, all made out of twigs. A small crystal fireplace had a tiny mosaic painting hanging over it.

From the rose section, I heard off-key singing accompanied by a guttural hum. I followed the voices to a section filled with a smattering of red, white, and pink roses. Dawn smoothed hair from her mother's brow. The frail woman sat half-slumped over in the wheelchair, lips drooping on the sides, hands curled in her lap on top of a rainbow-colored afghan. The woman's eyes were bright blue, her silver hair styled in elegant waves around her face.

"It'll be all right, Mama," Dawn said. "Everything will work out."

Dawn's mother lifted her curled arm toward her chest.

"Let me fix that for you." Dawn rearranged the bright blue scarf draped around her mother's shoulders. "I know you love having some color around your face. You're such a fashionista."

Her mother made a low keening sound and rested her head on Dawn's stomach. Dawn wrapped her arms around her mother and rocked her back and forth.

"Love is all we need," Dawn sang.

The tenderness Dawn showed her mother tugged at my heart. I retreated a few yards from the rose garden and called out for Dawn, not wanting her to know I'd intruded on their private moment.

"Hi, Dawn." I turned the corner and headed for Dawn and her mother. "This garden is a small piece of heaven. The facilities here are lovely and peaceful."

"I doubt you're here to check the place out for your grandmothers." Dawn gripped the handles of the wheelchair. "What do you want?"

Now that I was here, I felt bad about questioning Dawn in front of her ailing mother. There was no reason to upset the poor woman. "I need to ask you a question. In private."

Lucy uttered a sad moan.

"No," Dawn said. "We can do it here. My mom knows everything already. She thought I was making bad choices."

Tears filled the older woman's eyes.

Dawn pulled a handkerchief from a quilted pouch hung from the handles of the wheelchair and wiped her mother's eyes. "Nancy told me what she told you. We were desperate for money, but I still can't believe my husband would sell drugs to teenagers. I know he bought potpourri, but that was it. We had it out in the open. I swear I don't know how that stuff got under our store."

"Is it possible Chad was talking about setting the store on fire? Not selling drugs?" I asked.

Lucy rocked back and forth in the chair.

"How could you think such a thing?"

"Were you selling the building? Was oil discovered? There had to be a reason Chad knew your money troubles were over."

"I know the reason." Dawn gazed lovingly at her mom, a sad smile playing across her lips. "He didn't want my mom to worry about me. He adores...adored my mom and knew she was worried about us. My mom isn't doing well, and Chad didn't want our situation burdening her so he said that to make her feel better."

"That makes sense," I said.

Lucy's movements grew more erratic, almost pitching herself out of the wheelchair.

Dawn sank to her knees and wrapped her mom, wheelchair and all, in a hug. "What's wrong, Mama? Are you too hot?"

Lucy raised a curled hand and brought it forward and back like she was pointing at me.

"Is Faith upsetting you because of what she's saying about Chad?" Dawn set a look on me that could've frozen hell.

Lucy shifted her shoulders, moaning and raising her arm toward me.

I squatted down, meeting Lucy's gaze. "Chad planned to set the store on fire?"

Her mom moved her upper body back and forth, like a nod.

"No. It can't be." Dawn cupped a hand over her mouth as tears fell down her cheeks. "Felicity said she killed him. She started the fire. Why would she lie about that?"

Good question. "Could they have been working together?" As I asked, I realized it didn't make much sense, but neither did Felicity confessing to a crime she didn't commit. Felicity hated Chad. And it seemed the feeling was mutual. Had it all been an act? Charlotte had told Felicity I was planning on talking to Chad. Maybe she really came along to get me off Chad's case. The woman had gone off the deep end pretty quickly, with Chad goading her to take the jump.

Lucy continued making the rapid movements, adding in low moans and guttural noises.

"You want to go back to your room?" Dawn asked.

Lucy's eyes brightened.

Using the wheelchair, Dawn pushed herself to her feet, then fluffed her mom's hair with her fingers. "I'll give you a call later, Faith, so we can talk some more about this."

Lucy raised her crooked hand and tapped my cheek right under my eye.

"She wants to show you something," Dawn said.

A prickling sensation rushed across the top of my head and neck. I jumped up, spinning around. No one was behind me, but I still felt like someone was watching. This was a beautiful garden, so it was unlikely we were the only ones in it.

The sensation of someone spying on me intensified. Nancy had said the other nurses wouldn't be thrilled with my being there. I was known around town for asking questions and involving myself in police matters. Everyone was a fan of the truth until it revealed something they didn't want known.

Dawn set a fast pace down the halls to her mother's room. I wasn't sure if she didn't want anyone to see me going with her, or she wished to get the secret out of her mother's room. A large bulletin board stretched across the hallway wall. Poster boards were displayed, listing classes available for the residents: fire safety, internet scams, cooking, card making.

One of my grandmothers or I should talk with the director about doing a scrapbooking class, I thought. I bet the residents had wonderful stories to document and pass on to their children and grandchildren.

Lucy's room was the second to the last. Dawn unlocked the door and wheeled her mom inside. Yellow curtains with daisies framed the windows and a matching comforter was on the hospital bed. A plug-in fall fragrance made the room smell as wonderful as the garden. Bookshelves lined the walls, filled with childhood classics: *Little House on the Prairie, Black Stallion*, a Misty of Chincoteague collection, The Bobbsey Twins, and Nancy Drew.

"My mother is an avid reader of children's literature."

"She has great taste," I said.

"That she does." Dawn smoothed a lock of hair away from her mother's face.

Lucy swayed forward toward the bedside table. The only object on the surface was a picture of the Carrs and Lucy.

"What Mom wants to show you is in here." Dawn sat on the bed and opened the drawer. She pulled out a Bible, a stack of letters, a bank book, and an envelope.

Lucy didn't react to anything.

"Is there anything else in there?" I stepped close and peered inside. A few scraps of paper remained in the drawer.

"Nothing," Dawn said.

Lucy made a soft pained sound.

"Maybe it's written on one of these pieces of paper." I pulled them out, placing them on the bed. A stack of business cards were in the back corner.

When I took out the business cards, Lucy grew excited. She hummed and flailed her arms toward it. I flipped it over. Vulcan Catering. This was the third time I'd come across the card. "Was Chad planning on opening up a food business?"

"He never mentioned it to me."

I handed her the card. "This is for a catering company. From the decoration on the card, I'd say barbeque."

Lucy moaned in frustration.

"I love cooking and watching the food truck shows. Chad had been making some private phone calls he wouldn't talk to me about," Dawn said. "He must have wanted to surprise me."

"There's a number on here."

Dawn dialed the number. "It went straight to a voicemail that repeated the number, nothing else."

"Maybe Chad hadn't set it up yet."

Lucy slung her body toward her daughter.

"Mama, I'm trying to understand. I am." Dawn settled her mother back into the chair.

I swiped my finger on my cell screen and brought up a search engine. "Let's see if I can find anything about Vulcan Catering."

The first option was for Vulcan, Star Trek. The next one, Vulcan, God of fire and volcanoes. Lake's strange behavior played in my head, mixing in with Charlie's suspicion about the fires. There was nothing about a Vulcan Catering. Chad had told his mother-in-law he found a way to make money. And Dawn mentioned private calls. Had Chad turned to arson? Either setting it or arranging it for his store? "Is it possible Chad set Made With Love on fire?"

Dawn tore the card I held into shreds and shoved the rest into her purse. "I know Chad wasn't the hero I saw. But he's also not the villain everyone else claims. He didn't set those fires. And he didn't kill himself."

Lucy fixed her intelligent gaze on me. I could read in Lucy's eyes what her daughter refused to understand. Chad had set Made With Love on fire. He just hadn't planned on killing himself.

As I walked out of the facility, I called the number on the business card. Dawn needed to believe in her husband's innocence so much, I couldn't trust that she told me the truth. The phone rang twice before a message played with an automated voice repeating the number.

I knew my next step—filling Ted in on everything I discovered. My heart broke for Dawn. The ugly truth was going to destroy her.

"Go to the interview room and stay put. Don't move until Ted gets here," Bobbi-Annie greeted me when I walked into the police station. She readjusted her headset so the mouthpiece was closer to her mouth. "And don't tell anyone I told you to hide out back there."

"What—"

Bobbi-Annie pressed a finger to her mouth and shook her head, pointing down the hallway where the only rooms with doors were located. Most of the area in the station was an open bay, the exceptions being Chief Moore's office, the one interview room, a holding area, and the one restroom.

I'd argue with her, but since Bobbi-Annie wasn't participating in the conversation, I'd be quarrelling with myself, and I already did that enough. Since Bobbi-Annie warned me not to leave, I snagged a Diet Coke from the vending machine on the way to the room. Who knew how long I'd be there, and why Ted demanded I wait for him. Okay, technically Bobbi-Annie told me to hang out in there, but I was certain Ted issued the order.

Had Dawn called the police and informed them that I was on my way to disparage her husband's character rather than redeem it as she had asked me to do?

I took a seat on a metal chair, placing my purse on the table, and shifted in all different directions trying to find a comfortable spot on the chair. Not working. I moved to another seat and experienced the same problem. The room wasn't made for relaxation. The minutes dragged by. I dug my phone from my purse and opened a game. Might as well amuse myself until Ted arrived.

As I reached the end of my lives, the door opened.

"It's about time." I dropped my phone back into my bag.

"Nice of you to stop by." Officer Mitchell strode in.

I straightened my spine, hoping to exude confidence even though my insides quivered. "I came to speak with Detective Roget."

"About the Carr case, I presume." Mitchell leaned forward, bracing himself on the table.

"Presume what you want."

He grinned at me, a cross between full-out evil and a comeuppance was coming. "Trust me, I am. I'm sure you're here because you just happen to have information that is necessary for Roget to solve the case. Details, I'm sure, that take you squarely off the suspect list and put someone else on it."

"I'm not a suspect. Felicity confessed. Or haven't you been paying attention to what's going on in Eden?"

"I have been paying attention to what's going on in this, and how you seem to be smack in the middle of all of it."

"It's hard not to get involved when a police officer keeps

accusing you of being involved even though there is a suspect in jail for it."

"A woman who's confessing to a crime for the benefits it gives her, not because she actually did it." Officer Mitchell sat in the other chair, stretching his muscular legs out.

"What are you talking about?" I shoved the tremor out of my voice.

"Felicity couldn't have killed Chad Carr," he said. "But I'm sure you could've."

"She said she did it," I said. "And I wasn't there. I was at home."

"Alone. Right? Or were you with Steve Davis?" He leaned forward. "How about you tell me what happened that night? Did you find out Chad Carr was a drug dealer and was planning on letting you take the fall for it? He didn't go running to the police to tell them you weren't dealing Janie. That's a mighty good reason to kill him. Did you confront him Friday night? Maybe he tried making a move on you...forcing some unwanted attention your way and you had to defend yourself. You're not the type to sit back and let someone push you around."

Coldness shot through my body. Officer Mitchell was interrogating me, trying to give me an "out" for the murder he was certain I committed. I wasn't falling for that trick a second time. I was older, smarter, and had solved a few murders myself.

"I have nothing to say to you."

"That's unusual. You've had no problem talking about this case around town. Visiting Dawn and her mother. Talking with Charlotte Hanson and her daughter. Mrs. Barlow."

Calmly, even though my knees quivered, I picked up my purse and headed for the door. He couldn't hold me here.

"You're not the only one playing detective in town, Hunter. Karen has strong evidence to prove her cousin is innocent," Mitchell said.

SIXTEEN

The doorbell rang, sending my nerves into a frazzle worthy of a naughty child going to speak to Santa Claus. I knew I didn't do anything wrong. Okay, not really wrong, but I still feared that on the other side of the door was an officer ready to haul my butt to jail.

I peered through the peephole. It was an officer. I just wasn't sure if he was here to lecture me or arrest me. I cracked the door open and peeked at Ted. "Can I help you?"

"Let me in, Faith." He waved a takeout bag. "Hamburgers and fries from your favorite fast food place. I know you skip meals when you're upset. I want to know what Mitchell said to you."

Since he was here on a truce mission, and had food, I let Ted inside. "Mitchell thinks I'm the real murderer, even though the woman who confessed is behind bars."

Ted shut the door with his foot. "Kitchen or living room?"

"Living room." I cleared coloring books and pens from the coffee table. I collapsed onto the couch and waited for Ted to serve me.

He handed me a wrapped burger and a medium container of fries.

"Thanks." I tucked my feet under me and nibbled at my food.

"What else did he say? Bobbi-Annie said you hightailed out of the station like there was a crime you needed to solve."

I narrowed my eyes. His joke wasn't funny. "He had a whole bunch of scenarios on my motive for killing Chad, and he also knows who I've been talking to."

Ted wiped his mouth with a napkin. "That doesn't surprise me."

"What doesn't? That he's made a list of reasons why I'd want Chad dead? Or that he's been spying on me? He's certain Felicity's innocent. Said that she couldn't have done it and Karen will prove it."

Ted choked on his food. I whacked his back a few times to get everything unclogged from his windpipe.

"I'll be damned," Ted said, once he regained the ability to speak. "It's not Jasper."

"What isn't?" I was growing frustrated at becoming the "what" girl. I bet it was how Ted felt about me. Usually our conversations were Ted asking me what was going on.

"Jasper isn't the one leaking details of the case to Karen England. It's Mitchell. Considering Jasper is in love with Karen, we didn't probe too hard as we were certain it was him, and since he's out on medical leave, the chief thought it was best to let it be a bygone."

"He's going to be all right?"

Ted nodded. "Though he's going to be a little brokenhearted when he finds out Karen is taking up with Mitchell. Jasper could've been seriously hurt."

"Or killed." The words trembled out of me.

"I don't think they would've killed him."

"I haven't heard that the people responsible have been arrested."

"Unfortunately, there are a lot of tight lips in this community, and no one wants to admit which adults took part in the assault. Rutherford swears he was helping, and while the other parents acknowledge it, they won't tell us how he was involved. Jasper was attacked from behind, so he didn't see."

"Andrew Taylor was there. Rutherford blamed him for it."

"Rutherford meant Andrew was the one who posted on the team's Facebook page that Karen England and an officer were having a private chat with the kids at the high school."

"How did Andrew know?"

"Rutherford swears Andrew told him. Andrew swears that Rutherford texted him about it."

"Easy enough. Check his texts."

Ted rolled his eyes. "Thank you for sharing that brilliant idea. I'd never have thought about it. Andrew deleted the text. He never keeps any of them."

Since Ted was in a sharing mood, I decided to ask another question, hoping he'd go with the flow. "Why is Officer Mitchell certain Felicity is innocent even though the woman confessed? He has to have a reason, besides having a thing for Karen."

"I can't tell you, Faith."

"It's not like you're revealing something top secret. Mitchell already hinted at it. He said it wasn't possible that Felicity killed Chad. I don't know why he'd say that, since she did start a fire previously."

The look passing across Ted's face said it all. Chad hadn't been killed by the fire.

"Was Chad shot?"

"It's best you not know." Ted gathered up the trash. "I don't want you revealing it to anyone."

I clutched a decorated pillow against my stomach. "You don't trust me. You're afraid I'm going to tell someone and then the murderer will know."

Ted started to reply, growing quiet when the front door began opening. He motioned for me to hide behind the corner of the couch, placing a hand near the holster at his hip.

I shoved his hand away. "It's my grandmothers. I called in to work annoyed, and they're coming to make sure I'm not doing something lame-brained."

Instead of my grandmother walking in, it was Steve. My face flamed. Anger wormed through my entire body. I had forgotten to ask Steve for my key back, but after our talk on Saturday, he should've known popping in to surprise me was no longer appropriate.

Ted gathered up the garbage, turning toward the kitchen. "I trust you. Others not so much."

Did he mean Steve? I looked from one man to the other. Steve gave Ted a hard stare, which he returned.

"I'll just throw this out at my place." Ted changed direction. "It'll get me out of your way quicker so you can carry on with your night."

"Ted, wait." I placed a hand on his arm. He jerked away from my touch and walked out the door.

I slammed it shut and thrust my hand out. "Give me my key. You have no right to just walk in here."

"I saw Roget's car and figured the threat to arrest you was no longer just a threat." Steve dropped the key onto my palm. "I came to help you."

"There's no reason for them to arrest me."

"Chad Carr's murder."

"Felicity did it. Remember? She's in jail. Admitted to it."

"She lied," Steve said.

"She's recanting her statement?"

"She hasn't."

"Then I'm safe. There's no reason for you to barge into my home."

"Karen brought the police her cousin's medical records proving Felicity couldn't have bludgeoned Chad Carr to death. She has rheumatoid arthritis and wouldn't have been able to lift up an object heavy enough to crush in Chad's head."

My eyes widened. "Why would she lie?"

"According to Karen, it's so her son could go to college."

Felicity had been working at Polished on Saturday. She saw all the business coming Charlotte's way because they believed she killed Carr. "She thinks the only way her son can go to college is by confessing to a murder? That makes no sense."

Felicity overheard my conversation with Charlotte at Polished. Did Felicity really believe Allan would pick up extra insurance clients if she went to jail? Some people hadn't been very nice to

Dawn at church, but that didn't mean the town was going to support Chad's murderer.

My mind clamped onto the image of the business cards, swirling them through my mind. I had wanted to tell Ted about them but got sidetracked, and then Steve crashed in on us. What if it wasn't just because of her son—but to save her husband?

Allan insured all three of the businesses that caught fire: Lake's florist, Clive's pawnshop, and Made With Love. What if the business card wasn't a front for Chad but Allan? Had Chad been killed because he was going to tell the police about Allan and Vulcan Catering? Chad might've had all those extra business cards as evidence.

I prodded Steve out the door.

"Where are you going?"

"Not your concern."

Ted had to know. Tonight. Even if I was the last person he wanted to talk to.

A car glided down the street, slowing down, then jerking forward. Ugh. It was probably Mitchell spying on me. I'd have to convince Ted to meet me somewhere, or I could call him. If he didn't want to speak to me, I'd leave a voicemail.

Steve was almost to his house two doors down when the car screeched to a halt. *Whap! Whap!* Objects thumped near my window. Something slimy smeared down the wall. A hard object struck my arm, causing me to drop my cell. I heard the screen shatter.

"Hater!" Items were launched in my direction.

I hunched down, using my car for cover.

Teens leaned out of the passenger-side car windows. "Coach Rutherford rules."

Eggs and paint were heaved in my direction. They splattered on the roof of my car. The gooey concoction coated my hair, running down my face and back. Paint cans clattered to the ground. The car tore off down the road with the smell of rubber filling the air.

Steve ran across my grandmother's front yard. "Are you okay?"

Eggs dripped from my hair into my face. I wiped blobs of yolk from my eyes. "Yes."

Another glop of egg slithered from my head into my eyes. I lifted up the hem of my shirt. Nope. Half of my shirt was yellow, the other black, and neither of those were the original color. At least it was just a shirt. I wasn't looking forward to receiving the estimate to repaint my car blue.

"I'll call the police." Steve picked up my cell and tapped the screen. It remained dark. "I'll use your phone."

"I don't have a landline anymore." Maybe I should work it back into my budget. I had thought there was no need for it when I had my cell. Now I knew I was wrong.

"I'll call from my house, then stay with you until they get here."

Paint and egg dribbled down my forehead, causing me to slit my eyes closed as I Frankenstein-walked into my house. "I'm going to get cleaned up."

In record time, I de-egged myself and ran over to Steve's house. I didn't want him coming back over. Once Ted heard about this incident, he'd head over, and I had to talk with him.

Since Steve had no problem coming inside my house, I burst into his. When I saw his living room, breath whooshed from my lungs. The area was filled with boxes, packing material, and tape. Some boxes were sealed and labeled, while others were open and ready for filling. Steve was moving.

The fact stunned and angered me, flooding tears into my eyes. "You weren't going to tell me. My grandmothers."

Steve gaped at me, slowly putting the phone onto a charger.

I wanted to kick myself. It was apparent Steve planned on moving on from me, not just by ending our friendship, but removing himself completely from my life. That betrayal hurt deeper than finding out that all along he'd known about my past.

"I was going to tell you. Delaying the inevitable."

"Were you afraid I'd try talking you out of it?"

His shoulders heaved up and down, head lowering as he stared into the box. "I was afraid you wouldn't."

"I wanted to stay friends, Steve. You didn't." From the corner of my eyes, I saw a piece of eggshell in my hair. I picked it out. Patting the top of my head, I searched for more shells.

"Let me help." Steve gently took hold of a piece of shell, sliding it from the top of my scalp to the end of the strand resting just beyond my collarbone. His hand lingered, twirling the strand onto his index finger. Steve scooped the hair back from my face. Love and desire shone in his deep brown eyes.

Uncertainty tugged at my heart. Was saying no to Steve freeing myself from Adam, or giving him back control? Why had I decided Steve was off-limits? The past? Adam? Myself? Thoughts warred in my head and heart.

No. In a rational moment I had decided it was the best decision, and now I wasn't going to let longing change it. The last thing I wanted was to reconsider my decision, especially since Steve was leaving. "When are you moving?"

"The end of the week."

"That soon? How long have you been planning this?"

"Since Saturday. The furniture came with the townhouse, so it's only my personal items."

"But my grandmothers...the rent. What will they do?" My grandmothers were his landlords. They were getting by financially, but Steve's moving out might tip their finances into the red. "I know Cheryl's been standoffish. She'll come around."

"I have a month-to-month lease. I'm sure they can find someone else who'd like to rent the place." Steve went to stroke my cheek, only to pull his hand back when his fingertips were centimeters from grazing my skin. "It has nothing to do with Cheryl. It's too hard living so close to you."

"Where are you moving to?" I had broken up with Steve. It wasn't fair to expect him to stick around.

"You should go over and tell your grandmothers you're okay." Steve tipped his chin toward his living room window.

Two police cars with lights flashing stopped out front. Neighbors came out of their homes and stood on the sidewalks.

"That's a good idea." I inched by Steve, my body brushing his, and desirous feelings sprang to life.

I hurried out the door, not wanting Steve to know he still affected me. It was hard to get my brain and heart on the same page. Love wasn't so easy to turn off, even when you knew a man wasn't the right one for you.

SEVENTEEN

Keys? Check. Business card? Check. Broken cell? Check. Patience? Working on it. Last night, I had been torn between furious and sad when Ted hadn't shown up at my house. I knew he was irritated at Steve treating my home like his own, but Ted still should've been concerned about me.

My to-do list for the day started with buying a new phone and switching over my contacts. I had teenagers redecorating my house, a cop out to prove I was guilty of murder, and people to question about that murder, so a new cell was my highest priority. After that I was giving Ted the business card and telling him my theory.

Whether he liked it or not.

Stepping outside my house, I hit the automatic lock button. An engine hummed from down the street. Shielding my eyes I checked out the street, trying not to cater to the instinct of fleeing. Last night's dousing had me a little paranoid. A cruiser drove down the block. The lone occupant had red hair.

Ted was coming to check on me. Hours later.

He parked at the curb. I planted my hands on my hips and raised my chin, demonstrating my unhappiness. Unless he was bringing coffee. I'd change my attitude quick-like if he had caffeine.

Ted strode toward me, adjusting all the paraphernalia attached to his belt. No coffee. Considering he was wearing every police device manageable, this wasn't a check-on-me visit, it was business. The dark aviator sunglasses he wore hid his eyes from me, giving me no clue of his mood.

Well, here went nothing...or everything. I tugged the business card I found at the stadium from my back pocket. "I think Eden has an arsonist."

"What?" Ted lifted his sunglasses, resting them on top of his head.

"Lucy told me Chad had planned on burning down his business."

"Did she now?" Ted didn't look happy or like he believed me.

"In her own way. And since Chad couldn't have set his building on fire when he was dead, it means someone else did it. I found this card in the alleyway at the football stadium." I handed it over. "Chad was talking to someone and dropped it. Lucy had some in her night table. Chad had given it to her for safekeeping."

"Where is that card? And when did you speak with Lucy?"

"Dawn tore one up and took the rest. I talked with Dawn and her mom yesterday afternoon."

Ted tapped the card against his fingers. "Lucy Cooper died last night."

Oh no! "I'm so sorry to hear that." My heart twisted. Poor Dawn. First her husband, now her mom.

"How did Dawn Carr appear yesterday?" Ted asked.

"Normal. Well, as normal as a person could look when she knows her mother is dying, her husband was just murdered, and no one cares."

"Was Dawn Carr anxious?"

The use of Dawn's full name with every question settled into my mind, making me draw a horrible conclusion. "Lucy didn't die of natural causes."

"What makes you think that?"

"Your style of questioning. You're very predictable, Detective Roget."

A small smile flashed onto Ted's face, then quickly melted. "I'll remember that. Lucy Cooper overdosed on pain medications yesterday."

"And you think Dawn gave them to her mother?" I shook my head. "Didn't happen."

"Were you there last night?"

"No." I fiddled with the keys, accidentally setting off the car alarm. The Malibu blared and the headlights flashed on and off. I silenced the car and shoved the keys into my front pocket. "Sorry."

"Then how do you know that?"

"Because—"

I never finished my reason, as a car squealed to a halt just inches behind Ted's cruiser. Ted pivoted, shielding me with his body, hand resting on the butt of his revolver. I stayed behind him, not wanting to make Ted nervous, or have him feel he needed to unholster the gun to protect me.

Karen jumped out of the pale blue, almost silver Chevy Cruze. "When are you going to release my cousin? I gave you and the prosecutor's office proof she is innocent. I want her out now."

"Felicity couldn't have bludgeoned anyone." I rested my chin on Ted's shoulder to whisper in his ear.

"I swear I'm going to harm Davis. Severely." Ted stepped away from me, shoving the card into a small pocket in his vest. "It might be proof to you. But it's not to us."

"She couldn't have done it. You know it. Lucy's death proves it." Karen grabbed Ted's arm, forcibly herding him toward the cruiser. "You let her out right now."

"Control yourself, Miss England, or you'll find yourself in a cell next to your cousin."

"That woman killed her mother. Her own mother! If that doesn't prove the type of person she is, nothing will."

"Your cousin confessed to Chad Carr's murder."

"She couldn't have possibly done it."

"Then how did she know Carr died from a crushed skull?" Ted asked. "Did you tell her about that detail Mitchell passed on to you?"

Karen turned a deep red.

A door opened and Mrs. Barlow stepped outside in her faded flowered housecoat, videotaping Ted and Karen's battle of wills and words.

"That's what I thought," Ted said. "Adrenaline can give people a lot of strength."

Why would Dawn kill her mother? I replayed our conversation in my mind, bringing her image into focus. No. She didn't kill her mom. Dawn was devastated by her mother's illness and wanted her mom to fight. It was her mom who was ready to leave the Earth. The thought tumbled in my mind, latching onto the questions I had about Felicity's behavior. A mother would do anything for their child. Her love had no statute of limitations; it wouldn't lessen because their child was in their forties. Dawn stayed in Eden for her mom, and with Lucy gone, Dawn was guilt-free to flee and start a new life.

"She didn't kill her," I said.

"See, even Faith agrees with me." Karen sent a triumphant smile at Ted. "Now free my cousin."

"Faith isn't the judge and jury in this case. She doesn't get to decide." Ted's voice rose.

"I didn't mean Felicity," I mumbled.

"Then how come Dawn has disappeared? She's not answering her phone. No one has seen her. Where is she?" Karen asked.

If I were Dawn, I'd avoid Karen's calls too.

"Detective Roget." Mrs. Barlow shuffled across the road in her house slippers, the housecoat flapping open at her knees.

"Please let her be wearing something underneath." Ted sent his hope up into the sky.

Mrs. Barlow loved a man in uniform. Any uniform. Any man. One of Mrs. Barlow's hobbies, besides spying and gossip, was calling 911 in hopes a hot paramedic, fireman, or police officer would show up at her house. One day, after Mrs. Barlow kept sending the paramedics away when it wasn't the young guy she was crushing on, Bobbi-Annie answered the call to give Mrs. Barlow an official warning, and recorded it on her cell so Mrs. Barlow couldn't plead ignorance later.

"Detective, there's a missing person report," Mrs. Barlow announced.

"Is that so?" Ted lowered his head, tipping his sunglasses forward onto the bridge of his nose. He rubbed at his eyes and emitted a long-suffering sigh.

"I heard it on my scanner. Some guy..."

Another thing about Mrs. Barlow: it was hard to tell what part of what she said was reality and what was from the TV shows she watched. She had a habit of confusing police dramas with the happenings in Eden. And I'm sure living across from me didn't help her keep television viewing and her real life sorted out.

Ted hooked her arm through his. "How about I take you home and you fill me in?"

Mrs. Barlow beamed.

After making sure Karen wasn't following me, I drove over to Made With Love. I had a feeling Dawn was there. She wanted to prove her husband innocent, and knew I was no longer squarely in her corner. Had Chad been involved in setting the fires, or had he hired someone to commit arson? How was Felicity's husband tied into the mess? I had an inkling there was a double-cross somewhere in the scenario.

The only place that might hold the answer Dawn wanted was the store. I worried she'd find the final piece of proof and destroy her own heart and the evidence. With her mom passing, Dawn was probably more determined than ever to demolish the shadow of doubt hovering over her husband's memory.

And if someone was involved with Chad, they might be watching the store. Fixing my phone first might be the more prudent choice, but I intended to talk to Dawn before Karen arrived at the same conclusion I had.

I parked in the vacant side lot. Dawn wasn't going to make it easy. I walked toward the remains of the building.

A heavy scent, a cross between decay and fresh grass, hung in the air. The sun baked the ground, leaving the imprints the firefighters had made embedded into it. I hadn't noticed the footprints on Monday; then again, I spent most of my time trying to figure out why Charlie was interested in the circle the fire had burnt around the building.

A horde of flies buzzed around my face. I swatted at the annoying pests. The town needed to get this mess cleaned up before the bugs got worse.

I squatted down and focused on the circle. It looked like a barrier kept the fire away from the rest of the area. Had someone created a barricade so the fire didn't spread? There weren't any houses or businesses in close proximity. The closest neighbors of the Carrs were the tall trees, deer, and other critters living in the nearby woods.

I walked the perimeter of the dead grass, avoiding the lump of dirt right at the edge of the store property and the woods. Had the arsonist hoped to keep the flames down until the whole building, and Chad's body, were ashes? The other point of origin, bordered by a semicircle of rocks, was a few yards away from the main circle located inside of Made With Love. Counting off the paces, I carefully made my way through the debris, heading to the second point Charlie pointed out. If an ember from the teens' bonfire started this fire, it would've had to fly through an open window and land in the middle of the room

"Why am I not surprised you're here?" Ted clumped up the hill.

"I was looking for Dawn."

"At a crime scene?" Ted stepped over debris.

"It's the only place where she might find something to prove her husband isn't a drug dealer or a fire starter."

"Dawn has to face the truth. Her husband was guilty of selling Janie to the kids."

"You found more proof?"

Ted nodded. "In Lucy's room."

The bank book. "Chad was putting the money into an account in his mother-in-law's name. Right?"

Ted didn't confirm or deny. "I'd prefer you annoy me with

your Clue guesses rather than poke around the crime scene. You might not realize this, but a real police investigation isn't a murder mystery dinner show."

"I know that. Mrs. Barlow had your attention and there was no way I was going to mention Dawn might be here around her. And I was afraid Karen would come here and look for Dawn."

"Officer Mitchell has a close eye on you. If he was around, he'd arrest you."

"Doesn't that man ever sleep? I'm not doing anything wrong. There's no crime scene tape up. How was I to know it's still an active crime scene?"

Ted pushed a button on the walkie-talkie clipped to his bullet-resistant vest. "The tape is down at Made With Love. Find out who removed it." He turned to me. "Time for you to head home. I'll take a look around for Dawn. I'm sure you have better things to do."

"Not really."

Ted fixed a chastising stare on me.

I followed after him.

"Okay, I do need to buy a new phone."

A sharp crack filled the air. Followed by another.

"Get down!" Ted yanked me to the ground, shielding me with his body.

Crack!

I screamed. We were being shot at!

"Get behind the mound." Ted gestured toward the small pile of dirt at the edge of the property. "I'll stay here and draw their attention."

Tears rushed into my eyes. "No."

"Go. An engine is coming this way. I need you out of the line of fire." Ted drew his service revolver.

I couldn't let Ted get killed because of me. The only choice I had was taking cover. My long-ago Army training came in handy as I expertly low-crawled my way toward the mound. I gagged as a decaying stench wrapped around me. What died over here?

Another shot rang out. Ted returned fire. A large black truck with mounted roll bars and tinted windows sped by, swerving off the grass and onto the road.

"Stay there until I give the all clear," Ted yelled. "I have backup on the way."

I had to get away from the horrible smell. I sprang to my feet, catching the toe of my shoe on a root and tripping forward. My hands sank into the soft pile of dirt in front of me. There was something buried here. The dirt was recently turned over. I dug, not caring about the twigs and edges of sharp stones stabbing into my hands. "Ted!"

My hands worked on their own accord. Fingertips protruded from the dirt. I continued digging, revealing an arm. "There's a body up here."

Ted cursed.

My fingers exposed an ear. I brushed dirt from the person's face. Charlie Powell, the insurance investigator, stared vacantly up at the sky.

"Damn." Ted stood over me. He pressed the button on the walkie-talkie. "Found Powell. Send the coroner."

Sitting on the hood of Ted's cruiser, I wrapped my arms around myself.

"You okay?" Jasper handed me a foam cup of Home Brewed coffee, a white bag tucked between his elbow and waist. He had a black eye and a few other purple bruises on his face. "Dianne said raspberry mocha was your favorite."

"Thank you."

Jasper leaned against the side of the cruiser and opened the bag.

"Want a blueberry scone?"

"I'm not hungry," I said. "It's nice to see you back. Unless you didn't want to be."

"The doctor preferred I take a couple more days off, but I wanted to return to duty. Chief Moore needs me. With the fires,

Carr's murder, and now another one, every officer is running on fumes."

"I'm sorry you were in trouble because of me."

"You don't have to apologize. Want to tell me what happened?"

"Detective Roget knows." I fought back tears. I hadn't known Charlie long, but he seemed like a nice guy. Why had he come back to the scene? And more importantly, why had someone killed him?

"When did you talk with Charlie Powell?" Jasper asked. "It seems you're the last person who spoke to him."

I stared at him.

"Charlie Powell's boss called the station this morning." Jasper leaned against the car. "His wife hadn't heard from him all day yesterday and was worried. He always called home to read their daughter a bedtime story. It's something he's done since she was born. His daughter is eight."

Tears ran down my cheeks. "That poor little girl. When was the last time someone saw him?"

"There were sightings of him going into Scrap This and leaving with you," Jasper said. "After that, nothing."

Officer Mitchell would love this. One more reason to label me a murderer.

I watched the coroner van's pull up. "He was going to talk to the fire chief because there was something he found odd about the scene."

Jasper jotted down my statement. "Do you know what time he arrived?"

"I don't know if he even made it. He went to talk to Chief Ridley, and I went to talk to Detective Roget."

EIGHTEEN

"I don't need an escort." I exited my car and stomped toward my front door. I didn't know if my attitude resulted from holding back grief over Charlie's death, Ted ordering Jasper to go with me to replace my phone and then follow me home, or a combination of both. Ted had stayed at Made With Love to secure the scene and wait for the coroner to finish.

"I'd agree with you, except you keeping showing up in places that tick off Detective Roget. Powell's murder just complicated this case."

"*Now* it's complicated?" I unlocked the door.

"With Dawn's disappearing act, the public believes she had more to do with the sale of the drugs than just be being married to Chad. And you've been helping her. I'd advise you to stay inside."

I harrumphed a reply.

"I didn't hear a yes from you," Jasper said.

A shut door was my response.

I pressed my ear to the door, listening for Jasper to pull out of my driveway. I frowned. Nothing. What was the guy doing? I wandered over to the window and pulled back the curtain.

Jasper had walked over to Mrs. Barlow's house. Even from across the street, I could feel the happiness radiating from Mrs. Barlow as she bobbed her head up and down, a beaming smile decorating her face. Jasper hugged her.

Butterflies took flight in my stomach. I had just been had. Moments later, Mrs. Barlow exited her house with a small square black bag and a canopy sports chair. She set up the chair, angling it toward my house. Shrugging off the strap of the bag, she settled into the chair and leaned over to pull items from her bag. With a jaunty wave toward me, she placed a notebook and a pair of binoculars on her lap, and a water bottle went into the chair's cupholder.

I should've just promised Jasper I'd stay put. I sat in the chair near the window and picked up a book from the coffee table. I planned on reading a few pages, then checking to see if Mrs. Barlow had gone inside yet. She'd have to take a potty break sooner or later.

Hours later, I conducted another Mrs. Barlow check. She waved at me. I let go of the curtain. I hated doing nothing. There was no way I was getting out of the house without her squealing on me. I was sure if I said I was going out for a bite to eat, Mrs. Barlow would tag along. I didn't want her knowing what I was up to, and more importantly, I didn't want Ted finding out.

My whole being felt jittery, especially knowing Mitchell was building a case against me. This all started because the teens lied. I had to talk with Hannah. I glanced down at my sneakered feet. Walking was good for a person. I decided against calling Hannah, opting to make it a surprise visit. I'd grab a flashlight, then I was ready. I tugged on a hoodie, zipping it all the way up, and dropped the flashlight down the front. Pressing the flashlight to my side so it didn't slip out of my hoodie, I went out the back door. It might take me a few attempts before I made it over the back fence with one arm.

I was right. It took three tries before I got up and over the fence. Fortunately, I landed safely on the other side, and my neighbor had their Labrador in the house when I made my escape. I wasn't worried about the dog attacking me, just licking me to death. Howard was an overly friendly dog with no boundaries whatsoever.

The streets were quiet. I swept the light back and forth across the ground. At the next town meeting, I'd suggest sidewalks for all areas of town, not just ones in family neighborhoods. I walked as close to the trees as possible without becoming one with them. If Ted got wind of my "prison break," he'd send out a search party, and I was sure in his irritation, he'd dub Mitchell the leader. The trek was longer than I thought and the night had turned cold. When I headed out, eight blocks hadn't seemed that far, but after walking up the third hill, I was regretting my hasty decision of not calling.

After some more heavy breathing and exertion, I reached the Hanson house. There were lights on. Good. I wasn't disturbing anyone's slumber. I rang the bell and waited. I stamped my feet, trying to stay warm. I pressed the doorbell again.

The curtain moved back a sliver. Two blue eyes peered at me then vanished.

"Come on, I see you, Hannah." Or maybe it was Charlotte. Mother and daughter had the same color eyes.

I heard voices arguing in harsh whispers. I debated turning myself into a nuisance, but realized it ruined the whole plan of Ted not finding out. My trip might be in vain. I walked around on the porch. The air felt colder when I stood still.

Finally, the door opened. I rushed inside. "It's cold out there."

"I didn't hear your car." Hannah looked out the door. "Where is it?"

"I walked."

"Why?"

"Long story." Sooner or later someone would check up on me. It had been a long time since I snuck out of my house. The first and last time I had done it I was seventeen—and I got caught. "Why were you at Made With Love the night of the fire?"

Hannah drew back, opening and closing her mouth like an oxygen-starved fish.

"I don't have time for niceties. Karen England plans on proving Felicity lied. When she's successful, the police will come to ask you questions."

"I wasn't there," Hannah said.

"You were already there when your mom and I arrived."

"Why are you doing this to me?" Hannah ran into the living room and threw herself on the couch. School books, notebooks, and index cards slipped to the floor.

I felt a little bad for making her cry, but there was no way I'd go to prison to cover up for her. "I don't want to do anything to you. I'm trying to keep myself out of jail. Officer Mitchell has his sights set on me."

"I swear I had nothing to do with the fire or Mr. Carr's death. I wasn't there." Hannah raised her tear-stained face toward me.

"I saw you there. So did Detective Roget and Officer Mitchell. Try again." My patience and temper were being pushed beyond their limits.

"I got there after my mom. I took Brandon there. He told me his mom went to the bonfire to catch the kids with the Janie. He was worried the football players would hurt her. That stuff can make people crazy violent." Hannah gathered up the items on the floor, placing them on a pile of fashion magazines and catalogs for manicurist supplies.

A little bit of my sympathy returned for Hannah. She knew her friend wasn't physically able to help his mom, so she accompanied him. "Where were you when Brandon called? We went to find you."

"At Daniel's house." Hannah blushed and lowered her gaze to the floor.

"Daniel Burke? The volunteer firefighter guy?"

She nodded.

"At night?"

Hannah huffed out a breath. "Yes. I snuck out to spend a couple of hours with him. Daniel always takes me back home. I don't spend the night there."

Gee, that made it better.

"Daniel didn't want me at the bonfire. Said it would be nothing but trouble." Hannah sat cross-legged on the couch. The girl couldn't keep still.

"At least the man has some sense."

"When my mom saw I'd left, she called my cell. I told my mom

I was with Felicity at Made With Love, that I had promised to help find the drugs." She changed positions again, now slouching against the armrest.

"You have to tell your mom the truth." The web woven was growing thicker and thicker.

"I can't tell my mom." She bolted upright, kicking the stack of books, magazines, and catalogs to the floor. "She'll kill Daniel."

"I'm sure she won't." Hurt him, yes. Kill him, doubtful.

"She will."

The front door opened. "I will what?" Charlotte walked in, frowning at me.

"Give Faith a ride home. She broke down." Hannah rushed out the words.

I occupied myself with picking up the scattered items from the floor. Underneath an order form with a lot of cross-outs was a Vulcan Catering business card. My mind flicked back to the night this all started for me. Charlotte had said she was meeting with an insurance agent.

"I'll bring some pizza home," Charlotte said, motioning for me to move it along.

"Thanks, Mom." Hannah beamed at her. "See you later, Faith."

"So what's going on? Really?" Charlotte asked the moment my derrière touched the passenger seat.

"I wanted to know where Hannah was the night of the fire." I buckled up as the truck shot backwards.

"You have no right to question my child when I'm not home."

"It's because of you and your child I'm in this mess. Hannah let the police believe I brought the drug to the girls."

"Hannah fibbed. She was scared. Don't worry, no one thinks you're a drug dealer."

"Officer Mitchell does. And he thinks I'm a murderer. Karen says there is no way Felicity was capable of killing Chad Carr, and another man was murdered after Felicity was locked up."

"She could've done it beforehand." Charlotte weaved around a pothole.

"No. People saw me talking to the man on Monday. He worked for the insurance agency and was investigating the fires. The company was suspicious about paying out on three policies in this little area."

"I don't blame them. I'd look twice too." Charlotte glanced into the rearview mirror and frowned.

"Are we being followed?" I turned around. A dark-colored truck turned onto the crossroad.

"A little too close to my bumper. I hate tailgaters."

I shivered. Was it the same person who shot at me and Ted?

"You okay?" Charlotte fixed a concerned motherly look on me.

"I'm fine. All of this is bringing up bad memories."

"I'm sorry, Faith." She squeezed my shoulder. "I know trying to protect my daughter is costing you. I promise you won't go to jail. I won't let it get that far."

"Easy to say, harder to do when the time comes."

"We know you didn't kill Carr. I didn't kill him. Hannah didn't. And it seems Karen has enough to prove Felicity didn't. So that leaves..." Charlotte trailed off.

"Allan Sullivan. Felicity is lying either because she wants the hero's reward for killing the criminal, or she's protecting her husband."

NINETEEN

Nightmares had kept me tossing and turning all night. Every time I closed my eyes, Charlie's face—alive and dead—filled my head. Our conversation played over and over like a song on repeat. I tried grasping what my subconscious demanded I knew, but the lack of sleep hindered rather than helped. The one image that was a constant in every reenactment was Charlie's interest in the burnt grass circle. It was like the ring held the answer to finding the murderer and their reason for it.

I had taken some photos on my phone. A clue was in those pictures. Fortunately, the salesclerk at the cell phone store was able to transfer all of my data over. I sprang from the bed, unplugging the new cell from the charger, and raced to my office.

In a few seconds, I'd downloaded them onto my computer. I brought up the picture folder and enlarged the photos to fit the monitor screen. I tapped the mouse, going through each photograph. The circle around the building was nearly perfect. No way it had happened naturally. I didn't know much about starting fires, but I knew a Google search would tell me everything I wanted to know.

I scanned through the search results, stopping on one titled "Using Bonfires for Controlled Burns." As I read the article, fear and anger grew inside of me. During planned fires, a black line was created to reduce the amount of material consumed by the flames. Small fires—back burning—were created to "burn back towards the main fire."

The circle on the ground was the "black line" established to make sure the fire started at Made With Love didn't branch out too far from the building. Someone in the know set the fire.

My mind flickered to the business card I had found at the game after I spotted Chad talking to someone. Had someone stolen my camera because they were afraid I caught them meeting with him?

All the businesses that had burned down were insured by Allan Sullivan. Was that why Felicity turned herself in? To save her husband? It had to raise suspicions, especially in a small town, that one insurance agent sold the policies to all the businesses that sustained fire damage.

Saturday night, Jim Ryland had been upset when I opened his register. Had he been worried that I'd seen the Vulcan Catering business card?

I felt sick. Had Allan found a way to increase his income by causing a few fires in order to pick up more business clients? Was Allan working with someone in the volunteer fire squad? Or was I totally off-base?

God, I really hoped I was off-base. I liked Allan. I liked Felicity. It was easier to consider the people you didn't like as possible murderers.

There were two people who held some of the answers: Felicity Sullivan and Fire Chief Ridley. Only Felicity could tell me if she was afraid her husband was guilty—or knew he was. And Charlie had planned on talking to Fire Chief Ridley, so part of the answer must be at the firehouse. Did Charlie ever get there, or had he been killed before—or because of—his questions?

I decided to visit Chief Ridley first. Felicity wasn't going anywhere.

The fire station looked deserted when I pulled up outside the building. The fire department was manned by volunteers and didn't have someone there twenty-four/seven. Next door, the bowling alley's parking lot was almost at capacity. Ridley was probably helping his wife out with their business. I turned in the direction of the bowling alley, planning on asking him to let me in.

What if Chief Ridley had something to do with the fires?

I let the voice get to me and looked for my own way in. Five feet above my head were windows placed around the station like decorative flowers on a birthday cake. Every twelve feet there was another window. If I parked my car on the side of the building away from the alley, I could stand on the top and look inside; not as good as actually getting into the building, but better than nothing.

I glanced around the adjoining parking lots of the fire station and bowling alley. Only one other car was in the fire station lot. No time like the present. I parked my car right alongside the brick wall, the passenger side just inches from it. I climbed onto the hood, then stood on top of the car, bracing my hands on the windowsill. Leaning forward, I peeked into the truck bay, barely making out anything at all. I needed a little more height.

Standing on my toes, I stretched my neck farther, hoping to get a tiny glimpse of what was on the other side of the bay.

A shotgun racked behind me. "Don't move!"

I held onto the ledge for dear life, afraid to even flatten my feet to get better balance.

"The police are on the way."

"Can I sit? I might slip off the car." I hoped the person holding the weapon was a gentleman—and not the killer.

"Faith Hunter, is that you?" Fire Chief Norman Ridley peered into my face. "Wait until your grandmothers hear about this."

"I'd rather they didn't." If he intended to tattle on me, then he wasn't hiding anything.

"Too late," another voice joined in the conversation.

Ted. How did he always turn up when I was in an unexplainable situation? Or at least one I didn't want to explain.

"Get down from there." Ted held out his arms to help me down.

"I can manage."

I didn't want his help. It made it too easy for Ted to twirl me to place handcuffs on my wrists. I sat, inching my way down the front windshield and hood.

"You're lucky I didn't shoot you." Ridley unloaded the shotgun, pocketing the cartridge. "What in the world are you doing?"

I umm-ed and ahh-ed a non-response.

"Faith."

It had been a while since I heard Ted say my name in that warning tone. I still hated it. "I had an idea and wanted to explore it. I was afraid if I went to you, you'd get in trouble."

Ted groaned. "You need to stay out of this."

"It's hard to when a police officer and a reporter are determined to prove you're guilty of the crime," I said. "If you or Steve try helping me, your jobs are in jeopardy."

"If you wanted a tour, Faith, all you have to do is ask." Ridley's deep twang held a whole lot of amusement at my expense.

"Charlie Powell was coming to talk to you on Monday," I said. "I wanted to find out what you told him."

"That's not for you to ask." Ted's face turned a darker shade of red.

"I took that day off and spent some time at the casino in Rocky Gap. Me and the missus decided to overnight it there," Norman said.

"The whole day?" Ted asked.

"I know everyone in town thinks my life is just firefighting and bowling, but I use quality time to keep my woman happy." Ridley waggled his eyebrows up and down.

That was something Norman could've left off the police-and-Faith-need-to-know list.

"I'd like to take a look around," Ted said. "Charlie Powell was murdered, and I was told you were likely the last person he saw. He was headed over to talk to you."

Ridley shook his head. "I didn't talk to him."

"Are you sure?" I asked. "He was blond. A little over six feet tall. Sturdy build. Had a limp. He was a fraud and fire investigator for the company where Chad Carr bought his insurance."

"'Course I'm sure. As I said, I wasn't here on Monday."

"Charlie told me he was coming to talk to you. There was something about the Carr fire that bothered him," I said, my voice hinting at my frustration.

"I can handle this, Faith. You should head back to Scrap This," Ted said.

"I wish I'd been here. There's something been nagging me and Daniel about it too. Then there's...never mind." Ridley took a keyring from his pocket. "You're welcome to look around."

"You should tell us what's troubling you. It might be helpful," I said.

"He shouldn't tell you anything." Ted turned me around by my shoulder and gave my rear a little swat. "You should head off to work."

"I'm not a child."

I walked through the open bay door.

"Might as well let her come," Ridley said. "She'll just come back later on her own. Best to know what catches her eye."

"I suppose you're right about that," Ted said. "She'll cause less turmoil when I'm watching her."

I narrowed my eyes, wishing I could shoot laser beams to scorch his backside a little.

"Can I ask a question, Norman?"

"Sure, darling."

Ted groaned.

"How did you know I was out here?"

"Easy peasy. Daniel lives in the apartment complex up on the hill. He can see the station from here. He was out on his balcony and saw a car parking on the side, got curious, and used his bird-watching binoculars to get a look-see. Saw someone trying to get inside and gave me a call. I could get here a lot quicker, and Daniel doesn't own a gun."

Good to know. I might need to take some of those investigating classes Ted's brother Bob Roget taught. If I was the go-to girl for anyone getting in trouble in Eden, I needed to brush up on my butting-in tactics. A lot of people had an easy time figuring out when I was up to something.

Ridley walked around a large black truck parked in one of the vehicle slots. He kicked the tire. A clump of dried dirt dropped from the deep ridges of the tire. "Now, why did that boy park this beast in here?"

The truck looked like the one driven by the person who shot at us yesterday, and possibly the one I saw Saturday night at Piece A Pie. The look Ted fixed on me sent a shiver down my back, and not the good kind. He wanted me silent, and this time I obeyed.

"Whose truck is it?" Ted knelt down and picked up the wad of dirt. "Do you normally have personal vehicles in the bay?"

I sidled up to Ted and looked at it. The grass was dark brown, either from being burnt, or from no longer being in the ground.

"Hell no. Now I need to find out where the response vehicle is," Norman ranted. "Daniel sees Faith pull up, but can't see anyone swiping it? What's the good in paying him to keep an eye on things when he doesn't notice this?"

"I'd say whoever owns this truck is driving your missing car."

"That's the last thing I need, my no-good son-in-law trolling around town in my vehicle."

Ted forced out a smile. "Come on, Norm, that doesn't help me out. You say that about each of them."

"Andrew. The one I had to suspend off the squad a month ago. I told Debi to stay away from him. Knew he was no good from the day I met him."

Why would Andrew drive his own truck when he was going to shoot at the police? It was a good way to get caught, and quickly.

"Why are you interested in this truck?" Ridley's eyes widened. "Have anything to do with the man you're asking about?"

"A car similar to this one drove by and shot at me and Faith yesterday," Ted said.

Ridley worked his jaw back and forth, face reddening as he evil-eyed the truck. "When I got back, one of the gals working in the kitchen said Andrew called in sick on Monday. Drunk would be more the truth. I'm not that much of a danged fool. The last month, he's either been drinking or boasting. He's never at the place he should be. My daughter's calling her momma every night in tears because Andrew ain't home."

"And no one knows where he's at?" Ted asked.

"Nope, he's also not showing up for calls. The last call he came to, he was so drunk Wayne locked him in the fire truck."

"When was that?"

"The night Brandon Sullivan nearly died in the wreck. Wayne told me Andrew stumbled up to the scene on foot, tried yanking Wyatt away so he could do CPR on the boy. Andrew kept saying he needed to save Brandon. The next day, I wrote it up, and then suspended him from coming to the station or on any calls until he got himself straightened out."

"How did he get in here?" I asked.

"I keep an extra set of keys at the bowling alley. I bet he went in there and got them when no one was looking."

"Can I get a copy of the discipline report and any records of the calls? I want to check something," Ted said.

Ridley went over to a small office. "I'll give you the discipline report with no warrant, Detective, but I want to know why you want the other records."

I couldn't help it and butted in. "Maybe it's not the kids creating the bonfires but Andrew. The fires we've been having around town coincide with bonfire nights."

"Faith—" Ted issued another name warning.

"In that case..." Ridley opened the door and strode inside the office. "Damn it!"

Ted rushed in, blocking me from entering.

I squatted and peered between Ted's side and the door jam. The place was trashed. The computer was broken and empty file folders were strewn about. Burnt embers filled a metal trashcan.

All the evidence was gone.

Ted walked into the room, frowning as he took everything in. "I'm going to have Jasper come out and help me process all of this.

We might be able to get some fingerprints and find out who did this."

"It's your time to waste." Ridley stalked out of the room. "I know the answer already."

"I'm not quite sure about that. It's too—" Ted began.

"I know what you're thinking, Detective." Ridley grabbed a wrench from a toolbox, lifted up the hood of the truck, then removed something from the engine. "Thing is, Andrew isn't a smart one. The only brilliant thing he's ever done in his life was marry one of my girls, and the only brain-dead thing my middle girl went and done was marry him."

"Just because he's not the brightest color in the crayon box doesn't make him guilty of arson or murder," Ted said.

"I got more than that. Talk to Coach Rutherford too. There was a damn good reason the man threatened him away from the games and the bonfires." Ridley typed out a text, his movements almost violent. "Rutherford passed on some messages Andrew sent his daughter."

"What did the messages say?"

"Asking Whitney to meet up with him, that he needed to talk with her. The coach wasn't happy about them, but there was nothing written to make it a police matter. Coach thought I could put the fear of God into my son-in-law."

"And did you?" Ted asked.

"He stopped going to the bonfires."

No, he didn't. I'd show Ted the Instagram pictures later. "Why didn't you tell anyone?"

"Because he's family. I take care of my family's business."

"Is that what you just did?" I pointed at his cell phone.

"Yep. Told that SOB if he got near my girl again, I'd kill him."

"You shouldn't say that," I said. "If something does happen to him, Detective Roget will have to come to arrest you."

"As he should. 'Cause I guarantee if anything happens to that lowlife, I did it."

TWENTY

Ridley drove out of the bay, parking the long fire truck so it blocked the bay doors. Even if Andrew figured out a way to fix his truck, there was no way to drive it out.

"I need to run over to the alley and let my wife know what's going on." Ridley hopped out of the engine and slammed the door. "If Andrew comes in, I'll have him stalled and send word to you."

"I appreciate it." Ted halted Ridley with a hand placed on the man's shoulder. "I also need you not to mention this to your son-in-law or go looking for him."

"He can't be left to run around this town if he killed a man."

"We don't know that he had anything to do with Charlie Powell's murder," Ted said.

"Then why would he be shooting at you?" Ridley asked.

"If you're right, that's an even greater reason to leave this to me," Ted said. "Your daughters will be brokenhearted if anything happens to you. If Andrew is guilty—"

"I can guarantee it," Ridley said.

"If he's guilty, your daughter will need you even more."

"Detective Roget's right," I said. "Being married to a man accused of murder, especially a guilty one, tears you up. It's even harder when you're alone. People turn on you. Even ones who promised to have your back."

"No one here will do that." Ridley tapped his chest. "I'll always be there for my little girl. So will her momma and her sisters. The town loves her."

"Everyone sure seemed loving to Dawn on Sunday." Bitterness

crept into my tone. "Sometimes people are more willing to believe the bad about a person and hate them than look for the good and love them. She'll need you. Trust me."

Ridley and I entered into a showdown of the eyes. After a few minutes, Norman let out a grunt and raised his hands.

"Okay," Ridley said, punctuating the word with a nod. "If I see him, I'll call. I won't tell him nothing, or wring his drunk neck. I'll leave the justice to the legal system."

"I appreciate that," Ted said.

"Hopefully the town does too. Don't want anyone questioning my reputation because I didn't handle this the old-fashioned way." Ridley stomped off toward the bowling alley.

Ted took hold of my arm and hauled me to my car. "You need to stay out of this. I swear, next time I will arrest you for obstruction of justice."

"I'm not obstructing justice. I'm helping justice. Or at least trying to keep myself out of jail." I brought up Instagram on my phone and searched for the picture of Andrew talking to Whitney. Where did it go?

"Your attempts to find the murderer are likely to put you in jail rather than keep you out of it." Ted paused in the middle of the rant. "What are you doing?"

"I'm trying to find a photo I saw the other day. It was the night of the Made With Love fire. Whitney was talking to Andrew Taylor."

Ted leaned into me, looking over my shoulder at the small screen. My body felt like it was about to combust. "Where's the picture?"

"I don't know. It was on Kirstin's account the other day. She took a selfie and in the background were Whitney and Andrew Taylor. She tagged a few friends on the picture. I wonder if one of them made her delete it. I have a copy on my computer."

"Need any help?" Daniel strolled up to us. "Chief called and asked me to help the police search our office. He said reports were destroyed."

Ted nodded. "Jasper and Officer Glover are coming to process the scene. They can manage just fine."

"I did the majority of the paperwork since all the other guys hated doing it. I can tell the officers what's missing."

"Who else worked on the reports?" Ted asked.

"Andrew Taylor. He'd been ditching his duties before Chief Ridley kicked him out. I should've known he was up to something when I saw him hanging around the station the other day."

"When was this?" Ted opened the door of his cruiser and snatched up his leather notebook.

"Monday. He went into the bowling alley drunk and yelled at the staff. One of the cooks knows I live nearby and called me. I saw Andrew banging on the bay door, wrestled him into my car, and took him home."

"Was this out of the ordinary for him?"

"Getting drunk, no. Yelling, screaming, and picking fights with everyone was new. He was usually a calm, though boisterous, drunk. It's why everyone at the bowling alley let Norm handle it instead of calling the police."

"Andrew wasn't very gentlemanly when I left the police station Friday morning," I said.

Had Andrew been trying to set Allan up Friday night? Who better to shift the blame to than the man selling the fire insurance policies? It was a coincidence that Allan sold them all, but then again, the community knew about the Sullivans' financial struggles, and residents wanting to help them out made sense.

"What's your guess on his personality change?" Ted asked.

Daniel grimaced and looked at the ground.

"Say it," Ted said.

"I don't know if I should, Detective. It feels wrong."

"I need to know. Two men are dead," Ted said.

"Well, the last month has been rough for Andrew. Chief Ridley caught him hosting a party for the teens. From the dressing down I heard, Andrew had some of the synthetic marijuana and gave it to the kids. Chief also wasn't happy because Coach Rutherford gave him hell over Andrew's behavior. He expected the fire chief to keep Andrew in line."

Ted frowned. "Anything else?"

"He had a falling out with Coach Rutherford. He worships the guy, idolizes him. Andrew hates being on the coach's bad side. I think that's why he was so hotheaded the other day and went after Jasper. He wanted to earn Rutherford's respect back."

"The reason for this falling out?" Ted asked.

Daniel shrugged. "I don't know. I figured it had to do with the team. It's one of the things Rutherford actually cares about."

I sent Ted a text message: "Maybe Coach saw the picture."

Ted glanced at his phone, then nodded at me. Daniel headed into the station and Ted walked me to my car.

He held open my car door. "I'm going to talk to Coach Rutherford. I'd like you to come along in case he denies seeing the picture. He told me on Sunday that he monitors his daughter's phone on a regular basis, and that's how he knew about the meet-up."

"At the hospital he said Andrew told him." I slid into the car.

"That's what I thought. Coach Rutherford said I misheard him, that it wasn't what he meant."

"The coach is lying to you."

"Or having an extreme case of selective memory." Ted scanned the area.

"What if Coach Rutherford says I'm lying?" I inserted the key.

"That's when I'll mention I'll go through all the hard work of getting a warrant to pull the photos. Once a photograph has been posted online, it's hard for it to completely disappear."

"I'd love to help you." I smiled.

Ted leaned into my car. "Now let me tell you the conditions."

Ted parked the cruiser in the spot reserved for the resource officer, and I pulled into the one beside him marked for visitors.

"Remember, I ask the questions," Ted said.

"Trust me, I got it." I slammed the car door shut, the window rattling a tad. "I understood it the other umpteen times you said it. I'm not stupid."

"I'm not saying you're stupid."

"Okay, then stubborn. Interfering. Annoying." I rattled off a list of uncomplimentary words as I lead the way to the high school.

"Well..."

I about-faced and glared at him.

Ted pressed the buzzer by the front door. After the second bell, no one could enter the high school without getting buzzed in. I made sure to stand off to the side so the small camera only showed Ted. The office would open the door for him; me, probably not so much. I was sure Principal Hanover told the office staff I was an unwelcome visitor. A few minutes passed and no one buzzed us in, so maybe we were both on the thou-shalt-not-let-in list.

Ted hit the button again, and this time pressed his badge to the lens of the camera.

Principal Hanover yanked the door open. "I will not permit either of you to question any of the students."

"She's not here to talk." Ted took hold of my elbow and escorted me inside. "She's here as a witness."

"A witness?" Principal Hanover's features scrunched up in confusion.

"I need to speak to Coach Rutherford."

While Principal Hanover allowed us inside, he kept matching Ted's movements so we didn't get much farther than a foot into the high school. "He's teaching right now. I can't interrupt him or have him leave his class with no supervision."

"They're teenagers. I think they can be left alone for a few minutes," Ted said.

I held in a snort. Apparently Ted hadn't been around teenagers in a while. You had to keep your eye on them. Once a kid had keys to a car and the ability to drive it, they could be gone lickety-split.

"If there's a test today, Coach Rutherford's absence might encourage cheating," Principal Hanover said.

"If you monitor them, I'm sure the students will be on their best behavior," Ted said. "Two people have died. One might not be highly regarded, but the other was a good man with a young daughter. I've heard some rumors concerning a parting of ways between Andrew Taylor and Coach Rutherford, and want to clear it up before it gets any further."

When Ted said "before it gets any further," he set his gaze on me for a moment.

Principal Hanover nodded. "I see. You can wait for him in the teacher's lounge."

Principal Hanover escorted us to the teacher's lounge and went to get the coach. I took a seat at the end of the table and fixed my gaze on the warning signs in the kitchen. Either the principal didn't think too highly of his staff, or the State Board of Education was heading off any—and I mean any—type of potential lawsuits. I doubted the staff couldn't figure out that one must use an oven mitt or a spatula to take items out of the toaster oven.

The door opened, and an unhappy Coach Rutherford paused in the doorway.

"I was told a detective needed to speak with me, not the town's resident busybody."

"She's here for my protection and yours. Neither of us can claim we were threatened by the other."

"Like she's not going to side with you." Coach Rutherford came inside, the door slamming shut behind him. He walked over to the sink and grabbed a black mug with "EHS Football Champs" written in gold.

"Trust me, he's not on my nice list either," I said.

"Either of you want a cup?" Rutherford filled his to the brim.

We declined.

"Your loss. Wanda makes a great pot of coffee." He placed the mug on the table and sat down, leaning back in his chair. "What do the police believe my football players are up to now?"

"I'm here to find out about the argument between you and Andrew Taylor."

"He—" I pressed my lips together. Ted's eyes repeated his constant warning, which I felt was unwarranted.

"I had some words with him, but I wouldn't call it an argument," Coach Rutherford said.

"How would Andrew categorize it?" Ted asked.

I put my elbow on the table and cupped my chin in my hand, pressing my palm against my mouth. In this position, it made it a little harder for me to talk out of turn.

"I don't read minds, Detective." Rutherford blew on his coffee, then took a long draw.

If I'd done that, I'd have burned my mouth. Either the guy was super tough or wanted to singe his tongue, giving himself a good excuse not to answer any more questions.

"Care to tell me about this exchange of words?"

"No," Rutherford said.

"We can talk here or at the station." Ted stood. "Right now, I have reason to believe your argument might hold the key to solving this case. I'm here to see how your version compares to the one I already have."

Coach Rutherford pulled his cell from his pocket and placed it on the table; using his index finger he twirled it around. "I need you to promise me you'll leave my kids out of this."

Ted sat back down. "Sorry, Coach. I can't."

"Can the prosecuting attorney? I don't want this coming back to hurt Whitney."

"As I said, two men are dead."

"Hell, Detective, my daughter didn't kill anybody. I just don't want anyone thinking my daughter showed me."

I completely covered my mouth. Question after question begged to be released. I wasn't sure how much longer I could hold out, even with a physical barrier.

"Showed you what?"

"A picture." Coach Rutherford brought up the gallery on his phone and shoved it toward Ted.

The coach was going to show Ted the photo. I was

disappointed, and felt ashamed about my reaction. Before the phone reached Ted, I eyeballed the picture. This was a different one. Andrew held a cigarette pack out toward Brandon, who was taking one out. The other kids in the background were wearing t-shirt jerseys with numbers and EHS cheerleader shirts.

"When I found this picture, I forwarded it from Whitney's phone to mine."

"Why did this cause a rift between you and Andrew?"

"The time stamp." Coach Rutherford pushed away his coffee. "It was the night of Brandon's accident. Brandon swore up and down to me, his mom, and anyone who would listen that he hadn't taken any illegal narcotics. He didn't know what made him pass out. There was nothing in his system, so nothing to charge him with. His mom didn't believe he hadn't smoked anything, so she kept pushing. Whitney has a habit of leaving her phone lying around, and one of her friends saw the picture and shared it. It was brought to my attention that if you zoom in on the cigarette, you can see it isn't one from a tobacco company. It's hand-rolled."

"You believe Andrew Taylor tricked Brandon into smoking the synthetic marijuana." The nerve in Ted's jaw twitched.

"Yes." The coach's hand whitened around the phone. "The SOB tried to blame it on my daughter. I know Whitney had nothing to do with giving that cigarette to Brandon. She liked Brandon. They dated from freshman year until this summer."

"What happened this summer?" I asked.

Coach Rutherford glared at me. Ted gave me a "shut up" look, but repeated my question.

"Brandon took a liking to another girl."

Hannah was my guess.

"Why didn't you bring this to Chief Moore or Assistant Prosecutor Davis?" Ted asked. "Hell, or to anyone who worked in the police station or at the prosecutor's office?"

"I was covering my ass too." The coach cradled his head in his hands. "I knew what my players and the cheerleaders were up to at those bonfires. I knew they were smoking and drinking. No harm, no foul. Either I, Andrew, or any of Eden High's past football players acted as the kids' taxi service and took them home. I cut loose when I was a kid, and it didn't hurt my future, and some of those other guys had the same experience."

"Did Jasper act as a designated driver?" I asked before restraint emerged.

"No. Team loyalty comes third to him. Grandma first. The law second. Then the team."

"As it should," Ted said.

"I'm starting to see that," Rutherford said.

Ted had excused me from the meeting. There was some reason he didn't want to reveal the picture with Andrew, so I skedaddled out of there. With Ted occupied, it was the perfect time for me to have a chat with Felicity.

I drove over to the police station and parked in an overflow lot even though there were plenty of spaces out front, so neither Ted nor Mitchell would spot my car. I'd phoned Bobbi-Annie, and she told me Mitchell was out of the building. For now.

The original theory was that Felicity had confessed because Brandon's chances of getting a full-ride scholarship ended with his car accident. Felicity had stayed home to raise her son, and just when she started looking for a job to help with expenses, Brandon was paralyzed and needed his mom more than ever. Her son's condition and the medical bills piling up took a toll on Felicity. Over the last few months, she had lost weight and seemed in pain most of the time.

But what if Felicity actually confessed because she believed— or worse, knew—her husband Allan was guilty of setting the fires and murdering Chad Carr? Teens liked to share pictures, and there was a good chance Felicity and Allan saw the one of Brandon being handed the cigarette. Allan had been on the volunteer fire squad for a few months and knew something about their procedures; plus it wasn't too hard for an arsonist to find some tips on the internet.

I walked into the station. Bobbi-Annie rushed over, herding me toward the back where the visitor area was located.

"Felicity has been refusing to see any visitors, so don't get your hopes up on talking to her."

"Can you get a message to her that I want to talk to her about catering?"

"Catering?"

"If she doesn't come, I'll get my answer, and if she does, I will too."

"Okay." Bobbi-Annie ushered me into a small room with two round tables and four folding chairs. "Sit wherever you'd like. I'll need your purse and your cell phone. I'll hold them up front for you."

I handed them over to Bobbi-Annie and waited. And waited some more.

I checked the time on the wall clock, feeling instant guilt that I had essentially taken the entire day off from work. My grandmothers would easily forgive me, as yesterday had been rough, but I had to find a better balance between working at the store and proving to Officer Mitchell beyond any doubt that I was innocent.

Just as I was about to call it a day, an officer escorted Felicity into the small room. She shuffled over and dropped into a seat across from me. She had dark circles under her eyes and her hair looked lackluster. The officer remained by the door.

"I'm guilty," Felicity said. "It's as simple as that."

"I don't think so."

Tears glittered in her eyes. She leaned forward, her stomach pressing into the table. "Let me have this. Please."

"Your son needs you."

"He needs his dad."

"If you think Allan has something—"

Felicity cut me off. "My husband is innocent. I don't care what the police think. It was nothing more than a coincidence that Allan sold those policies to the businesses right before they burned."

"I thought Allan sold car and house insurance."

"After Brandon's accident, we needed some extra income, and my arthritis doesn't allow me to work much. About two months ago, Allan participated in a family event at the nursing home. It was an afternoon question and answer session for the families of the residents. They had a representative from the hospital, fire department, an estate planner, and they asked Allan to give a talk about insurance policies."

Lucy Cooper. "Did the Carrs ask about business insurance?"

"When Allan got home, he said that Chad had asked about getting a policy for his business. He wasn't thrilled about the company he was with and wanted to use someone local. I told Allan I thought it was a great idea. Now I wished I hadn't."

"Why did you agree to see me?" I asked. "Bobbi-Annie said you've refused all other visitors."

"I was curious because you said catering. What do you know about it?" A flash of pain entered into her eyes.

My heart pounded. Was the anguish because of the pain of her arthritis, or that we were close to discovering her husband's crime? "What do you know?"

"You're the second person who has come to talk to me about catering."

I scooted to the edge of my chair. "Who was the first?"

"Assistant Prosecutor Davis."

When I finally arrived at work, my grandmothers assigned me the job of scrapbooking for Mrs. Barlow. She was struggling in putting together Lake's album and had come to my grandmothers for help. The three of them brainstormed a "perfect solution." I would arrange the photos and embellishments in different patterns, Mrs. Barlow would offer her own suggestions for changes, then I would adhere everything to the page for her.

Somehow they decided that this complied with Lake's instructions for Mrs. Barlow completing the album herself, and I was back to being her scrapping minion. She sat beside me for three hours, instructing me on photo, ribbon, and sticker placement. I tried convincing her that fabric die cuts added a more elegant look, but she would have none of it. With my grandmas giggling in the background, I placed owls, dogs, and football stickers in the exact spots Mrs. Barlow dictated.

Now in the cover of night, I was standing on my front porch, discreetly watching Steve. What did the prosecutor's office know about Vulcan Catering? I'd go over and ask, but I had enough sleuthing experience to know the car parked at the end of the block was Officer Mitchell observing me.

I stretched my body and took another look over at Steve's house. Fortunately, the light from the full moon allowed me to keep my porch light off. I wasn't sure I wanted Steve knowing I was spying. He made another trip from his townhouse to a truck. He was really leaving.

My phone trilled. I tugged it from my back pocket, almost dropping it in my haste to silence it. Ted's picture flashed on my screen. Why was it that the man always knew when I was up to something?

Oh, that's right—Officer Mitchell.

"What?"

"I wanted to warn you that Andrew Taylor hasn't been found yet. Stay inside your house with your doors locked."

"You think he's after me?"

"He knows you've been asking questions. If you hear any noises, give me or even Steve a call. He can get to you quicker."

"Not for much longer. He's in the process of moving out. Like right now."

"Call me if anything weird is going on. Don't check it out yourself."

"I won't."

Andrew sure hadn't covered his tracks well. My mind kept playing Norman Ridley's words over and over again: Andrew wasn't very bright. Coach Rutherford had a lot of people keeping an eye on the parties, so why hadn't one of them said anything to him about Andrew hanging around his daughter that night?

The car finally left the spot down the street. Steve walked out of his house carrying two more boxes. My heart clenched. This was it. He was really leaving. I started for my house when my cell rang again. It was the nursing home.

"This is Nancy. We haven't seen Dawn since Lucy died." Nancy's voice dipped. "I'm worried about her. I understand her not wanting to come around, but she hasn't answered any of our calls either, and arrangements still need to be made for her mother."

That wasn't like Dawn at all. "Maybe she needed a few days away. It's been tough for her lately."

"If she hadn't been arguing with that man on Monday, I wouldn't be worried."

"What man?"

"I didn't get a good look at him, but the truck he was driving had an Eden County volunteer fire department license plate on the front."

"What color was the truck?"

"Black. He and Dawn were standing beside it. He sped off when I walked outside to see what was going on."

An alarm sounded in the background.

"I have to go." Nancy hung up.

Dawn was in trouble. I hoped she was hiding out and not another victim. I called Ted.

"You got yourself into trouble already?" Ted asked.

The man told me to call him if anything weird came up and now he was acting put out. "No. But Dawn might be." I relayed everything to him.

Ted stayed quiet until I was finished. "I'll go over to the nursing home and talk with them. I'll also put an APB out on her. There might be a good reason she left town without a word. Stay inside."

Steve crossed the lawn, tossing his keys from hand to hand. "Talking with Detective Roget?"

I stuck my hands into my pockets. I didn't want Steve to see them shaking. "Maybe."

A smile inched across his face. "I'm sure you were. You two never just talk to each other, you argue. It can't be healthy."

I wanted to tell Steve not to concern himself with the friendship I had with Ted, but instead I kept quiet. I wanted to spend a little bit more time with Steve, not chase him off. Besides, he was right. Ted and I argued an awful lot, about pretty much everything. We seemed to know which buttons to push to get each other riled up.

Steve came up the stairs slowly, pausing momentarily on each one. My body yearned to lean forward, feel his arms around me again. I tightened my muscles, blocking myself from doing anything. Steve took the last two steps at once and reached out.

My body trembled. My lips tingled, hoping for a kiss. When would my head and heart be on the same page?

"Here you go." Keys glittered in the moonlight as Steve dangled them near my face.

My emotions froze. I took the keys.

"I was going to give them to your grandmothers, but they aren't home," Steve said.

"It's Bunco night." I gripped the keys, the edges digging into the palm of my hand. "What do you know about Vulcan Catering?"

Steve pivoted, walked to the truck parked next to the curb, and got in. Without a wave, or even a glance in my direction, he drove away.

TWENTY-ONE

Sunlight poured through the window of Scrap This, bouncing off the wrapped Christmas-themed three-ring binders I pulled from our delivered order. Most people didn't like seeing Christmas items displayed before Halloween, and definitely not before October, but last year I'd made the mistake of waiting until after Thanksgiving to bring out our holiday items, and most of the merchandise went on our clearance table. A lot of crafters started their holiday projects before Thanksgiving, and after Black Friday, it was time to start wrapping presents and decorating the house rather than crafting. Whatever handmade gifts and decorations weren't complete by then were stashed away to become next year's Christmas gifts.

A few customers browsed around the store. I glanced at the front door every few minutes, certain I'd get whiplash by the end of the day, wishing I could stop Ted's warning from playing in my head. I could do paranoia by myself; I sure didn't need Ted planting ideas in my head.

Marilyn was at the front windows, cleaning off toddler-sized fingerprints. The culprit and his mother had wandered to the back where there was much temptation. I logged into Facebook on the front desk computer. Social media seemed to be the key in this case, and I hoped to find something about Vulcan Catering. There was the possibility someone in the community mentioned it on the town's page. Nothing.

Next, I looked at Dawn Carr's page. She was a regular poster, at least four times a day for the last three years, but there was nothing from the last two days. I dialed Ted.

A screech, followed by a clatter, came from the back of the store where we displayed our embellishment packages on clips attached to the wall.

"I'll take care of it," Marilyn said.

"Detective Roget." He answered right away. He must've been waiting for a key piece of information or confirmation on one he already had.

"I'm worried about Dawn."

"And this is?"

Gee, way to make a woman feel good about herself. "It's Faith. I checked Dawn's Facebook page and she hasn't posted."

"We've noted the concern about her whereabouts. Remember, she is an adult and doesn't have to check in with anyone."

"What about the argument in the parking lot?"

"Dawn was seen later that night at the convenience store stocking up on snacks and bottled water."

"She wouldn't be going on a trip. Her mother died. She'd stay here to plan the funeral."

"Goodbye, Faith."

I slammed the phone down. Dawn's husband was recently murdered. You'd think the police would act a little more concerned about her disappearance. Someone else might be interested that the widow of the murdered suspected drug dealer has vanished.

I dialed Karen's direct line.

"Karen England."

"This is Faith. Dawn Carr is missing. The police aren't taking it seriously."

"What are you up to?"

"A woman whose husband was murdered hasn't been seen in the last two days since her mother died. Don't you find it odd and a little concerning?"

"As a matter of fact, I don't," Karen said. "Her husband was a drug dealer, and her invalid mother died of a drug overdose. Not surprising at all she took off. What I am fascinated by is the fact that the police aren't following up on it. Dawn should be a person of interest, if not in the drug distribution, than at least in the death of Lucy Cooper. Once again, the police are letting feelings overrule legal procedures. I'll get right to work on this story."

Ted was going to blow when Karen called him, and more than likely it'd be directed at me. "The police aren't letting her get away with anything."

"Detective Roget defended her in church. He's allowing his sympathy for her being a widow to overshadow the facts in the case."

"No, he's not."

"Then maybe it's listening to a certain wannabe investigator he wants to hook up with."

"That's not true either. I'm the last person Ted pays attention to."

"Keep telling yourself that, Faith."

Karen hung up.

If she had witnessed how Ted treated me the last few days, she'd know I was right.

Brandon was our only answer.

A woman tugging a squirming little boy behind her approached the counter. The little boy clutched the end of a strip of stickers. A trail of superheroes stretched four feet behind him.

"Got them all! Got them all!" the little boy sang, giddiness clear on his face.

His mother, on the other hand, didn't look happy about the parade of superheroes going home with her.

Another shopper picked up the tail end of the sheet and draped it over the little boy's shoulder. "Don't want them to get stepped on."

The boy shook his head.

The mother let out a long-suffering sigh and placed three packages of 3D amusement park stickers on the counter. "Also the stickers my son is holding."

"I'll need to count them."

The mother took hold of the end of the strip resting on the

child's shoulder. The boy's lip quivered, tears welling in his bright blue eyes.

From the corner of my eye, I caught Marilyn waving her hands frantically over her head. Once she knew she had my attention, she used her fingers to tell me the number. Twenty-three.

"Twenty-three superheroes." I punched the correct keys into the register. Fortunately, those stickers were a big seller, so I knew the SKU by heart. If not, I'd have had Marilyn bring me the number. No way did I want anyone else wailing and gnashing teeth in the store. I was doing enough of that myself.

Mrs. Barlow pushed her way between the mother and the customer who had saved the superheroes from being stepped on. The mother took her change and left.

The customer behind her poked Mrs. Barlow in the back. "I'm next."

Mrs. Barlow held the woman's prodding hand. Pushing her glasses back up the bridge of her nose, she brought the customer's hand to her eyes for closer inspection.

I rubbed my forehead. Mrs. Barlow was in her intense social butterfly mode, where she believed everyone was her best friend and craved physical contact. Some days, she was able to control her urges and allow people their personal space, other days—like today—not so much.

The woman sent me a panicked look.

"Mrs. Barlow, no touching the customers. We've had this talk before."

"I'm looking at her nails. I've never seen such an exquisite shape. They're completely natural." Mrs. Barlow thrust the woman's hand toward me.

The customer's stomach pressed into the counter and an oof puffed out.

"Mrs. Barlow, please stop." I shouted my plea, hoping to draw the attention of my grandmothers, who were working in the back office.

"You wouldn't understand." Mrs. Barlow released the

customer, then grabbed my hand. "Short. Uneven. You have chipped nail polish."

I pulled away and hid my hands under the counter. "I've been busy this week."

"I know, dear, you're a working woman and a detective." She stuck her hand into her oversized faux leather tote, then slapped a thin catalog onto the counter along with a small packet of sample nail wraps in a leopard print. "That's why these would be perfect for you."

I didn't think so. "No, thank you."

"They have other designs, and some are even craft-related. It'll be like having nails done at a fancy shmancy spa."

"I don't go anywhere where I need fancy nails." Heck, I didn't go anywhere where I needed fancy anything.

"Maybe if you took some time to do yourself up, that would change," Mrs. Barlow said.

"Those are lovely." The customer offered me a sympathetic smile. "Mind if I take the sample?"

"Please do." Mrs. Barlow handed her a catalog and a postcard. "I'm hosting a party tonight at my house. You should come. I'll nominate you for the hand model position. Your nails are breathtaking."

"I can't," the woman said. "The elementary school's PTA meeting is tonight."

Mrs. Barlow pulled out her cell and tapped across the screen with a stylus. "No, you're free. The meeting has been rescheduled to next week. Mrs. Rider is ill."

The woman took out her iPhone and checked her emails. "Oh, you're right."

Mrs. Barlow grinned and winked. "I know everything that happens in this town. The Eden public network system begins and ends with me."

That was it! Mrs. Barlow kept records of all the calls she heard on her scanner, and recorded the calls that came through on the nights when she was at Bunco or taking part in one of her other community gossip research activities. She hated being out of the loop.

"I'll come." I picked up a postcard. "Mind if I bring someone with me?"

"No men."

I rolled my eyes. "Trust me. There isn't one I'd want to hang out with right now."

The front porch of Mrs. Barlow's house was lit up from all angles like she was protecting her area from invading marauders. I squinted and tried to find the doorbell through the unnatural brightness. I touched a prickly piece of plastic. Once my eyes adjusted, I saw a green plastic wreath with neon yellow, off-white, and rust-colored fabric flowers attached to it. Mrs. Barlow had hung up the same wreath every fall since I could walk and talk. I hoped she'd exchange the monstrosity for the gift I brought along.

"Was all this really necessary?" Charlotte juggled two bags of muffins from Home Brewed while she stood behind me and stamped her boots. Mrs. Barlow had decided to spruce up her garden and sidewalk before the direct sales party. Small pieces of mulch covered the sidewalk, making it a little slick and coating the bottom of our shoes with debris.

"Mrs. Barlow loves presents and hates giving out her documents. The key to the truth rests in the records of the calls to the fire station." I shifted the bouquet of cut flowers and the fall wreath into one arm. Gossip she'd unleash without any encouragement, but if we wanted the actual proof to back up the statements, bribery was in order. And a lot of it. Buying some nail wraps wouldn't cut it.

"You can't know that."

"Why did Andrew—or whoever's guilty—destroy them? If Karen hasn't visited Mrs. Barlow yet, she will. Her task is to get her cousin out of jail, even if it means your daughter or I get arrested. Unless—" I almost let "Hannah gives her real alibi" slip out.

"Unless?"

A war waged inside of me: to tell or not to tell. Hannah didn't want me to mention it to her mother—but she never said I couldn't tell Ted. And Ted would make sure Charlotte didn't land in jail for assaulting Daniel. Charlotte would be furious I spoke to Ted instead of her, but I hoped one day she'd forgive me.

"Faith..."

I rang the doorbell and took a step to the side, gesturing for Charlotte to close ranks. "If Snickerdoodle gets out, Mrs. Barlow will be furious."

"Then she needs to train her dog."

"Don't call it a dog, it's her baby."

"I'm sure her daughter loves that." Charlotte plastered a smile on her face. "I can't believe you talked me into attending a direct market sales pitch for the competition."

"Maybe it's something you can add to your store."

"That'll help increase my income...a cheaper way for women to get a manicure."

Barking erupted from behind the door.

Charlotte knocked. The barking grew more frantic. The dog sounded like he was scurrying from one side of the door to the other. "You think she's okay? It's taking her a while."

"She's old," I said. "Her pep isn't what it used to be."

Melinda called me monthly to check up on her mom and make sure Mrs. Barlow wasn't driving the community too crazy. While she worried about her mom, Melinda wasn't so worried she wanted to move back to Eden. She enjoyed her own life in Florida and the improved relationship she had with her mother by not living in the same town.

"I'm surprised she wasn't waiting by the door." Charlotte adjusted her hold on the bags of muffins. The movement released some of the aroma trapped in the bag.

My stomach rumbled.

"She wouldn't want us to know she was. She's all about the dramatic delay."

"Be there in a few," Mrs. Barlow sang. "Had an important call to answer."

I smiled at Charlotte. "See?"

Charlotte rolled her eyes. "How would she know it was important?"

"Caller ID," I said.

Mrs. Barlow opened the door with a flourish. "Come in, come in."

Snickerdoodle, a black Scottish terrier, bolted past us. Charlotte pulled off a small chunk of blueberry muffin and held it by her leg. The dog skidded to a halt and trotted up to Charlotte, sniffing away. She led him into the house.

Mrs. Barlow narrowed her eyes at Charlotte. "Don't give him that."

"I was stopping him from becoming one with the road." Charlotte shoved the morsel into her coat pocket.

"He wouldn't have gone far. Snicker doesn't like being far from Mama. Do you, baby?" Mrs. Barlow clapped her hands on her thighs and the dog sprinted to her. His sturdy body trembled with glee as Mrs. Barlow caressed his head and back.

"We brought you some presents," I said.

Mrs. Barlow's attention was diverted from the dog. She eyed what I carried, then what Charlotte held in her hands. "Since those snacks were made by Dianne, you can place them on the table to serve tonight. I have a vase in the kitchen I can use for the flowers. Would you mind hanging the wreath on the door, Faith?"

"Not at all." Opening the door, I made sure I kept my smile toned down. I didn't want Mrs. Barlow to know how pleased I was about the changing of the wreath. Now if there was only a trashcan I could sneak the old one into, everything would be perfect.

"Anyone pull up behind you?" Mrs. Barlow peered around me.

"Not yet." I closed the door and debated how to ask about the wreath. "Where is the trash?" seemed a little harsh.

"You can leave it by the front door. I'll hang that one out when the weather gets really bad. I don't want to ruin my new one."

Now there was an idea. Why hadn't anyone in the neighborhood thought about it sooner? The next time we had a bad windstorm, I'd snatch the wreath and then commiserate with Mrs. Barlow when she woe-is-me'd about the storm taking off with her decoration.

"Why don't you girls have a seat and a snack. I need to make a few quick calls. Lake should've been here by now, along with my other guests."

Besides an uncomfortable-looking wooden rocking chair, the only other place to sit was an oversized couch with large floral pillows. It looked like the type of furniture that swallowed a person whole.

"After you." Charlotte pointed at the couch.

Choosing to sit at one of the ends, I sank into the cushions, keeping hold of the armrest in case I needed out. With my feet dangling off the floor, I felt like a little kid sitting on a piece of furniture meant only for adults.

Charlotte chose to sit on the opposite side. I figured she wanted an armrest too.

A few minutes later, Mrs. Barlow returned, looking crestfallen.

"What's wrong?" I wrestled myself out of the couch.

"Looks like it's just us." Mrs. Barlow dabbed at her eyes with a lace handkerchief. "Even Lake Breckenridge can't make it tonight, and she's the consultant."

"Why?" I asked.

"Lake's at the police station to answer some questions. The detective didn't care she had a prior commitment." Mrs. Barlow looked even sadder.

I was getting the feeling it wasn't the fact no one showed up that bothered her, but that some awesome drama was happening right under her nose and no one told her about it. If Lake had told her earlier about having to go to the police station, Mrs. Barlow would've bailed on her party too.

I had a way to cheer the woman up. "Since no one is coming, you can help Charlotte and me solve a mystery."

Mrs. Barlow's pale blue eyes lit up. "A mystery?"

I glanced around secretively. Mrs. Barlow loved a good drama. "Did you know the fire station was broken into and all their records stolen?"

Disappointment flooded her face. Of course she knew; she listened to all the calls.

"I have a hunch the bonfires might have been staged to burn down businesses."

Squealing, Mrs. Barlow fluttered her hands by her face. I had her now. "Oh my goodness. That's why Lake is at the police station and didn't tell me. The police think she was up to something unscrupulous."

Or if she wasn't, Clive Murphy had been. His shop had also sustained damage in the same fire. "Charlotte and I would like to take a look at your records. I know you keep detailed notes of the calls you've heard."

Mrs. Barlow crossed her arms and studied both of us. "I should've guessed you were here to pump me for information. Charlotte has her own nail place."

Heat flashed across my face. I felt a little guilty about using the elderly woman. "Well, um..." My brain wasn't working fast enough to come up with a solid alternative reason.

"Yes," Charlotte blurted out the truth.

Mrs. Barlow grinned and grabbed our arms. "This is the best day ever. Come on, I'll take you to my office."

She hurried us down the hallway with Snickerdoodle hot on our heels. She opened a door with a grand flourish. "Ta-da! Here is my sewing room and command center."

Charlotte and I gaped at the set-up. It was quite the display, and I wasn't just referring to the lovely embroidery and high-tech sewing machines Mrs. Barlow owned. Her police scanner was a sight to behold. Heck, I didn't think Eden's police department had one as nice and elaborate as hers. On the wall was a map of Eden, showing the town divided into polling districts.

"What fires would you like to know about?" Mrs. Barlow sat in a leather office chair and turned on her computer. "I keep records of all the calls and the order in which the trucks go out."

"Does that matter?" I hovered behind Mrs. Barlow, taking notes on an app.

"I'm not sure it does to the general public, but I like knowing who's going out on a call," Mrs. Barlow said. "The fire station will have a more detailed record, as they keep the names of the members who showed up for the call; they don't always need everyone. I know who's assigned to each truck."

That's how she knew if she should cancel her emergency. She'd hear which truck was coming, and knew whether it was one with a hot fireman or one of the older guys who didn't appeal to her. And that explained her phone calls to Bobbi-Annie, trying to find out what officer was on duty. She was working on her chart for the police station.

"Chief Ridley gave you his roster?" I asked.

Mrs. Barlow blushed. "Let's just say that Norm forgot his anniversary one year and to get even with him, Hildie gave me a roster of the squad, including which emergency vehicle they were assigned to."

"The volunteers don't get into whatever one is there?"

"No. The ladder truck can't be driven by everyone, and neither can the ambulance. There also needs to be a paramedic onboard before the ambulance leaves."

"Can we get a copy of the roster and a list of all the fire calls on the Thursday nights before home football games?" I asked.

"I don't usually share." Mrs. Barlow tapped her chin and gazed off thoughtfully into the distance.

"In novels, the sidekick of the sleuth always shares with her," I said.

Mrs. Barlow beamed. "I'm your sidekick."

I had a feeling I'd regret this later, but for now, I needed the information. "Absolutely. You helped me on the Belinda Anderson case by telling Detective Roget about the car driving by my house."

"I did. Well, since we're working together..." Mrs. Barlow

typed in the find field and brought up a couple of pages of data, then hit print. "There you go. Keep those safe and make sure you don't show them to anyone else."

"We won't. Trust us," Charlotte and I said in unison.

Charlotte and I pored over our copy of the report. I wanted to take a look at it right then and there in case I had any questions. Andrew was a dangerous man. I didn't want Mrs. Barlow actually getting involved in the investigation. The less I went to her for help, the better. The report revealed that Officer Mitchell had been the first to arrive at Made With love, and reported the volunteer firefighters who arrived at the scene rather than heading to the station. Andrew showed up five minutes after Mitchell, even though he was suspended from the squad. The majority of the crew arrived fifteen minutes later, with Daniel showing up last.

"Have you figured out the culprit?" Mrs. Barlow plopped down so close to me she was almost in my lap.

Jim Ryland had a Vulcan Catering card. It was Thursday. There was a home game tomorrow—bonfire night. I checked the time on my phone. Piece A Pie should still be open. "No. But there is someone we have to go talk to." And a fire to stop.

"Who?" Charlotte asked.

"Jim Ryland."

Mrs. Barlow opened a desk drawer and pulled out a binder. She flipped through it and put bright yellow Post-it notes shaped like arrows on the corner of the page. "If I don't hear from you girls in an hour, I'm putting together a cavalry to come get you."

TWENTY-TWO

Before we left Mrs. Barlow's house, Charlotte and I decided to take separate cars. She'd park on the grassy field to the left of the restaurant, and I'd park in the parking lot. Since Jim knew I saw the business card, I'd question him while Charlotte stayed in the shadows and recorded the exchange on her cell phone.

The Piece A Pie lot was empty. Did Jim park in the back, or had his wife dropped him off? Charlotte and I should've planned better. We never took into account that he might have closed early. The restaurant was supposed to be open. I made my way to the front door, scanning the parking lot for any lurkers. A handmade sign on the door said, "Closed. Family Emergency."

I texted Charlotte the information, tugging on the door in case the sign was a diversion. Nope. It was locked. Now what?

A noise came from the back of the store. Hunkering down, I crab-walked my way to the corner of the building and peered around. Jim tested the doorknob a few times, a lone box at his feet. He picked something up and tossed it at the safety light. It plinked off the fixture.

Standing, I gripped the side of the wall and angled myself farther out.

"Come on." Jim threw another rock. "Hit it." It missed.

In the soft light, I strained my eyes, making out a gas can and the edge of a photo frame sticking out from the box. A pit formed in my stomach. Jim planned on burning down the pizza joint tonight, with or without the arsonist's help.

The smell of smoke drifted to me. Crop it all. There might not be a suitable place for a bonfire behind the restaurant, but from the smell of it, there was a perfect clearing in the woods. At least tonight, they set the fire far enough away so an "improperly put-out bonfire" couldn't be blamed for Piece A Pie going up in flames. But the teens were in danger if Jim, or the arsonist, spotted them. The murderer had already killed two people. What were a couple more?

A sharp breath drew my attention back toward Jim. He stared at me for a long moment. The box clattered to the ground, and Jim sprinted toward the trees. I snapped some pictures, hoping they'd come out.

"Get the kids out. I'm after Jim." I prayed Charlotte heard me, or the kids. I didn't really care what made them leave the premises.

Fortunately, I was younger and in better shape than Jim. He slowed, his huffing and wheezing reaching my ears. He found some reserves of energy and put on a burst of speed, crossing toward the parking lot.

"I know it's you, Jim," I called out.

He stopped and bent over, presumably to catch his breath.

Cautiously, I walked over to him. I didn't think I had anything to fear from Jim, but no one liked getting caught almost committing a crime. I remained a few feet away. "Why were you going to torch your place?"

"The bills are killing me. My blood pressure is high. I can't sleep. My head always feels like it's going to explode. It's taking all my time. Take your pick. They're all true."

"There are other ways."

Jim sank to his knees, covering his face with his hands. "My wife has cancer. I don't want to spend her last months at this damn place. I want to be with her."

"I'm so sorry." The anguish in his voice tore at my heart. I blinked away tears.

"I tried selling the place. This was the only way to get out from under the business."

"You hired Vulcan Catering to set the fire. That's the real business model...not cooking barbeque."

"Yes." Jim rubbed his eyes. "I know it's horrible. I was so lost."

"Who gave you the card?"

"I don't know."

"You really expect me to buy that?"

Jim lumbered to his feet. "I don't care what you believe. I found the card on my windshield after I attended a meeting at the nursing home. I thought whoever was opening the catering business was interest in buying Piece A Pie and left their card on the windshield. I had told everyone I was selling it."

"Why wouldn't they just talk to you?"

"I figured they wanted to talk to the presenters who were available that night."

"Your wife is a resident?" Was that how Chad received a card? Did someone else overhear him confiding to Lucy?

"No, I was talking to Norm one day, and he said I should go to the family information seminars. Thought it would be helpful. And since my wife might have to move in, I figured it was a good way to see what's offered. I asked a few questions, especially about resources available, as my income had taken a hit."

"Do you remember who was there?"

"Allan Sullivan. Lake Breckenridge. Daniel Burke."

"Lake?"

"She was given a flower-arranging class."

A car tore out of the woods. Burnt rubber filled the air.

Charlotte and the teens. I hadn't heard anything from them since I ran after Jim. Did the arsonist finally show up? I raced off, heading toward the smell of the smoke.

Waves of red and orange flames danced a few yards ahead. I tried calling out, but either panic or being out of breath was working against me. The knot in my stomach tightened. At the very least, I had expected to hear Charlotte dressing down the kids.

I peered through a few branches. Hannah and Brandon were the only ones at the bonfire. A little ways behind them was a fallen tree covered with fleece blankets, a few filled grocery bags resting against it. Charlotte wasn't there. Nausea rose in me.

"I told you this was a bad idea," Hannah said. "All we've done is cause more trouble."

"I'm not leaving," Brandon said. "You can't make me."

I stepped out of the shelter of the branches. "Where's your mom?"

Letting out a startled squeak, Hannah spun and nearly toppled into Brandon's lap. She recovered quickly.

"My mom?"

"She came with me. I went to talk to Jim, and she was coming to check out the bonfire." I was proud of myself for keeping my panic under control.

Hannah shrugged.

"We didn't see her," Brandon said. "Haven't seen anyone else."

Why wasn't Hannah concerned? Was she lying to me about her mom's whereabouts? Had I mistaken where the sound had come from and Charlotte was the one who'd driven off?

"I want answers, not more lies. There are enough stories floating around and innocent people are getting hurt." I planted my hands on my hips and glared at the only teens—Hannah and Brandon—at the bonfire. Either they came out for some alone time or they were up to something dangerous and stupid.

Hannah lowered her gaze to the ground and shoved some dirt around with her foot. The well-maintained blaze cast an orange glow onto her face. The bonfire was contained between large rocks.

"I want one of you to start talking." I fixed my fiercest gaze on them.

"We don't have to talk to you," Brandon said. "You're not the police. Not that I'd have to talk to them either. We're not doing anything wrong."

"Then why are you hiding out back here?" I asked.

"We're not hiding. We're at the pre-game bonfire," Brandon said.

Hannah remained uncharacteristically silent.

I heaved out an I-wasn't-born-yesterday sigh. "Where's everyone else?"

Brandon and Hannah exchanged a look. He maneuvered his wheelchair closer to her.

I stepped onto the only clear patch of ground, blocking him from Hannah. I felt a little bad doing so, but I wanted the truth, not a plotted excuse.

"I'm not saying anything." Brandon glared up at me.

"You better start explaining to *me*." Karen stepped out of the shadows and into the firelight. "Because if not, I'll call your dad and you can enlighten him. He told you last night when he got home from talking to the police to let us handle it. We *will* get your mom out of jail."

Brandon groaned. "I should've known you'd be here. Why can't you just back off, Aunt Karen?"

"Because nosing around in this murder investigation can get you hurt." Karen stomped over to Brandon. "Don't you get that? Your mom would be devastated if something happened to you. She'd never forgive herself."

"I'm devastated. Today. Yesterday. Tomorrow." Tears glittered in his eyes. "Don't any of you understand that? Mom won't even see me. I don't want her doing this for me."

"She isn't—"

"Don't lie to me!" Brandon screamed. He yanked the rims down, jerking his chair forward. "It is about me. She thinks the only way I can have a life is if she gives up hers. I don't want one that way. I'd rather live here the rest of my life, work at a fast food counter, and never have enough money than have my mom in prison."

"Honey, I've tried. She won't listen." Karen's breaking heart was in her voice. "She doesn't want anyone's help."

Felicity's stubbornness was destroying her son and making me like her less and less. Her decision made no sense to me, unless she knew the next most likely suspect was her husband. But why would Allan allow his wife to go to jail in his place?

"My mom is crazy." Brandon pressed the lever on his chair. The wheelchair gave a jerky start, stopping when the wheels caught on a root half buried under the ground. "Tell her I won't quit until she's out of jail."

"We won't let her go to prison for this," I said. "Even if that is what she wants."

"How? We need proof." Brandon settled back onto solid ground.

"My mom's going to get it," Hannah said.

"Now?" I asked. "Where?"

Hannah refused to meet my gaze.

"She could be in danger," I said. "A vehicle zipped out of here."

"I'm not, but someone else likely is." Charlotte stepped out from the woods and sent a scathing look at her daughter. It was the first time I ever saw Charlotte show any displeasure with her daughter. "Did you get a good look at the car?"

"No, I was too far away," I said.

"There was no one back down by the creek," Charlotte said.

"I swear I saw a flashlight coming from there." Hannah's voice trembled. "Someone was out there."

Brandon held Hannah's hand. "I saw it too, Ms. Hanson. There was a light coming toward us, and Hannah called out saying she was glad they could make it. Whoever it was left."

Charlotte crossed her arms and began a staredown with her daughter. "When are you going to stop trying to make things better by sneaking out and agreeing to elaborate plans that are only going to get you into trouble, or worse, hurt?"

"That's not going to happen."

"You think this," Charlotte waved her arms around, showcasing the bonfire and the bags of food and drinks placed near the downed tree covered with blankets, "was a smart idea?"

"I wanted everyone to come," Brandon said. "The team has never skipped a bonfire before, especially when the food and drinks are free."

"You're lucky none of them came," Karen said.

Brandon backed up the wheelchair then moved forward again. After a few times, the chair rolled over the root.

"You told them not to, didn't you? I can't believe you did that."

"I didn't speak to any of the players or cheerleaders. I interviewed Coach Rutherford this morning, and told him I thought it would be best if his players refrained from the bonfire tradition until after the murders were solved. Some of our rivals would love to use the fires against us and get our team banned from playoff games. Coach Rutherford agreed. And what the coach says goes. You know that, Brandon."

With the firelight, I saw wetness on his cheeks. "I do. They were my friends when I was winning; now they have no use for me. And they did this to me." Brandon punched the armrests of his chair.

"What do you mean?"

Karen sat on her heels and wrapped her hands around her nephew's fists.

"The cigarette I took from Whitney. It wasn't tobacco."

"From Whitney?" I blurted. "The pictures showed you getting it from Andrew Taylor."

"Whitney told me she'd hold them in her thermal bag since we were playing with water guns. They'd stay dry in there. She must've given them to Andrew to bring to me."

"I'll take care of this." Karen shot to her feet.

"I'll handle it, Aunt Karen. I want them to know I can take care of myself."

"Did your mom know about Whitney?" I asked.

Brandon shook his head. "I didn't tell her. I didn't believe I was high. It wasn't until school started that I found out about the picture."

"How? Who?" Karen's voice rumbled like thunder.

"Kirstin showed it to me," Hannah said. "I told Brandon about it. I promised him we'd take care of it. Whitney wouldn't get away with ruining his life."

"Why didn't you tell Coach Rutherford?" I asked. "Principal Hanover?"

"Because Coach Rutherford is an upstanding member of the

community," Hannah said. "My mom isn't. You really think someone would believe me over Whitney? Not going to happen."

"I believe you. My grandmothers would. Steve would. Detective Roget would. And a lot of other people."

"Keep living in your fantasy world," Hannah said. "We'll handle this on our own. Once we get the solid proof, we'll show everyone."

"No, you won't," Ted's voice boomed in. "I'll take this matter over from here."

We all turned. Ted stood with a group of men. Jasper, Wayne, and Wyatt were in the middle of the pack, with Ted and Steve at the ends. Each of the men had arms crossed, scowls on their faces, and blocked the only clear exit from the clearing.

"What are you guys doing here?" I focused on Wyatt, who seemed the least annoyed.

Charlotte sidled over to me. "We forgot to keep track of time."

Mrs. Barlow had kept her word. She rustled herself up a cavalry to come out and save us. Now that it was apparent we didn't need saving, our rescuers were highly ticked off.

Karen, Brandon, and Hannah drew closer to us. There was safety in numbers.

"I think you know why we're here," Ted said.

Poor Mrs. Barlow. She'd love to have been here to see all these guys lined up side by side. Of course, she'd have liked it better if they were all in uniforms, though an assistant prosecuting attorney didn't really have a uniform, unless you counted a suit.

"Someone sent out a premature distress call," I said. "As you can see, we're fine. We just came to check out the bonfire."

"I'm sure you only came here to tell these kids why this was a bad idea." Ted tipped his chin, indicating the fire. "Wayne and Wyatt, I'd like you guys to put that out. Hose it down good and make sure there's no way anyone can say this fire started another one."

"I hope this isn't one of Felicity's new plans to frame herself," Steve said.

"Frame herself?" Karen left the safety of our circle and approached Steve.

"Don't play stupid, Karen." Even though Steve addressed Karen, his eyes were on me. "You know that the other common factor is that Allan sold all of the insurance policies to the businesses that burned down. The police would find out."

"Shut up, Davis," Ted snapped.

"Why can't he tell the truth?" Brandon rolled toward Ted. "You guys were going after my dad. I told you he was home with me, but you all think I'm a liar. My dad volunteered as a firefighter but quit after my accident. So what? That doesn't make him an arsonist or a murderer. He quit because being responsible for people's lives made him anxious, and Mom needed him at home to help with me."

"And once Karen proves Felicity's innocence, it'll be harder for the police to charge Allan. It'll look like they're targeting the Sullivan family," Steve said. "So she rounded up her three most probable suspects right here. At a fire."

Karen drew in a sharp breath. She looked crestfallen at what Steve accused her of. Part of me believed it was a possibility, but the other part knew Karen well enough to know she'd have publicly tarred and feathered Allan if it was true.

"Davis, don't make me tell you to shut the hell up again."

"Your theory is baseless," Karen said.

"I wouldn't be so sure of that." Steve smiled at her.

Karen's eyes widened.

Steve talked to Felicity about Vulcan Catering. Had Dawn spoken to Steve or the police recently about it? Was that why Ted shrugged off my concerns?

Ted's radio crackled.

"Emergency at Barlow's." The dispatcher sounded furious. "Not an admiration call. Someone actually attacked her."

TWENTY-THREE

I had reached our block after the police cordoned off the street, and now was stuck on the wrong side of the tape. Ted was allowed past the barricade along with Wayne, Wyatt, and Steve. Charlotte, Hannah, Brandon, and I were instructed to remain behind the tape.

"Why can't I go home?" I pointed across the street. "You know where I live."

Officer Mitchell ignored me. The lights on the ambulance swirled and pulled out of the driveway.

My grandmothers were huddled together on their porch, watching the ambulance transport Mrs. Barlow to the hospital. I wanted to comfort and be comforted by my grandmothers. Who would hurt Mrs. Barlow?

"My grandmothers need me," I pleaded.

"Davis went home. He'll take care of them," Mitchell said.

Ted walked over to the tape, lifted up an edge, then nodded at me and Charlotte. "A word with you two."

"I disagree, Detective." Mitchell blocked our entrance. "We shouldn't give them permission to interfere in this investigation."

"I'm questioning Miss Hunter and Ms. Hanson, not inviting them to play a round of Clue."

I scooted under the crime scene tape. "I wasn't here."

"You were sometime today," Ted said.

"You think they saw Mrs. Barlow's attacker?" Mitchell grabbed my arm, yanking me fully to my feet. "Or they directed the assailant to her?"

Ted placed a warning hand on Mitchell's shoulder. "Watch the roughness."

"I don't want the accomplice to get away," he said.

"Accomplice?" I looked at Charlotte. She scanned the area like she was preparing a plan to bolt. I hooked my arm through hers. No way was I being left to face this alone.

"How else would the attacker know when Mrs. Barlow walked her dog at night, and where she kept all the notes she takes on what's going on in the community?" Mitchell asked.

Ted stayed uncharacteristically silent. He usually had no trouble adding in a word or two when it came to my shortcomings.

"I don't know when Mrs. Barlow takes her dog out at night. She's the one who tracks everyone's comings and goings," I said.

Charlotte kicked me in the shin. I guess she didn't approve of my commentary.

"And you probably didn't like that one bit," Mitchell said. "Is that why you went over to her house tonight? To tell her to stay out of your business?"

I fixed my gaze on Ted. The expression on his face either meant, "You're getting what you deserve" or "Where is Mitchell pulling these theories from?"

"Mrs. Barlow was having a nail wrap party. She invited me this afternoon, and I asked Charlotte to come along."

I searched for Steve. Even though we weren't together anymore, and he'd moved—I drew in a deep breath. Steve moved. Why had he gone into the townhouse? Did he have another set of keys?

"A weird choice, considering Charlotte owns a nail salon," Mitchell said.

Ted still remained silent, gaze wandering off in the direction of my grandmothers. Was he worried Cheryl would come over and give Mitchell a browbeating?

"I wanted to check out what my business is competing against," Charlotte said.

Good. I didn't want to do all the talking.

"In searching Mrs. Barlow's home, we didn't see anything party or nail related. Am I right, Detective?"

"That you are," Ted said.

"That's because the consultant, Lake Breckenridge, never showed up," I said. "She was being questioned at the police station."

Ted strode forward, breaching my personal space. "And how do you know that?"

"Mrs. Barlow told us."

At the end of the road, two small eyes glowed from the police cruisers' headlights.

"Where's Snickerdoodle?" I strained my eyes to get a better look at the critter jogging down the road. "You said Mrs. Barlow was walking her dog."

"The dog wasn't there," Ted said.

I crept forward. "I think I see him."

The men turned. In the dark, all we saw were the glowing white eyes moving closer.

"Come here, baby," I sing-songed, tiptoeing forward. "That's a good doggie."

Yapping, the dog bolted behind what was once Steve's house. Or maybe still was. I ran after Snickerdoodle.

Why would Steve lie about moving? I saw the boxes he'd packed.

"Faith, stop," Ted said.

"We can't let Snickerdoodle get hurt."

Mrs. Barlow loved her dog. He was her companion. Her best friend. Her heart. Now was when she'd need him most. There was no way I'd stand back and let her come back to a Snickerdoodle-free home.

A round furry object veered around the fence that separated my grandmothers' and my yard from Steve's. Snickerdoodle circled around, heading straight for me. I opened my arms...and landed flat on my face as Ted tackled me from behind. Grass tickled my nose and almost became my dinner.

"I almost had him." I pushed myself up on my elbows and tried wiggling out from under Ted.

Ted snagged my waist. "Go home. I'll finish asking what I need there."

"What about Charlotte? No questions for her?" I finally escaped from Ted's grasp.

"Officer Mitchell is taking her to the station." Once again, his arm was around me, bringing me close to his body.

I was having trouble breathing and the world suddenly turned hot. "Aren't you afraid of being accused of favoritism? Why did you stay behind to question me and send Charlotte off with Mitchell? My interview is being conducted in my cozy home and she's being dragged to the station."

"I can't argue that this isn't cozy," Ted's words whispered across my cheek, "but I disagree with your assessment that Charlotte was dragged anywhere."

"Unhand me," I said.

"I'm not letting you run away from me."

"What's going on out here?" Steve strode over, Snickerdoodle cradled in his arms.

"We were chasing after Mrs. Barlow's dog." I smiled. "And you found the little rascal. Thanks."

"It's easier to locate a fugitive when you're not rolling around in the grass." Steve stared at Ted's hands clasped around my waist.

I slipped away from Ted. "You gave me the keys to what had been your place. How did you get in?"

"What are you talking about?"

"Officer Mitchell said you went home. You don't live there anymore. You gave me your keys."

"He was mistaken." Steve placed the dog in my arms, murmuring into my ear as he drifted a kiss across my cheek, then left.

Fear filled me at his parting statement. "For everyone's sake, let this go."

*   *   *

I couldn't. Mrs. Barlow had been hurt because of this case. Because of me. I brought her into this mess and shouldn't just sit safe and sound in my house while her attacker roamed free. I knew the police were looking for the person who assaulted her, but I was also responsible. I had to do something to quiet some of the guilt roaring through my head and heart.

The most important thing I needed to do was check on Mrs. Barlow. She was probably scared, and her daughter was a fifteen-hour drive away. There was no way Mrs. Barlow should spend the night alone in the hospital. After putting Snickerdoodle in my bedroom, I snatched up my keys and ran out to my car.

As I sped down the road, I remembered a car had left the woods near Piece A Pie. What if that had been the arsonist? The person probably saw us and took off before they could be identified. But why would they go after Mrs. Barlow? The person had to know she had information they'd want kept quiet. That meant the arsonist had to be someone local and knew Mrs. Barlow kept an ear on everything going on in Eden.

The parking lot was surprisingly full considering how late it was. I recognized a few of the cars. I should've known my grandmothers and Gussie would show up at the hospital. I was also sure the dark-colored sedan was Ted's unmarked squad car. I doubted he'd think I was only here to find out about Mrs. Barlow, and I wasn't in the mood to deal with him. Instead of going into the emergency room, I went inside the main area and over to the nurse manning the receptionist station.

"I want to check on a friend of mine. She was brought in recently."

She smiled at me. "I'm sorry. I can't give that information out to you."

I was sure her gentle smile was to soften her answer. "I'm a neighbor."

"I'm sorry. Family only." The nurse turned her attention to a stack of papers on her desk.

Drat. I should've guessed I wouldn't receive any information. But I bet Gussie would've found a way to get it. I was going to have to gather up my courage and sass and just go into the emergency room. I couldn't let Detective Ted Roget scare me away. Besides, with my grandmothers and Gussie there he wouldn't jump all over me too much. Then again he might not have to, as it was likely my grandmothers knew what I'd been up to early in the evening.

If a comeuppance was the only way I'd learn about Mrs. Barlow's condition, it was worth it. I headed for the emergency room, stopping in my tracks when I heard sobs coming from inside the women's restroom.

I stepped inside. Lake straightened, wiping her face with paper towels.

Lake had Mrs. Barlow working on her scrapbook for an insurance adjuster who was arriving in town. Charlie. She was supposed to have been at Mrs. Barlow's house, but had cancelled because the police took her in for questioning. Had the attacker mistaken Mrs. Barlow for Lake? Or had Lake lied about the reason for not coming?

"Are you all right?" I rested a hand on her shoulder, deciding to take a more subtle approach to get some answers.

"I'm fine." Lake shrugged off my hand and reached for the door handle.

I blocked the door. "Something has you upset."

She huffed out a breath. "Of course I'm upset. A friend of mine was hurt tonight. Who wouldn't be upset? Besides you." She punctuated the last statement by fixing a haughty look on me.

"I've moved past the upset stage into anger. Whoever hurt Mrs. Barlow will not get away with it."

"They better not."

"I'm glad you agree because I need your help." Did I really want to involve someone else? Too many people had already been hurt. I had to. I was certain Lake had some of the answers. And if she hadn't told the police, now was the time.

Her eyes widened. "I can't help you."

"You can help Mrs. Barlow. You have to tell the police the truth."

"I don't know what you're talking about."

"You hired someone to set fire to your shop."

She paled and grew unsteady on her feet. She drew back, placing a hand on the sink. "How can you accuse me of such a thing?"

"The pictures you gave Mrs. Barlow to scrap were taken the day before the fire."

"Just a coincidence," she squeaked out.

"I don't think so. And I don't think the investigator believed it either. That's why Charlie Powell came to Eden. He was working on your and Dawn Carr's claim. There was a business card for Vulcan Catering mixed in with your pictures. Vulcan isn't a new food business in town."

Tears filled her eyes. "It was a coincidence. I had nothing to do with that man's murder."

"I don't think you did it. But I do think you have information that will help the police find the person who is responsible."

She shook her head.

"I can't. If I know the person responsible it means I committed a crime. I'll go to jail."

"Tell Detective Roget everything. He'll understand. He'll help you."

"If I did hire someone to burn down my store, do you really think it would matter that I was losing money because people are buying their flowers at the box store and my health insurance premium takes up most of my income? If I'm going to have enough money to retire I needed to unload it. No one is interested. Jim's having the same trouble. No one wants to buy a business located at our end of town."

"Two people were murdered. Mrs. Barlow could've been killed. This person needs to be stopped and you possibly have the information to stop them."

Lake pushed me out of the way. "I have nothing to say to the police. I already made that clear to Detective Roget. I'm not going to jail."

"It's better than being dead." I hated myself a little for it but knew it needed to be said.

She paused with her hand on the door handle.

"What if the person who hurt Mrs. Barlow had actually thought it was you they were attacking? I'm sure Mrs. Barlow had told practically everyone in town about her nail party. You don't think this person wants to keep their identity a secret? How can they trust that you'll keep quiet?" Every question I asked made me feel a little bit worse. "But there's no need for you to worry about it. Right?"

Lake hightailed it out of the restroom.

TWENTY-FOUR

Light seeped past my eyelids, mingling with the muddled images in my mind: Felicity arguing with Chad, the aftermath of the fire, Dawn and her mother, Charlie's murder, being shot at, Mrs. Barlow bruised and bloodied, Steve's warning, threatening Lake.

Grimacing, I stretched my neck, working out the kinks from sleeping in the recliner all night. The notebook and reports Mrs. Barlow printed out for me slipped from my lap, cascading onto the floor.

A car door slammed across the street. Was someone bringing Mrs. Barlow home? I knelt on the chair and turned around, scooping back a corner of the blinds with my index finger. Ted and Jasper hauled cleaning supplies from the back of Jasper's car. There was something I could do for Mrs. Barlow. I hurried upstairs, making myself presentable to the world, then headed out the door.

Ted glanced in my direction. I was too far away to get a read on his expression. He didn't like me getting involved in solving crimes, but his attitude toward me was even brusquer than usual. I wished I knew what the problem was.

Ask him. I slowed, giving myself more time to turn over the command in my head. There were some times I shouldn't listen to my instinct, and I believed now was one of those.

"I'm here to help," I said.

"Right." Ted stretched out the word.

Jasper looked at Ted, then me. "We could use it. Mrs. Barlow has woken up and might be released this weekend. The doctor is limiting her visitors right now to immediate family. My grandmother is heading over hoping to sweet talk the doctor—she's friends with his parents—into letting her in because Mrs. Barlow's daughter won't be here until this evening. She doesn't want Mrs. Barlow to be alone."

I smiled at Jasper. "Thanks for letting me know."

He patted my shoulder. "No problem. I know you've been worried. You've always kept an eye on her."

The small amount of good mood in me crumbled. "Except for last night."

"That wasn't your fault." Jasper opened up the front door. "Mrs. Barlow has always stuck her nose into everything. She had plastered photos of Andrew Taylor at the bonfire all over her blog last night."

"I should read her blog. I bet she keeps a detailed list of everything going on in the community."

"And whatever she thinks is happening. Stay out of it, Faith." Ted shoved a mop and a bucket at me. "Why don't you go swab the deck?"

"I'll take care of the deck." Jasper removed the items from my hands. "You and Faith can take care of inside."

"I think it'll do her some good," Ted said.

"And I think you'll regret it." There was a sharp edge to Jasper's voice.

"Nothing else that's happened has made a dent in her stubbornness," Ted said.

"You can take up my insubordination with Chief Moore." Jasper headed to the back. "There's no way I'm letting her clean up that mess. And if you weren't so angry this morning, you wouldn't let her either, Detective Roget."

The mess out back. Mrs. Barlow's blood. I felt a little queasy. I pressed my hand to the doorframe, steadying myself.

"Jasper's right. That's not something I should've asked you to handle."

"Why do you hate me?" The words tumbled out before I regained my equilibrium.

Without replying, Ted headed down the hallway to Mrs. Barlow's office.

I went after him, wanting an answer, and also to see what damage was done in there. With Ted's behavior and what he'd said, I knew the attack on Mrs. Barlow had everything to do with Chad and Charlie's murders and the fires. "I asked you a question."

"Were you in this room yesterday?" Ted opened the door. "We've dusted for prints, and I'd like to know whose I might find."

He was dodging the question. Fine. I wouldn't care anymore. Let him act however he wanted. "Charlotte and I were in this room for a little while yesterday. Mrs. Barlow was showing us all her gadgets since Lake Breckenridge had to cancel the nail wrap demonstration because she was having a chat with someone at the police station. I wonder what about."

"Not for you to know."

"Of course it isn't," I said. "According to you, nothing is for me to know, including the reason for your obvious hostility toward me."

The CPU unit for Mrs. Barlow's computer was missing, the file cabinet drawers were empty, and a portion of the rug was cut out.

"That wasn't gone yesterday." Ted squatted down. Using the end of a stylus, he lifted up a corner of the cut rug.

"I didn't hear anyone come back last night," I said.

"You might not have since your room is on the second floor in the back."

"I slept on a chair in the living room near the window," I confessed. "I wanted to be able to hear—"

"If the attacker returned so you could go deal with him." Ted slapped his hand onto the wall. "When are you going to learn? This is dangerous."

"If Mrs. Barlow came home," I corrected him. "Contrary to your belief, I'm not an idiot. If I'd heard something, I would've called the police, not tangled with the person one on one."

"I don't think you're an idiot. I just think you're a little too headstrong and you feel the need to be everyone's hero."

"What's wrong with wanting to help?"

"Nothing, except you take it too far and put yourself in danger." Ted continued to check out the rug. "It's exhausting worrying about you all the time."

"Nobody asked you to."

"You think it's something I can consciously control?" Ted pulled out his cell and sent a text. "It's time for you to go to work. Get a cup of coffee. Do anything except hang around a crime scene."

"I'm not hanging around a crime scene. I'm cleaning up a friend's house."

"It's a crime scene," Ted said. "I'm formally requesting that you leave."

"Fine." I had other things to do today, like go to work and conduct an impromptu get-well-soon-card party. Mrs. Barlow would love to be showered with cards. It'd perk her right up to know that everyone took time out of their day for her and that she was the talk of the town. I whipped out my cell phone and posted a message on the store's Facebook page.

"And stop interrogating people."

I twisted to stare at him.

"I know you spoke with Lake."

His attitude today hinted that she didn't tell him the truth. If she did, he'd be a step closer to solving the case and that was a good thing. "Did she tell you about a scrapbook Mrs. Barlow was making for her?"

"Not for you to know. By the way, I don't hate you," Ted said. "A guy wants to be the first choice, not the default."

My heart went into freefall, then ricocheted back up, getting stuck where my conscience resided. My emotions had always tumbled when I was near Ted, tempting me. I had always drawn back, reminding myself I had chosen Steve. The safer bet. The man I believed would never make me doubt his feelings for me, who'd always put my best interests first, who wouldn't challenge me. I wanted to feel safe, on even ground all the time. I wanted a relationship where I was in firm control and could adjust the intensity at my will. What I wanted, and thought only Steve could bring to my life, was security and calmness. When I realized that would never be the reality again between me and Steve, I ended it. I had fallen for an illusion and couldn't only blame Steve for creating it.

Ted wasn't safe. Ted challenged me. He was the one who pushed me past my comfort zone and made me see a life alone was one controlled by Adam, not by me. Ted made me break down my walls, try my hand at living a fuller life, even if it meant I fell in love with another man. He argued with me. Consoled me. Counseled me. Ted made me face the world, rather than allowing me to hide from it and wallow in the past. He wanted more from me—and for me. The truth dumped on me felt like a bucket of ice water. I trusted Ted with my insecurities and found myself being truly one hundred percent me around him more than anyone else in my life. Ted had encouraged me to open my life up, to take a chance on Steve. I looked over my shoulder, meeting Ted's gaze.

"You were never the default."

The Silhouette Cameo machine hummed and chugged along, making a slight clicking sound as it cut another base for a pop-up box card. I had gathered a mix of embellishments and placed them on one of the cropping tables along with the bases. Three customers had already arrived and were working on making either a swing-style or box explosion card. We had decided Mrs. Barlow deserved something with pizzazz for her get-well cards.

An older woman clutching a cane hobbled up to the counter and held out a pop-up box. A little dog resembling Snickerdoodle waved a sign saying "Get well soon," while the other slots for the pop-ups were filled with other types of dogs, a cat, and a baby. Wobbly hand-drawn line-stitching details highlighted the bright blue cardstock used as the base of the card. "How does this look? Heather loves babies and cats. You know, blue is her favorite color and you don't have many blue squares."

"I'll be sure to cut some more." I gingerly took her creation from her, giving it the reverence it deserved. "It's beautiful. She'll love it."

"I also brought her some magazines." She motioned for the young woman sitting at the table.

The girl stopped working on her Biology homework, carried over a sealed brown paper bag, and handed it to me. She stepped back out of eye range of the older woman and mouthed "don't open." Knowing Mrs. Barlow's love of men in uniform, I decided not to see what type of reading material was being gifted to her in a sealed package.

"I'll give it to her." I placed the reading material into my large tote and made a mental note to save it for last. I wanted to be out of the room when Mrs. Barlow started browsing through her magazines.

The bell above the door jingled and jangled. "Welcome to Scrap This," Marilyn said.

Allan Sullivan had walked into the store. He swallowed a couple of times, sweat beading his brow. He glanced around the room, taking in everything and everybody, before his gaze settled on the card-making supplies on the table.

"We're making some get-well cards for Mrs. Barlow," I said. "I'll be taking them over in a little while."

"Is it all right if I tried putting one together?"

"Sure," I said.

Staring wide-eyed at all the supplies, Allan sat down. He chose the base for a swing card, opened it, turned it over to the side, then put it right back. Next, he picked up the base for the pop-up box card, again studying it from every angle, and then placed it back on the table. The man looked lost.

"I think he needs help." Marilyn walked behind the counter and nudged me. "You should go."

"Why don't you? You know how to make them."

"Because I have a feeling he didn't walk into Scrap This to make a card. He's not on our mailing list."

I took a good long look at the man. He seemed despondent, not like he was ready to engage in a battle, and regardless of what Ted thought, I had learned lessons from the other murders I solved. One should never confront a murder suspect without some sort of a plan, even out in the open. I patted my pocket. My cell was in reach.

I headed over. "Need some help?"

He held up both bases. "Do you have anything less complicated to make?"

"They're easy once you know how they go together," I said. "We can make the pop-up card."

I picked up a base and a scored and cut piece of cardstock, and used a bone folder to press the folds to make sure it folded easily. I chose two matching blue strips to glue inside the base for our pop-up elements. I flattened it and dragged over some choices of pattern paper toward us. "Glue a piece of cardstock onto the front of the card, and then a long strip of cardstock is glued onto the inside part of the card that acts as the backdrop for the pop-ups."

Allan chose a few pieces, and I closed my mouth. It was his card. The patterns weren't ones I'd mix together, but this was his creative endeavor and I didn't want to discourage him. The world needed more male scrapbookers and card-makers.

"How's this?" He held it up.

"Great. Open up the box and glue in the strip to either side of the card. Add some chipboard pieces or die cuts onto the strips." I pointed to each pile.

"Felicity would love to make these. But with her arthritis, all the folding and cutting would be hard on her," Allan said.

"I can make some kits for her. All she'd have to do is glue them together."

He smiled and placed the explosion card in the palm of his hand. "I appreciate it. It upset her when she had to stop hand-making Christmas cards."

"Did you want to talk to me about something? I have a feeling you didn't come to stock up on crafting supplies for your wife who's in jail."

Allan reddened and sweat beaded on his forehead. "I had nothing to do with those fires."

That was a popular statement lately. I remained quiet, allowing him to continue.

"After the Made With Love fire, I told the police I had insured all of those businesses. I was worried because it looked like someone was targeting my clients. Lake. Clive. Chad. When Charlie Powell arrived and told me some of his findings, I got even more concerned. An hour before the fires, all three clients used our online option to purchase an increase in their coverage."

Disappointed flooded me. Clive was involved. "What's going to happen to them?"

"I don't know, since it looks like their accounts were hacked."

"Are you sure?" Happiness was restored. Clive wasn't guilty of insurance fraud. I kind of liked the old guy.

"The IP addresses were traced to the fire station."

"Who told you this?"

"Karen. She got a hold of one of the police reports."

"Why did Felicity confess?"

"Because she wants to help our family and thought it was the best way."

"She was afraid the police would suspect you?"

"She hadn't known I'd already brought my concerns to them. I gave them a list of the stores I insured and also the ones who had filed claims. Detective Roget hoped keeping it quiet might make the arsonist slip up, that they'd get cocky. He didn't want them on guard. Felicity was under so much stress between her illness and Brandon's medical issues, I hadn't wanted to give her one more thing to worry about, so I didn't tell her. Now I wish I had."

"What's her connection to Andrew Taylor?"

Allan rubbed his eyes. "She made threatening calls to Andrew. She found out that while Chad sold the drugs, Andrew was the one who handed it to Brandon."

"She had a motive to kill Chad and set up Andrew."

"My wife's biggest regret is she couldn't have killed Chad for ruining our son's life. Since no one else wanted to claim it, she did."

"She couldn't have killed Charlie. She was in jail."

"But she could've told Andrew Taylor that Charlie Powell was going to prove he killed Chad, and that set the murder in motion."

"Why would she put another man at risk?"

"She didn't think she was. She doesn't really believe Andrew's a murderer, but she wants him to suffer too."

I heaved my overfilled bright pink tote bag onto my shoulder, squeaking my way across the hallway in the hospital. Mrs. Barlow was at a room at the end of the hall being guarded by Gussie. The police might not have thought the elderly woman needed protection from her attacker, but her friends had.

If I ever needed a bodyguard, I'd feel safe knowing Gussie was nearby. She might not be young and spry anymore, but she packed a wallop, and had such a fierce expression it wouldn't surprise me if she literally turned a bad guy into a frozen block of ice.

"Bearing presents and get-well cards." I struggled to lift the bag up higher and show it to Gussie.

"She'll be thrilled."

I tapped on the door.

"It's Faith."

"Come in."

I opened the door and was hit by the overwhelming smell of flowers. There was a mix of roses, gardenias, carnations, and even pine in the room, making it look like Mrs. Barlow decided to open a flower shop in her hospital room. Vases of flowers filled every spare inch of table or window space. Balloons were tied onto the visitor chairs and the head of the bed.

Mrs. Barlow swatted one away from her head. "I didn't want them blocking the television. Now I'm afraid one of them might strangle me in my sleep. I didn't have the heart to turn away any gifts."

I retied the balloon so it wasn't threatening to wrap around

Mrs. Barlow's throat. "You could donate them to the pediatric floor. I bet the kids would love them."

She beamed and raised the head of the bed. "That's a terrific idea. It'll make me happy to know the balloons are appreciated."

"I hope you don't mind, I have more gifts." I plopped my bulging tote onto the bed. "I have cards, chocolates, and magazines."

"What type of magazines?" She peered into the bag.

"I don't know. A friend of yours gave them to me in a sealed brown paper bag."

"Thank you." Blushing, Mrs. Barlow tucked the package under her pillow. "I'll take a look at those later. It'd be very rude to thumb through a magazine while I have company."

"How are you feeling?" I sat in the closest visitor's chair.

"Better." She held her hand over the bandage on her left temple. "Just a little headache and my arm aches some. The doctor says it's fortunate I didn't break anything when I fell."

"You fell?" Had we all been mistaken about what happened to Mrs. Barlow? My phone rang. I turned it down and set it on the bedside table, letting the call go to voicemail.

"Not on my own. I took Snickerdoodle out for his before-bed potty time. He started whimpering, so we went back inside to put his booties on. He doesn't like it when the ground is cold. I checked my messages, and you girls hadn't called yet, so I had to make some calls. I was worried."

"Sorry about that. We had a bonfire to break up."

"I wish I had known. I called Detective Roget, Steve, Daniel, Officer Jasper, Wayne, and Wyatt. I hate the fact I sent them on an unnecessary call. No one is going to take my calls seriously if I call for nothing. To think, I might have gotten you girls in trouble because no one wanted to head out until I told them exactly why I was worried. That detective was the crankiest of the lot."

"That's not a surprise."

"While I was talking to all the men, Snickerdoodle kept trying to get the muffins from the buffet, so I put those away and then put all my records away and made a backup of all my data. I hadn't done it in a week, and with everything going on, I thought that would be a good idea."

"Where do you keep it?" My phone buzzed and skidded around the table.

"Shouldn't you answer that?"

"I'm more interested in your story."

Smiling, Mrs. Barlow settled herself more comfortably against her pillows. "I hide the memory stick under my mattress."

My heart sped up. There was evidence.

Mrs. Barlow bopped my nose with her fingertip. "Now, don't you get too excited. I already told that detective where I kept it."

Drat. Well, I should be happy since the police had the evidence. They were the ones who really needed it.

The door flung open. Melinda, Mrs. Barlow's daughter, stood in the doorway, trembling from head to toe. "I want you gone."

Mrs. Barlow wagged a finger at her daughter. "That is no way to treat my company."

My phone buzzed again. A text message flashed on the screen. I scanned it.

"I want you to stay away from my mother." She jabbed a finger at the door. "If I find out you ever get her involved in your messes again, I'll slap a restraining order on you."

Holding my head high, and my cell phone clutched in my hand, I hurried out the door. I was less worried about Mrs. Barlow than the text I'd just received.

"I'm going after the evidence." Dawn had typed.

I texted Dawn back. "Call the cops."

"Can't."

My fingers flew over the keys. "It's too risky. You have to tell them. Or I will."

"If you do, I'll be dead. It's one of them."

TWENTY-FIVE

Leaves crunched under my boots as I made my way past the remains of Made With Love toward the wooded area where Dawn said the evidence was located. A chill worked its way through my body. Even as I tried avoiding the mound where Charlie had been buried, my gaze kept skittering toward it, almost searching for it. My emotions felt as scattered as the leaves on the ground. A cop was the murderer. I didn't want to believe it. Even after my bad experience with the law, I still firmly believed in justice and the men and woman who risked their lives for their communities.

I couldn't see it. Not in Eden. And not any of the officers I knew. Well, there was an exception: Officer Mitchell. He was feeding Karen information and doing his best to make me the suspect.

"Dawn," I stage-whispered. No reply. I called out again, this time a little louder.

Where was she?

I stood still and listened. Off in the distance, I heard twigs snapping. Ducking under low hanging branches, I moved deeper into the woods, careful of where I stepped. Dawn better show herself soon, or I'd call Ted.

An arm wound around my upper body as a gun was pressed to my temple. Trembling, I snuck a glance over my shoulder. Andrew Taylor. Twigs and leaves were stuck in his hair, and dirt coated one side of his face.

"Let's go." He waved the gun toward the woods. "It's time for a reunion with your friend."

"No one else is here."

"I'm not that stupid," he said. "I know Dawn Carr is here. And I know what you are both up to."

"It's just me."

"Stop lying and move." He jabbed the gun into my back.

I examined the world around me, taking mental notes and making an escape plan. Fortunately, there were plenty of downed branches, so I had my pick of weapons. I only needed to wait for the right moment. I had parked in a spot perfect for a getaway and left the keys in the ignition. I could get us out of this alive.

"You're stalling. Let's go. And no funny business."

If he was going to boss me around, I wished he'd be a little more original. Then again, Ridley said Andrew wasn't bright. So what did that say about me for getting captured by a person I believed wasn't a blade sharp enough to score a piece of paper?

"Hurry up." Andrew grabbed my arm and yanked me forward.

"It'll take longer if you make me break my leg. There's a lot of debris around here." I stepped over a fallen tree branch.

Andrew flattened himself against a tree, pulling me to the side. A crackling sound broke the stillness of the woods. I peered through the trees and spotted Dawn.

She was brushing leaves away from the trunk of a tree. Large roots stuck out from the ground, creating a little cave at the base of the tree.

He rested a finger against my lips. "Say one word and I'll shoot her. Got it?"

There was nothing I could do but nod.

"Don't think," he added to his warning, and pointed the barrel of the gun through an opening between the branches. He had a clear shot.

Dawn must've heard something. She spun around, fear on her face, and tried to shield the nature-created hiding spot.

"Move." Andrew shoved me.

I fell forward, tumbling onto the ground a few yards in front of Dawn.

"What in the world?" Dawn squatted down beside me.

Flipping myself over, I sat up and pointed at Andrew. "Watch out!"

"Think I wouldn't find out what you were up to?" Andrew walked forward, gun aimed at Dawn. "You took my accountability tag and are hiding it."

"Your what?" we asked.

"My fire department ID," Andrew said. "I have to have it or I'm not allowed on calls."

There was a nice size branch, perfect for clubbing, a few feet away. I angled my heels to the right, then brought the rest of my feet over. A few more of these moves, and I'd have it in my hand.

"Why would I take it?" Dawn shuffled backwards.

"I was showing it to the kids. Chad took it and wouldn't give it back. He gave it to you."

"Chad didn't give to me," Dawn said. "I didn't even know what was hidden here. I swear."

"Then how did you know where to look for it?"

"I'm not telling you."

Andrew's trigger finger twitched. I wasn't sure now was a good time to start showing an attitude.

I tried distracting Andrew with a question. "Did you tell the police Chad took your ID?"

"Hell no. I wasn't going to say I was out here the night of the fire. I knew people would think I killed him." Andrew turned the gun on me. "Stay still. I'm not as dumb as everyone thinks."

Dawn hugged herself.

"You should've told them," I said. "It would've made you a hero. No one really cares that Chad was killed."

Dawn drew in a sharp breath. Tears glittered in her eyes. I snuck a glance at the branch and then back at her. I repeated the movement again, hoping she'd understand.

"My husband didn't deserve to die like that."

"And I don't deserve to be set up for his and the other guy's murder," Andrew said.

"We're not framing you." I pointed at myself. "Mitchell has been trying to pin it on me."

"And there's your reason for saying I did it."

Unfortunately, he had a point. "I promise we're not trying to frame you. Maybe what Dawn came to find isn't about you."

Andrew looked doubtful.

"Let me take a look. Please," I said.

Andrew hooked an arm around Dawn, pressing the gun to the back of her head. "If you try anything, I'll shoot her. Understand?"

Perfectly. I lowered myself to the ground and stuck my hand inside the cave the roots formed. I felt around. After a few minutes, my hand closed around two cards. One firm and one flimsy and soggy.

"Did you find something?"

"No. But I can't reach all the way back. My arms aren't long enough."

"I'll do it."

I discreetly placed Andrew's accountability tag and the barely held-together Vulcan Catering card under my derrière.

He motioned with his gun. "Move it."

I scooted on my rump, dragging the evidence with me, and praying I didn't destroy either piece.

"I mean stand up." He eyed me suspiciously. "What are you doing?"

"Moving. My legs are a little shaky, so it's hard to stand," I said, running through options for hiding the cards.

"Lean on your friend. Just stand up."

"Why? Where are we going?" I asked.

"No questions, Miss Sherlock Holmes. From now on, you listen. You've run your mouth all over town long enough," Andrew said.

"If you're mad at me, let Dawn go." I flattened my hands on the ground. "No reason to make her stay."

"I didn't do anything," Dawn said.

Andrew pointed the gun at Dawn. "You know everything."

"I don't." Dawn clasped her arms around her quaking body. "I'm trying to figure it out, but I know nothing."

"She doesn't know anything," I said. "She had no idea Chad paid someone to burn the place down."

"Yes, she does. She's keeping it quiet, making everyone think it was me." Andrew roamed the barrel toward me. "Now stand up."

I dug my fingers deep into the loose dirt. I scooped up a handful and threw it in Andrew's face.

"Run!" I snatched up the evidence in one hand, grabbing Dawn's arm with the other. I ran.

She stumbled behind me.

Andrew screamed, "I'll kill you for this!"

Not if he couldn't catch us. Once we made it to the main road, we'd be fine. There wasn't a lot of traffic down this portion of Route 220, but with the high school game starting in an hour, there'd be a steady stream of cars.

"Stop! I'll shoot you."

I listened for the sound of the gun, wanting to know which way to feign. Nothing. Dawn cried out. My arm jerked down.

"I twisted my ankle. Bad," Dawn said through gritted teeth.

"We can make it," I said.

"You go."

"I'm not leaving you." I helped Dawn to her feet, directing her in front of me. She half-ran, half-limped.

"I'll shoot. This is my last warning." Andrew's voice came from a few feet behind us. "I mean it!"

"We're almost to the road." I hoped my encouragement pushed her through the pain.

Dawn used the trees to pull herself along. "Almost there. Almost there."

"Stop ignoring me. I will kill you," Andrew wearily threatened.

Then why hadn't he already? The man had had plenty of time to shoot us at least three times. Why keep threatening it? Because he couldn't kill a person. I stopped and faced him.

Andrew skidded to a stop, pointing the gun at me.

"Good, you finally listened. I won't have to kill you."

"You wouldn't have killed me," I said. "You're not a murderer."

He lowered the gun. "Now someone believes me."

This was quite the conundrum.

"Faith," Dawn called out to me.

"It's okay. He's not going to hurt us."

"I wouldn't be so sure." Dawn hobbled back to me.

"I am." I crossed my arms and glared at Andrew. "Start talking. Why were you at the bonfire last Friday night? Coach Rutherford told you to stay away."

"Because someone had to look after the kids."

"They're teenagers. They don't need a babysitter," I said.

"Coach didn't know about this one. He wouldn't be there to make sure the kids didn't drive high."

"Weren't the other monitors there? Wouldn't they snitch on you?" I asked.

"It was game night. Most of them were out drinking with their friends, and Mitchell was on duty."

"If Coach Rutherford—"

Andrew cut me off. "I know. He'd have lost it, and I'd have been run out of town. But I couldn't do nothing. Not after what happened to Brandon."

"Did you know you handed Brandon Janie the night of his accident?"

Andrew's arm slackened. The gun dangled by his leg. "No. But I was the adult. I should've known something was up. Brandon was acting real weird when he left. I should've insisted on driving him home, but the kid wanted to be alone."

"Why? Did Brandon get into a fight with someone at the bonfire?" I asked.

Dawn shifted some leaves with the toe of her dirty sneaker. "It was because he saw Hannah with Daniel Burke."

I stared at Dawn.

"The night of the accident, I left Made With Love late because I was working on the books," Dawn said. "I saw Daniel and Hannah sitting in his truck, making out. I heard someone behind me and turned. It was Brandon."

"Why didn't Chad stop the kids from driving?" I asked.

"He told me it wasn't his responsibility." Andrew tapped the barrel against his leg. "He was providing the place. He never admitted he sold the Janie, but we all kind of knew, but as long as we didn't *really* know—"

"You didn't have to tell the police. No one wanted the players getting busted." I worked on locking up my disgust. I was close to the truth, and didn't want my attitude shutting it down.

"But that night, I knew Chad was angry," Andrew said. "When Brandon drove off, Chad said maybe now Felicity Sullivan would get off his back. Chad had rolled all the cigarettes and was filling up the empty packs the kids brought him."

"You liar." Dawn charged Andrew.

She was slowed down by her ankle, so I easily snagged her around the waist and stopped her. "He has a gun."

"He won't shoot us."

"Maybe not on purpose."

Dawn removed my arms from around her waist and sank to the ground. "I can't believe my husband would purposely hurt a child. Is that why Felicity set him on fire?"

"She didn't have the strength to kill him," I said. "Chad was dead before the fire."

"Who set it?" Andrew asked. "I didn't."

"Where were you when Made With Love burned down and Charlie was murdered?" I asked.

"With my wife. Norm keeps telling Debi to roll on me. Give the police what they want. I didn't do it. I killed nobody."

I pulled the cards out of my pocket. "Who would want to set you set up, Andrew? I found these under the tree."

"I don't know. My father-in-law don't like me much, but I can't see him burning down places and people so I'd go to prison."

I couldn't muster even an ounce of conviction for that theory either.

Andrew turned the business card over. "Is this a new place? I've never heard of it."

"What about your truck? It was in the bay at the fire station, and I know it was the same one used when someone shot at me and Ted," I said.

"I reported my truck stolen Monday night," Andrew said. "No one believed me."

"Why?" Dawn bunched her legs toward her chest, resting her chin on her knees.

Andrew blushed. "Because it was always getting stolen, or moved, as Norm called it. I was always leaving my keys on the counter at the bowling alley. My father-in-law or Daniel would take my keys and move my truck on me so I couldn't drive home."

"And we're supposed to believe that," I said.

"That's exactly what the police said. I swear it's the truth. Someone did steal my truck that night." With sad eyes, Andrew looked at Dawn. "I don't know why you and your husband hate me so much. I don't deserve to be blamed."

Dawn rose. "My husband didn't deserve to be murdered. The day Faith talked to me and Mom at the nursing home, I found a map showing this spot. I was helping Mom organize her closet and it was shoved in a pocket of her winter coat."

"You've been searching for the evidence since then?" I asked.

"I wanted to, but my mom needed me. It wasn't until she died I started looking for it. I knew it had to do with Chad's death. Someone snuck in when I went out for food and gave my mom an overdose of her pain medication. I was afraid I'd be killed next."

The murderer killed Lucy. She was defenseless. She couldn't hurt whoever it was. Why Lucy? She wasn't a threat to anyone. Fury boiled through me.

"Whoever did that deserves to be set on fire," Andrew said.

"I hid, but Detective Roget found me," Dawn said. "I told him everything, and he promised to keep me safe."

"You were staying at Steve's old place," I said. That was why Ted tackled me. He was afraid I'd see Dawn.

"Not at first. But someone broke into the first place the detective arranged for me. Steve Davis was worried there was a leak somewhere in the police department. So he offered to use his place as a safehouse for me."

"My grandmothers—"

"They were safe. Chief Moore would keep an eye on them, and Officer Jasper stayed with me."

With all the police presence in my neighborhood, how did Mrs. Barlow get hurt? "Mrs. Barlow was attacked last night."

Dawn tucked her hair behind her ears and cupped her hands around the back of her neck. "The person who hurt her had to know Chief Moore hadn't arrived yet, that your grandmothers were still at the store, and that there was an incident at Piece A Pie. That proved to me Steve was right about there being a leak."

"The assailant knew Mrs. Barlow was vulnerable," I said.

I replayed the conversation I'd had with Mrs. Barlow. She had listed Daniel Burke as one of the men she called as part of her cavalry. He didn't show up at Piece A Pie. The criminal on the inside wasn't a police officer with insider knowledge. It was a firefighter. Charlotte—Hannah—had had a Vulcan Catering card. When I went to talk to Charlotte Tuesday night, someone had been in the house with Hannah. My guess was Hannah's boyfriend Daniel.

"You two stay here where you're safe. I'll call you after I have a chat with someone." Hannah had to tell her mom and the police the truth.

"I think I should go with you." Andrew scratched the side of his head with the barrel of the gun.

Norman Ridley was right. His son-in-law wasn't very bright. "Give me the gun."

Andrew passed it to me without an argument.

"If I bring someone else, Hannah will bolt. She trusts me," I said. For now.

Since I'd been back home, I worked hard at protecting friendships. I made some stumbles and had sworn to myself I'd never do it again. The problem with promises—even those made to yourself—was at times you had to break them.

"You two stay here while I sort this out. Last thing you guys want is to get caught by the man trying to set one, or both of you, up for murder."

TWENTY-SIX

My nerves were raw by the time I made my way through the slow traffic and reached Polished. I hoped Hannah was still there and didn't find the hang-up call I'd made too unnerving. I didn't want her to know I was coming. What was I going to do if Daniel was there? I fingered my phone, wishing Ted would've picked up. He needed to get a cell he'd answer even when on duty. For all I knew, he had one and hadn't given me the number. I mulled over calling the station but if Mitchell was on duty, he was more likely to arrest me and tip Daniel off at the same time. Daniel would be out of Eden, and likely the country, before I'd get Mitchell to trust me.

I slowly drove past Polished. Through the windows, I watched Hannah and Charlotte clean, and a conversation began playing in my head. Charlotte had said she was going to the game tonight. What made her change her mind?

I decided on parallel parking in front of Scrap This so people saw my car. I opened the console between the driver and passenger seat and pulled out the report Mrs. Barlow made about the fire calls, along with her chart of who went in what vehicle. The last person on the majority of calls was Daniel Burke, the volunteer who lived closest to the station. Granted, the man probably didn't hang around his house all night, but why was he consistently the last one to show up at the station when there was an out-of-control bonfire? Every other type of call, Daniel was the first one at the station.

I called Ted again. Still no answer. His voicemail clicked on. "It's Daniel Burke." It was the shortest message I ever left Ted.

While I wanted Dawn and Andrew out of my way, I also

wanted them safe. I couldn't rely on Andrew saving himself and Dawn if trouble showed up there. The only person I could count on right now was Karen. She had a vested interest in this, and wanted solid proof her cousin had nothing to do with Chad Carr's death.

Karen answered on the second ring. "Mrs. Barlow told me you chatted with her, then took off like Dianne was handing out free baked goods and coffee."

"I got a text from Dawn about going after evidence." I quickly explained the outcome of that situation.

"I'll head over there and interview them," she said. "Be careful."

"The volunteer fire squad always attends the game in case anything happens. I figure I'm good for a couple of hours," I said.

Charlotte tapped on my window.

"Have to go." I ended the call and rolled down the window.

"Did you break down or run out of gas?" Charlotte asked. "You've never parked out front before."

"I need to talk to Hannah."

The smile slipped from her face. She cast a look over at her store, wrapping her arms around herself. "How about we talk in Scrap This? It's a little chilly out here."

"It's important I speak with her."

"You have to get through me to talk with Hannah." Charlotte opened the car door.

"Okay." I knew my voice sounded hesitant. I wasn't quite sure why Charlotte wanted privacy; I hoped the trust I placed in my friend wasn't my downfall. I unlocked the door to Scrap This and entered, with Charlotte tagging along behind me. After she was inside, I locked the door. No sense taking any chances on unwanted visitors.

"Hannah wasn't with Brandon and Felicity the night Chad Carr died. She was with Daniel Burke." I wasted no time getting to the heart of the matter.

"No, she wasn't."

"Yes, she was. Hannah told me."

"Hannah lied."

"What?" This twist was making my head hurt. "Why would she lie? She told me you'd kill Daniel if you knew she snuck out to see him."

"Felicity texted me that Hannah had snuck into Brandon's room through the window."

"How do you know Brandon didn't text you on his mom's phone? Maybe he was covering for his best friend."

Anger flashed in her eyes. "My daughter wasn't with Daniel that night. Felicity didn't like leaving Brandon alone. She wanted to know if it was all right if Hannah just stayed there with him because she had an errand to run."

"The errand being getting evidence from Made With Love."

"Yes."

"And the kids followed her there?"

Charlotte sighed. "Yes."

Daniel Burke had been the last one at the fire. Hannah lied to me to give Daniel an alibi.

Charlotte looked around the store, a confused look on her face. She sniffed a couple of times. The smell of smoke wafted toward me. Where was it coming from?

I rushed into our employee lounge to check if someone left something in the toaster oven. While the smell still lingered in the air, it wasn't as strong. The smoke wasn't coming from Scrap This.

Polished. I ran for the front door, finding it open and Charlotte gone. Smoke billowed from the nail salon, an orange glow snapping from inside the building. Charlotte ran into her store.

I dialed 911 and told the dispatcher about the fire.

"Stay on the line please," the pleasant voice said.

"Can't. Two people are inside."

I grabbed a scarf from my backseat, tying it around my mouth and nose, looking more like an ill-suited attempt at a bank robbery than a rescue. I wasn't sure how much smoke the sheer material would block, but it was better than nothing. I gingerly reached for the doorknob of Polished. It wasn't too hot.

Why hadn't Hannah come out herself? Or Charlotte with her?

After drawing in a few breaths of clean air, I pushed the door open and went inside. A gasoline smell almost overpowered me and forced me to retreat outside. Fighting the instinct, I continued forward, squinting through the haziness of the smoke. Slumped over in one of the pedicure chairs was Charlotte, her head lolling to the side.

Something heavy struck my shoulder and the side of my neck. I screamed and pitched forward. Shooting my hands out, I broke my fall for a moment before I found myself facedown on the ground. A throb worked its way from my shoulder blades down to my wrists. I started to roll over, but a foot pressed into my back, keeping my face pressed to the floor. The scarf was untied. The smoke burned my lungs.

"I hate that it's come to this." Remorse filled Daniel Burke's voice.

I eased my head a few inches from the ceramic floor and twisted my neck to the side. Pain arced down my spine.

He cradled a two by four in his arms. He spread his arms apart and the wood struck the small of my back, then he tipped over a metal shelving unit.

I covered my head as shampoo and conditioner rained down on me. Heavy bottles struck my arms and the unprotected parts of my head. Smoke and pain made tears course down my face. Where was Hannah?

I looked around the room as best I could. Two gas cans were near Charlotte, along with a box of matches. Small flames leapt past the lip of a metal trashcan.

"It won't work," I choked out. The police and fire department should arrive soon. I had to stall Daniel from unleashing the inferno he planned.

"Simple plans always work." Daniel's form entered into the mist.

"Then why do I know you killed Chad Carr and Charlie Powell?"

"I didn't plan those," Daniel's disembodied voice reached me. "They gave me no choice. Chad said he'd tell the police about my side job helping failing businesses if I told them he sold Janie to the kids."

"You mean arson for hire."

"I was using my skills to help people. Not like Chad. He told me he wanted to start a new life and stop dealing. Chad lied. He was going to keep selling Janie. I had to stop him. And Powell...well, he had it almost figured out."

"Talk to Ted. He'll help you." I tried to roll over, but pain arcing down my back left me immobile. Daniel poured gas onto the ground. I struggled harder. There wasn't much time to get free. I hadn't heard a sound from Charlotte. Had he killed her?

"You both know too much." Daniel walked away.

Both. He didn't know Hannah was in the building. I pushed and twisted with all my strength, ignoring the pain rocketing through my body. The metal shelf slipped from my legs. The good thing about the constant pain was it made me numb to it.

I had to find Hannah. Get her out of here.

Daniel returned wearing an oxygen mask, a small tank worn on his back. He dropped Charlotte beside me. He lit a match, flicking it toward the pedicure area. Flames crackled to life.

"Hannah. She's here." The words wobbled from my throat. I wasn't sure if it was pain, smoke, or the soul-crushing truth that I was about to die that made me sound so pitiful and hopeless.

Daniel turned. "No, she's not."

Flames danced up the walls.

"I saw her. It's why Charlotte wanted to talk at Scrap This."

Daniel swallowed hard, horror passing over his features. "You're lying."

"I'm not. You're going to kill her too."

Hannah crept up on Daniel, a broom clutched tightly in her hand. She swung it at his head. "No one hurts my mom!"

Daniel blocked the blow, sending the broom straight into a gas can. It tipped over, spreading toward the controlled fire.

"Hannah, run." All I wanted with every fiber of my being was to know Hannah was safe. Smoke filled my lungs. I coughed and inched out from under the board, heading for Hannah.

The building creaked and groaned. Plaster flaked from the ceiling. Snapping came from above my head. Beams and tiles bowed toward us, one of them directly above Hannah. I scrambled forward, desperate to reach her. "Hannah, the ceiling!"

Daniel braced his body over Hannah as tiles slipped from the metal grates above, raining down on them. Hannah reached for her mom. The gray smoke turned black. The crackling of the fire morphed into a roar.

Daniel rose to his feet, heading toward me. We were all going to die in here, unless I got us out of the impending inferno. I grabbed a piece of beam and heaved it at his head. It connected with a thwack, and he slumped forward.

I crawled toward Hannah and Charlotte, ignoring the spasms clenching my back. Quickly, I searched Daniel, figuring he brought something to help himself that I could use for us. I pulled out a small pack from his pocket. Fire blanket. I ripped it open, draping the thin silver blanket around Hannah and Charlotte.

"Keep it around you," I said. "It'll protect you from the flames."

"My mom isn't moving." Coughs and gasps stole Hannah's breath. "We're going to die."

"No, we won't. I'll help you bring her out. Make sure the blanket stays over her."

"Daniel?" Hannah caressed the man's cheek, grief and uncertainty contorting her features.

"Once you and your mom are safe, I'll help him." I didn't want to kill Daniel, even though I put him out of commission for the time being.

Hannah placed an arm around her unconscious mom's waist, wiggling her from the debris.

Moaning, Daniel's hand inched toward Hannah's wrist.

I hit his hand. "Don't touch her."

Daniel took off the mask and placed it on Hannah's mouth and nose, slipping off the straps from the oxygen tank.

The door started to open.

"No!" Daniel screamed, gathering us toward him. The air whooshed into the building, churning up the flames.

Hannah curled her body into a tight ball, gasping for air. I held her against me. Daniel drew us further underneath his body, rearranging the fire blanket around us.

"I never wanted this," he whispered into my ear. "I wanted to protect Hannah. Chad almost killed her best friend. He could've killed her next time. Save Hannah. I'll get Charlotte." Daniel lumbered unsteadily to his feet.

A figure crawled toward us. I squinted. Andrew. "It's time to go, Hannah." I pushed and prodded the sobbing girl toward the rescuer. Andrew clasped her wrists. He inched backwards, Hannah disappearing from my view.

The smoke grew heavier. I didn't know how we'd ever find our way out the door.

Daniel picked Charlotte up and placed her in a rolling chair. Her body pitched forward. "Hold her. Roll her out."

I kept one hand on the back of the chair and the other around Charlotte.

Andrew had returned, and now pushed and shoved items out of my way, making our path clear. Daniel snagged a fire extinguisher and squirted it in our direction. The flames leapt behind him.

The moment I stepped into the fresh air, water smacked me in the face, taking the little breath I had away. Screaming sirens bore down on us. They would save Daniel. He didn't need to die. A wheel of the chair hit the groove at the front door. Charlotte tumbled out, and I took a nosedive over the chair, knocking the remaining breath out of me.

People ran toward us. I scrubbed at my eyes. Smoke and tears made everything blurry. Strong arms effortlessly lifted me up. Feet pounded away from the building, away from Daniel.

I saw Hannah with Dawn. Where was Andrew?

I struggled to free my legs. "Daniel's in there. And Andrew. He saved us."

"You ain't in any condition to get either of them out, Faith." Wyatt deposited me into the backseat of a car. "You got her, Ma?"

"She ain't going nowhere, baby boy."

Wayne tenderly carried Charlotte toward an ambulance pulling to a stop.

Wyatt, without any fire protection, headed straight for Polished.

"Mommy!" Hannah's wail hit me in the heart.

Karen and Andrew were using the Buford's plumbing hose to fight the fire. The fire trucks started pulling in. Chief Ridley jumped out of the ladder truck and stared at his son-in-law for a few moments. Ridley motioned to his crew. "Help them out!"

The volunteer fire department members gathered around the unlikely pairing of Karen and Andrew, training their hoses onto the flames threatening to destroy the whole shopping complex.

The flames danced from the roof of Polished over to Scrap This, then sashayed over to Home Brewed. A ladder truck from a neighboring town pulled in, sirens and lights going full force. Cars pulled into the lot. It looked like half the residents showed up at the fire from the game. Squad cars pulled into the parking lot.

"Is Scrap This locked?" Gussie asked.

"The front door is open."

"You stay here."

I knew what Gussie had planned. She was going to save some merchandise so my grandmothers weren't financially ruined. I stood on unsteady legs.

"I'm helping too."

Gussie looked ready to argue then nodded. "Let's go."

We ran for the building.

"What are you crazy women doing?" Ted's desperate voice called out to us.

We ignored him and continued with our mission. People

formed a chain in front of Scrap This and Home Brewed, waiting for the flow of items.

The neighboring town's fire engine trained their water on Scrap This, while another town's ladder truck arrived and aimed their hoses at Home Brewed.

Buses pulled to a stop at the end of the parking lot. Both football teams and sets of coaches charged out of the buses.

"Get the large items, but if Chief Ridley says git, you git. Got it?" Coach Rutherford said.

"Yes, Coach!" the boys responded in unison.

The other team pulled out blankets and bottled water from their bus and set up a makeshift shelter. One teen walked over to Hannah and draped a blanket around her shoulders.

Quickly, products and tables came out of Scrap This.

"The game," I said.

"Community first, football second," Coach Rutherford said. "What's the point of being a winning team if the town we represent is destroyed in the process?"

TWENTY-SEVEN

The fire crews rolled up their hoses, boots splashing in the water filling the parking lot. Polished had sustained quite a bit of damage, but was saved from total destruction. It would take Charlotte months, and a lot of money, before her store reopened. Scrap This wasn't unscathed, though our loss was minimal compared to Polished. My grandmothers and I had started adding up the inventory ruined, quitting soon after we started. None of us wanted to face it tonight. There was plenty of time tomorrow to sort and tally it all up.

I drew in a deep breath, setting off a coughing fit as smoke still lingered in the air. More residents pulled out of the lot, heading back home. Our town had really pulled together. Warmth trickled into my heart. I needed to trust and have more faith in my community. We had our problems, created some along the way, but when push came to shove, Eden residents rallied. The football teams had gone over to Piece A Pie to share a meal. Coach Rutherford had returned to the shopping complex, delivering pizzas and drinks to the firefighters and helpers. He told us that the parents and teens of Eden had chipped in and bought the food, wanting to make the first move in patching up the relationship between them and the police.

Ted brought me a Diet Coke and a slice of pizza. "What you and Gussie did was dangerous."

"Not that dangerous. It was safe to go in when we did. If the building was on fire like Polished, we wouldn't have done it."

"Shouldn't have done it anyway. A fire can get out of hand quickly."

"It's my grandmothers' livelihood." I sat on the hood of my car. "Besides, it was Gussie's idea. I figured if it was that bad of an idea, Wayne and Wyatt would've been dragging their mom away, or else would have come over to hose down Scrap This. Those guys would never let Gussie face danger without them."

"Fine, I'll scold Gussie too."

A small laugh escaped me. "Good luck with that."

Ted dumped some water onto a napkin. "You know, your grandmothers would much rather have you."

"I want them to have both. To have it all."

"I wonder if anyone ever can." He stroked my face with the napkin, soot turning it from white to gray.

"Some can. It just depends on the way you go about it," I said.

"It was still risky."

"I'm willing to take risks when I need to."

"Is that so?" He leaned forward, bracing himself with his hands on either side of me.

I was trapped. His green eyes locked onto my brown ones. My heart thumped out a frenzied beat I wasn't quite sure of the reason for. Was I nervous, scared, hopeful, or anticipating something? Unfortunately, or maybe fortunately, my grandmothers ran up to me.

When Ted drew back, my heart rate returned to normal. I swear some disappointment skittered through me. I slid off the car.

"Are you sure you're okay?" Hope pulled me into a hug. "We heard you coughing. I was trying to find out some information from Randall. No one has said anything about Daniel Burke being under arrest."

I looked over at Ted. His eyes traveled toward an ambulance where a sheet was placed over a body. My grandmothers followed his gaze.

Steve joined our group. "Burke didn't make it. Wyatt got him out, but it was too late."

With the way Ted averted his gaze, I had a feeling Daniel's death wasn't from smoke inhalation or the flames. Daniel had found a way to take his own life. His conscience had caught up with him.

"I don't know what to think," Cheryl said. "He tried to hurt my granddaughter."

"He changed his mind," I said. "He helped me and Charlotte escape."

"He wouldn't have had to help you if he hadn't started it," Hope said.

She was right, yet I felt a need to defend Daniel. He wasn't the good, upstanding citizen everyone believed, yet he wasn't an unfeeling, evil monster either. He truly believed he had to kill Chad, knowing the man planned on disappearing and finding a new city to set up base and sell synthetic marijuana to teens.

Charlie. Charlie was the stumbling block in my willingness to forgive Daniel.

"He had good intentions when he started," I said. "Once he made the first choice, he found himself tied to it and had to follow it through."

"I think that's true with most mistakes we can't recover from," Steve said.

"That's no excuse," Cheryl said.

"It's not an excuse all the time." Steve pocketed his hands and let out a resigned breath. "People sometimes make choices with the best of intentions. Like Faith getting involved in solving murders. She doesn't want to annoy the police or interfere in a case; it's not what motivates her, yet it's one of the outcomes of her actions. She wants to make things better for people, and sometimes trying to make things better hurts people worse."

Cheryl snorted. "Maybe that's because the person was actually thinking more about themselves than the person they say they were helping."

With his head lowered, Steve walked away.

"Grandma, that's not fair."

Cheryl hugged me. "Sweetie, I'm not talking about you. I know your heart. You truly do want to help."

I pulled back some, not enough to hurt my grandmother's feelings, but enough to let her know I was drawing a clear line. "You're not being fair to Steve. He made a mistake. I don't think there was malice intended in not telling me earlier about Adam. It hurt me when I found out. I felt stupid. Betrayed."

"Come on, Cheryl." Hope took hold of her arm.

"Where are we going?"

"To apologize to Steve. I don't want him run out of town, and neither does Faith. And if she doesn't, you shouldn't."

Cheryl studied me for a moment. She smiled softly and tweaked my nose. "Fine. I'll do it for Faith. But that man still aggravates me, and I don't think I'll put him back on my Christmas cookie list."

Well, at least he was back on the Christmas card list. "Thanks, Grandma."

"What I do for our girl," Cheryl muttered as Hope led her away.

Ted leaned against the car. "So, you and Steve? You two are back together?"

"My marriage to Adam did a number on my head and heart. I need him out of my life once and for all. To have Steve in it is to have Adam in it."

"The question you should ask yourself is do you love the man. If you do, don't let a murderous thug dictate the relationship."

I planted myself in front of Ted. "Why do you keep pushing me at Steve?"

"What?" His eyes widened.

"This is the third time you've encouraged me to date Steve."

"Is not."

"Is so," I said. "First time was when my lockbox was stolen. You told me you'd be okay if it was because of Steve that I let my past go. Second time was after I got shot. You said it was a fact Steve and I would get through this issue. And now, here you are again, telling me I should be with Steve."

"I'll be damned." There was regret and surprise in Ted's voice.

I placed my hands on his shoulders and looked him right in the eye. "I'm not the one who said you were a second choice, a default. You did."

"What does that mean for us?" Ted linked his arms behind my back.

Slowly, I drifted my hands down and covered his, unwinding his fingers. I slipped out of the loose embrace. Smiling, I inched my way to the driver's side door, opening it. "Depends on the risk you're willing to take, Detective Roget. You like to plead Steve's case. How about you try your own for a change?"

"I find you infuriating. Stubborn. Sassy. Opinionated. Protective. Beautiful. I want the best for you. I want you safe. Most of all, I want you to have happiness and hold onto it, even if what makes you happy irritates the hell out of me." Ted's voice took on a raw edge that tripped my heart, and I found it extremely sexy. "I've think I've fallen hard for you, Miss Hunter."

"That's a good start."

CHRISTINA FREEBURN

The Faith Hunter Scrap This Mystery series brings together Christina Freeburn's love of mysteries, scrapbooking, and West Virginia. When not writing or reading, she can be found in her scrapbook room or at a crop. Alas, none of the real-life crops have had a sexy male prosecutor or a handsome police officer attending.

Christina served in the JAG Corps of the US Army and also worked as a paralegal, librarian, and church secretary. She lives in West Virginia with her husband, children, a dog, and a rarely seen cat except by those who are afraid or allergic to felines.

**The Faith Hunter Scrap This Mystery Series
By Christina Freeburn**

CROPPED TO DEATH (#1)
DESIGNED TO DEATH (#2)
EMBELLISHED TO DEATH (#3)
FRAMED TO DEATH (#4)

Available at booksellers nationwide and online

Visit www.henerypress.com for details

Henery Press Mystery Books

And finally, before you go...
Here are a few other mysteries
you might enjoy:

ARTIFACT

Gigi Pandian

A Jaya Jones Treasure Hunt Mystery (#1)

Historian Jaya Jones discovers the secrets of a lost Indian treasure may be hidden in a Scottish legend from the days of the British Raj. But she's not the only one on the trail...

From San Francisco to London to the Highlands of Scotland, Jaya must evade a shadowy stalker as she follows hints from the hastily scrawled note of her dead lover to a remote archaeological dig. Helping her decipher the cryptic clues are her magician best friend, a devastatingly handsome art historian with something to hide, and a charming archaeologist running for his life.

Available at booksellers nationwide and online

Visit www.henerypress.com for details

FIT TO BE DEAD

Nancy G. West

An Aggie Mundeen Mystery (#1)

Aggie Mundeen, single and pushing forty, fears nothing but middle age. When she moves from Chicago to San Antonio, she decides she better shape up before anybody discovers she writes the column, "Stay Young with Aggie." She takes Aspects of Aging at University of the Holy Trinity and plunges into exercise at Fit and Firm.

Rusty at flirting and mechanically inept, she irritates a slew of male exercisers, then stumbles into murder. She'd like to impress the attractive detective with her sleuthing skills. But when the killer comes after her, the health club evacuates semi-clad patrons, and the detective has to stall his investigation to save Aggie's derriere.

Available at booksellers nationwide and online

Visit www.henerypress.com for details

MURDER IN G MAJOR

Alexia Gordon

A Gethsemane Brown Mystery (#1)

With few other options, African-American classical musician
Gethsemane Brown accepts a less-than-ideal position turning a
group of rowdy schoolboys into an award-winning orchestra.
Stranded without luggage or money in the Irish countryside, she
figures any job is better than none. The perk? Housesitting a lovely
cliffside cottage. The catch? The ghost of the cottage's murdered
owner haunts the place. Falsely accused of killing his wife (and
himself), he begs Gethsemane to clear his name so he can rest in
peace.

Gethsemane's reluctant investigation provokes a dormant killer
and she soon finds herself in grave danger. As Gethsemane races to
prevent a deadly encore, will she uncover the truth or star in her
own farewell performance?

Available at booksellers nationwide and online

Visit www.henerypress.com for details

THE SEMESTER OF OUR DISCONTENT

Cynthia Kuhn

A Lila Maclean Mystery (#1)

English professor Lila Maclean is thrilled about her new job at prestigious Stonedale University, until she finds one of her colleagues dead. She soon learns that everyone, from the chancellor to the detective working the case, believes Lila—or someone she is protecting—may be responsible for the horrific event, so she assigns herself the task of identifying the killer.

More attacks on professors follow, the only connection a curious symbol at each of the crime scenes. Putting her scholarly skills to the test, Lila gathers evidence, but her search is complicated by an unexpected nemesis, a suspicious investigator, and an ominous secret society. Rather than earning an "A" for effort, she receives a threat featuring the mysterious emblem and must act quickly to avoid failing her assignment...and becoming the next victim.

Available at booksellers nationwide and online

Visit www.henerypress.com for details

FINDING SKY

Susan O'Brien

A Nicki Valentine Mystery

Suburban widow and PI in training Nicki Valentine can barely keep track of her two kids, never mind anyone else. But when her best friend's adoption plan is jeopardized by the young birth mother's disappearance, Nicki is persuaded to help. Nearly everyone else believes the teenager ran away, but Nicki trusts her BFF's judgment, and the feeling is mutual.

The case leads where few moms go (teen parties, gang shootings) and places they can't avoid (preschool parties, OB-GYNs' offices). Nicki has everything to lose and much to gain — including the attention of her unnervingly hot P.I. instructor. Thankfully, Nicki is armed with her pesky conscience, occasional babysitters, a fully stocked minivan, and nature's best defense system: women's intuition.

Available at booksellers nationwide and online

Visit www.henerypress.com for details

www.ingramcontent.com/pod-product-compliance
Lightning Source LLC
Chambersburg PA
CBHW060536260626
47161CB00003B/926